Murder in Wax

Holly Copella

ISBN: 1947694103
ISBN-13: 978-1-947694-10-1

To Crystal Koch

ACKNOWLEDGMENTS

Copella Books: First Paperback Edition 2018
Cover Artist: Fantasyart
SelfPubBookCovers.com/ Fantasyart
Printed by CreateSpace, An Amazon.com Company

PUBLISHER'S NOTE

Chapter One

The once charming stone bridge had seen better days. Considered impassable by cars for years, it was mostly used by young lovers embarking on romantic interludes. Despite its reputation for kids in love, it had been dubbed 'lover's leap' decades ago. Although not a fantastic drop, the shallow water below and many rocks meant certain death to anyone attempting to jump from it. Despite its nickname, only two kids had ever committed suicide by jumping from the bridge in its one hundred or more years in existence.

Not far from the infamous bridge, a young woman just barely eighteen walked through a nearby meadow filled with lush grass and wildflowers. She carried her sandals and a small bouquet of flowers. Chelsea Smyth was a raving beauty with long, golden blonde hair. She had a flawless, makeup-free complexion, sparkling blue eyes, and a radiant smile that almost certainly indicated a woman in love. Despite her ample curves, she dressed conservatively in jean shorts and a tank top covered with a button shirt, which she left open on the warm, sunny afternoon.

Chelsea's perfect afternoon was quickly ruined when she heard the sounds of girls' giggling from nearby. The smile disappeared from her face at the familiar sound. She glanced across the meadow and saw four girls, all sixteen years of age. Her younger sister, Jamie, was the ringleader while Tamara, Paula, and Christine were her devoted minions. Chelsea was in too good of a mood to deal with her narcissistic and possibly sadistic sister. She ignored them and headed across the meadow toward the woods, hoping to avoid a confrontation.

"Looks like someone has a hot date," Jamie teased while they followed Chelsea.

"Go away," Chelsea scoffed without looking back at the menacing four.

Jamie was attractive in her own rights, although she couldn't quite compete with her older sister. She shared the same long, blonde hair as Chelsea, but her beauty came from layers of makeup rather than naturally. Her three friends were also attractive young ladies with the same flair for makeup, which seemed to be their signature trademark. Chelsea ignored her sister and continued on her path for the woods.

"Does mom know you're out here meeting boys?" Jamie continued while pursuing her, now at a faster pace to catch up.

"I'm not meeting boys," Chelsea insisted without looking at Jamie. "Leave me alone."

Jamie laughed with what could only be described as a banshee war cry. Developing the fake laugh took a few years to perfect.

"Not meeting boys, huh?" Jamie continued as her friends giggled from a few feet behind. "Judging by that radiant glow, I'd say you've been doing a lot more than just *meeting* boys. Wait until mom finds out you gave up your virginity."

Chelsea spun and faced her sister. Her look was now enraged as her eyes narrowed. "I'm being preached to by the town slut?" she hissed.

On cue, Jamie's friends mocked her with cackling laughter. Jamie sneered at the insult and snatched the flowers from her sister.

"She doesn't care what I do," Jamie snapped then raised her sinister brows. "You, on the other hand, are her little angel. Wait until she finds out just how dirty you are."

Chelsea glared at her sister and attempted to reclaim her flowers despite that there was an entire meadow filled with them. Jamie pulled them back, keeping her from having them.

"Give them back," Chelsea snarled becoming angry to the point of lashing out at her sister.

"Are they from *him*?" Jamie teased while grinning. "Are they from your *lover*?"

"Give them back," Chelsea cried out and again attempted to snatch them.

Jamie carelessly tossed them over her shoulder while her friends watched them scatter and fall.

"Dinner tonight should be fun," Jamie announced with her signature giggle. "I can't wait to see the look on mother's face."

Chelsea just glared at her sister, silently seething, although avoiding a physical altercation. Jamie turned to her friends while grinning mischievously.

"Come on, girls," she ordered and snapped her fingers as she walked past them, being certain to trample the discarded flowers.

All three obediently fell in line and followed her, making certain to trample the discarded flowers as well. Chelsea frowned and attempted to pick up the flowers. Most had been crushed by her sister and her minions as they trampled them when they left. Chelsea threw the bent and broken flowers down with disgust then picked up the remaining, unharmed flower. She stared at the flower a moment, and her smile returned. Even Jamie couldn't ruin her mood entirely.

Chapter Two

As Jamie led her friends through the woods, she was silently seething despite her obvious victory over her sister. The three remaining girls talked and giggled about things only important to a teenage girl. Jamie could hear someone else rustling around in the woods and held her hand up to her friends.

"Shut up," she ordered, silencing all three.

They looked around the woods then saw a man in the near distance walking along a different path. Although he wore a baseball cap, concealing his identity, what little they saw of him, they were certain he wasn't from town.

"Who the hell is that?" Paula suddenly chirped.

The man was too far away to hear or notice them. Judging by his old jeans and dirty jacket, he was possibly a drifter. His age was unclear, although he was almost certainly in his early twenties.

"I suggest we don't find out," Christine muttered. "He looks scary."

"You're such a wuss," Jamie snapped back at her friend.

Once he was out of sight, the four continued on their way through the woods. The three girls resumed their earlier conversation.

"Why were you called into the principal's office?" Tamara finally asked Christine.

"It was stupid," Christine explained while rolling her eyes. "Someone keyed Mr. Rowling's car in the parking lot, and the principal questioned me about it." She shook her head in disgust. "As if I'd vandalize a teacher's car. I'm not that stupid."

Jamie suddenly stopped and spun to face her friends. She glared at Christine. "What did he ask?" she demanded.

"He just asked where I was during lunch," Christine replied then shrugged. "Uh, in the cafeteria. Where else would I be?"

Jamie's eyes widened with horror then anger as she stared at her friend. "You idiot! You were supposed to tell him you were with me cleaning up in the gym after the pep rally."

"Relax, Jamie," Christine groaned. "He knows you didn't key Mr. Rowling's car."

"How does he know that?" Jamie demanded.

"Because he asked if you were in Mr. Paterson's room helping him clean his classroom," Christine remarked. "You're in the clear."

"You stupid bitch," Jamie cried out in rage, surprising all three friends. "I told you to tell anyone who asked that I was with you in the gym!"

"What's the big deal?" Christine asked with surprise. "He knows you didn't key that car. You were with Mr. Paterson. He'll give you an alibi."

Jamie suddenly slammed her palms against Christine's shoulders and cast her backward. "He wasn't supposed to know I was with Mr. Paterson in his room," she cried out in anger. "That was supposed to be a secret!"

"What?" Christine gasped. "Why?"

"Because I was flunking history, and he gave me passing grades in trade," she cried out and again slammed her palms against Christine's shoulders.

Christine stumbled backward and fell to the ground. She looked up at Jamie with surprise while Tamara and Paula stared at their enraged friend, uncertain how to react to the outburst.

"The principal was already suspicious," Jamie cried out. "That's why you were supposed to tell anyone who asked that I was with you in the gym!"

"I didn't know," Christine cried out. "You didn't tell me why you wanted me to lie."

"You ruined everything," Jamie screamed and kicked Christine in the side.

"Jamie," Tamara gasped with surprise and attempted to stop her.

Jamie pushed Tamara aside.

"I didn't know," Christine cried out while cowering on the ground.

"Now I'm going to be expelled, and Mr. Paterson will lose his job," Jamie screamed and kicked Christine in the head. "Everyone will know I slept with my teacher!" She kicked her in the head again. "My mother will know I slept with my teacher. She'll throw me out of the house!" Jamie kicked Christine in the head again.

She was about to kick her again when Paula stopped her. They stared at their friend on the ground. She was bleeding from the head and wasn't moving.

Paula suddenly gasped. "Is she--?"

All three stood motionless while staring at their fallen friend. Jamie placed her hand to her mouth and took a step back. Tamara rushed to Christine's side and gently nudged her.

"Christine?" she choked on her words.

There was no response. Tamara looked up at her friends with horror.

"I don't think she's breathing," Tamara gasped.

"I think you're supposed to check for a pulse or something," Paula cried out while running trembling fingers through her hair.

Tamara touched Christine's neck and felt around in several places. She sprang to her feet and looked at her friends as the color drained from her face.

"She's dead," Tamara gasped.

"We need to call an ambulance," Paula cried out while sobbing.

"She's already dead, you twit," Jamie snapped.

"We have to tell someone," Tamara announced while nervously rubbing her chilled arms.

Jamie was silent a moment while her friends sobbed. "Shut up," she cried out. Once they both silenced, she glared at them and pointed a warning finger. "No one can know about this."

"What?" Tamara gasped. "It was an accident. You didn't mean to kill her."

"That's not going to matter," Jamie lashed out. "They're going to throw me in jail for it." She eyed each of her friends with an unpredictably psychotic look. "You don't want me going to jail, do you?"

There was a moment of silence.

"Do you?" Jamie cried out.

"No, of course not," Tamara announced while Paula just shook her head.

"We'll move her off the path, cover her over with leaves, and pretend this never happened," Jamie informed them.

"Pretend it never happened? Her parents need to know," Tamara protested as tears streaked her face. "They'll want to bury her."

"She'll be found," Jamie replied then considered the comment. "Eventually."

"Won't they be able to tell how she died?" Paula asked then looked at her friends. "On all those forensic shows, they're able to find cause of death."

"That's true," Tamara agreed. "They'll figure out she'd been kicked in the head. They'll be able to tell it was a girl's foot from the size of the bruises or something like that."

"Then we'll need to make sure they can't do that," Jamie informed them.

Tamara and Paula gave her a strange look.

"Help me move her," Jamie ordered and indicated an area off the path where no one traveled.

Both girls reluctantly helped her pick up their dead friend and move the body into the secluded area. Jamie walked the area and looked around.

"Find branches and things to toss over her," Jamie informed them.

Tamara and Paula exchanged frowns and did as they were told. A strange cracking sound was heard. Both girls spun around and watched in horror as Jamie struck Christine in the head with a large rock. She hit the dead girl repeatedly in the head until her skull split open. Tamara and Paula held back their cries. They heard a startled gasp. All three turned and saw Chelsea standing on the path staring at them. Chelsea stared at the bloodied rock in Jamie's hands and then Christine's mutilated head. Jamie dropped the rock and stared at her sister, unable to speak.

"What have you done?" Chelsea gasped as the flower fell from her hand.

"You aren't going to tell anyone," Jamie lashed out in anger. "You're going to keep your mouth shut!"

Chelsea stared at her sister with horror clearly on her face. She shook her head. "You're a monster," she suddenly gasped then took off through the woods.

"We need to stop her," Jamie cried out and ran after her. She paused and looked back at her friends.

Tamara and Paula just stared at her.

"And do what?" Tamara suddenly asked with surprise. "Kill her?"

"You're already screwed," Jamie informed them with anger showing in her eyes. "If I go down; you're going down with me. Now get her!"

Jamie took off through the woods and ran down the path after her sister. Tamara and Paula exchanged frightened looks then ran after them.

Chapter Three

Chelsea ran through the woods and into the meadow with Jamie closing in behind her. Chelsea's sandals weren't helping gain traction in the grass. She managed to kick them off while she ran and was able to pick up speed. Jamie continued her pursuit with her friends several yards behind screaming for her to stop. Chelsea ran across the stone bridge with Jamie directly on her heels.

Jamie tackled her sister, knocking her into the crumbling half wall on the bridge. Chelsea hit the stone with force. It crumbled slightly under her weight. She attempted to pull away. Jamie grabbed her by the shirt with her blood-covered hands and slammed her back against the crumbling wall. She glared into her sister's eyes.

"You're not going to tell anyone about this," Jamie screamed in anger. "I want to hear you say it! You won't tell anyone, or I swear I'll kill you!"

Chelsea struggled against her sister's grip and attempted to break free. Jamie again slammed her against the half wall. Tamara and Paula slowed when they saw Jamie slamming her sister's back against the stone wall with increasing force.

"Say it," Jamie screamed like a mad woman while nearly ripping the shirt clutched in her hands.

On the fourth time she'd slammed her against the half wall, the stone gave away, and Chelsea slipped backward from the bridge, her shirt slipping through Jamie's clenched fists. Paula and Tamara ran onto the bridge and peered down to the creek that was barely a trickle. Chelsea lay in an awkward position, bent and broken, below the bridge near the bank among the rocks. Blood trickled from the corner of her mouth as she lay motionless. The three stood on the bridge for several minutes, unable to move or look away from the horrible image.

"You killed your sister," Paula finally gasped, snapping them out of their trances.

Jamie spun to face her friends. "It was an accident," she insisted. "She fell."

"We have to do something," Tamara announced while panicking and pacing the bridge.

Paula attempted to run across the bridge to get help. Jamie ran after her and caught her.

"No," Jamie shouted while shaking Paula by her shoulders. "We aren't going to do anything. We're going to stick to our original plan."

Tamara stared at her with horror. "You're just going to leave your sister there?"

"When she's eventually found, they'll assume the wall collapsed, and she accidentally fell to her death," Jamie informed them then glared demandingly at her friends. "Are we agreed?"

As she glared at Tamara and Paula, a sobbing Paula slowly nodded. Tamara couldn't take her eyes off Chelsea lying motionless below the bridge. Jamie grabbed Tamara's arms and shook her until she made eye contact.

"Are we agreed?" she cried out in anger.

Tamara stared into Jamie's nearly psychotic eyes and nervously nodded as well.

§

Several hours later. It was early evening as Sheriff Carter stood on the bank of the stream below the bridge and watched the paramedics strap the motionless eighteen-year-old girl onto the stretcher. Chelsea wore a neck and back brace to keep her immobile while they moved her. She was alive but had yet to regain consciousness. As the paramedics carried her up the bank, Sheriff Carter watched and shook his head.

Sheriff Carter was in his mid to late forties. Considering the low crime rate of his town, he remained physically fit, which only made his six-foot-two stature all the more impressive. He was a serious-looking man with short, light brown hair and a neatly trimmed beard. His much younger deputy, Havens, frowned while watching the paramedics remove the critically injured girl.

Deputy Havens was in his mid to late twenties. Despite his tall stature, he was more lanky than muscular. He was considered adorable by the women in town. What barely constituted as a mustache on his upper lip may have had something to do with that. There had been plenty of debate as to whether or not the few hairs on his chin were meant to be a goatee.

"I'm surprised she's alive after a fall like that," Deputy Havens remarked.

"She's not out of the woods yet," Sheriff Carter reported while maintaining his frown. "Something about this stinks, Havens."

"You don't think it was an accident?" his deputy asked with surprise while turning to face him.

"She had blood on her shirt," the sheriff reported while remaining in his own world. "I'm no expert, but I don't think that blood will turn out to be hers. Apart from a few scrapes on her legs, she didn't have any cuts. The blood on her shirt looked almost like--" He placed his hands out in front of him and reached for the deputy's jacket. "Almost like hands grabbing her."

The deputy stared at him with horror. "You think someone pushed her?"

The sheriff didn't respond to the question. "Did you find her shoes?"

"No, they weren't anywhere near the bridge," Deputy Havens informed him.

"Spread out the search," the sheriff announced. "I want to know where she lost her shoes. It could be important."

"Sheriff," a deputy called from beyond the bridge. "We found her shoes!"

"Where?" Sheriff Carter called back.

"In the meadow," he announced. "Quite a distance from here."

"Show me!"

The sheriff and Deputy Havens followed the other deputy into the meadow where he indicated the shoes discarded haphazard several yards from each other. Sheriff Carter paused within the meadow to pick up several crushed flowers and stared at them. Both deputies watched him with bewildered looks.

"I don't like this," Sheriff Carter announced then looked around with genuine suspicion. "I'd like to search the entire area."

"What are we searching for?" Deputy Havens asked looking lost as if he missed what the sheriff obviously had seen.

"The blood on her shirt could be from whoever pushed her," the sheriff informed him, "but how did our perp get blood on him. She didn't have any blood on her hands.

That was a lot of blood. Seems unlikely she injured him during the attack, or she'd have blood on her." He eyed his deputies. "I think someone else could be injured. We need some dogs. Asap."

§

Jamie paced the hospital waiting room while her mother, Dorothy, sat on a nearby chair and sobbed into her handkerchief. Another woman clung to Jamie's mother and spoke softly and reassuringly. Jamie's mother was possibly a fine catch in her early years, but with little regard for makeup or even a decent hairstyle, she looked more like an old-fashioned librarian. Her long, slightly graying hair was worn in an old granny bun, and her clothes suggested old-fashioned in every sense of the word.

"She's going to be okay, Dorothy," the woman announced. "I know she'll be fine. The Lord will take care of her. We need to pray for her."

Jamie listened to the conversation and fidgeted. Each time a doctor or nurse appeared from the emergency room, she jerked with fear that her sister was somehow going to survive. The doctor finally approached Dorothy. She sprang to her feet and stared at him with anticipation. Jamie twitched while nervously wringing her fingers together.

"Mrs. Smyth," he announced in a soothing yet concerned tone. "Your daughter is currently in stable condition."

Dorothy sobbed with relief and hugged her friend. Jamie's expression dropped as all color drained from her face.

"We need to talk," the doctor informed her and escorted her to a private area.

Jamie trembled and started to pant. Her face was nearly white, and her palms were sweating. Sheriff Carter approached her, practically appearing out of nowhere. She jumped when she saw him. He offered a sympathetic smile.

"How's your sister?" he asked.

"Uh, the doctor just showed up to talk to my mother," she informed him. "If you want to talk to her--"

"Actually, I'd like a word with you," he announced and indicated the nearby chairs.

Jamie slid into the chair almost unable to maintain her balance as she trembled.

"When was the last time you saw your sister or your friend, Christine Marion?"

"Uh, I hadn't seen Chelsea since we'd left for school this morning," she informed him as her voiced cracked. "Paula, Tamara, and I were with Christine after school. Last time I saw her, she was heading home. Paula, Tamara, and I decided to go to town rather than head home." She stared at him a moment. "Why are you asking about Christine? What does she have to do with Chelsea falling from the bridge?"

"Jamie," he announced timidly while staring into her eyes. "Christine was murdered in the woods not far from the bridge where we found your sister."

Jamie stared at him unable to move while managing to wipe her sweaty palms on her pants. Everything was unraveling faster than anticipated.

"We believe someone killed her, and your sister may have witnessed it. We found a flower from the same meadow where we found Chelsea's shoes on the path not far from Christine's body," the sheriff announced then drew a deep breath. "We believe the killer then went after your sister to keep her quiet."

"I--I don't know what to say," she gasped while trembling. "Do, uh, you know who did it?"

"Did you happen to see anyone near the woods when you and your friends left Christine?" he asked. "Did she have a boyfriend?"

"No, she didn't have a boyfriend," Jamie immediately announced then fumbled for something to say. "But, uh, there was--" She suddenly looked at the sheriff as her eyes lit up. "We saw some guy near the woods. We'd thought he'd left. It could have been him."

"Anyone you know?"

She shook her head. "No, I'm sure he wasn't from town," Jamie replied. "He was dressed sort of grungy and wore a dirty green jacket and a black baseball cap. I really couldn't see his face."

"Maybe your friends got a better look at him," Sheriff Carter announced. "Why don't you check on your sister? I'll stop at Tamara and Paula's houses later and see what they remember."

Jamie nodded and watched Sheriff Carter walk away. Once he was gone, she bolted up from her chair and hurried to a nearby payphone.

Chapter Four

Seven years later. The small town of Fairview Glen was comprised of tiny homes with fenced yards and quiet streets. Beyond the small town, there was farmland as far as the eye could see. Some farmers grew crops while others raised cattle or sheep. Just beyond the vast farmland was a newly constructed resort area containing large, impressive hotels with swimming pools, nightclubs, and restaurants. Although the town attempted to distance itself from the booming resort area, the younger generation embraced the idea of a new, modern world at their doorstep.

Nestled somewhere between town and the resort area was a large, out of place, newly constructed museum surrounded by a lush cornfield. Scaffolding surrounded the left, front corner of the building where workers were completing the finishing touches on the building's exterior. A large, historic home resided just a short walk from the museum. Apart from the house and museum, the only other building residing among the never-ending farmland was an old funeral home just on the other side of the cornfield.

A jeep pulled into the secluded museum parking lot early that morning and stopped near the main entrance. Two young, attractive women in their early twenties, Devon Vincent and Ivy Jennings, looked out the jeep's windshield and stared at the large and impressive museum. Both immediately cringed when they saw the words 'wax museum'.

"You didn't mention it was a wax museum," Ivy announced while displaying her distaste. "Those places are creepy."

Ivy's strawberry blonde hair was meticulously styled and her makeup perfectly applied with just the right shade of lipstick. She was dressed to kill in a conservative, yet flattering thin-strapped dress, which revealed just enough of her cleavage.

"The owner didn't mention it was a wax museum either," Devon remarked then drew a deep breath and collected herself. "I hate interviews."

Devon was the typical girl-next-door with a classic tomboy appeal. Her long dark hair was worn up in a simple ponytail, which she'd actually taken time to make it neat. She usually didn't wear makeup, but today she wore a little eyeliner and a little lipstick. She was dressed even more conservative in a simple blouse, revealing none of her ample cleavage, and black dress pants usually reserved for church. She wore a pair of black dress boots to complete her conservative, job interview outfit.

"You'll be fine," Ivy insisted then frowned. "I'm the one who should be nervous. You're going to make me late for my audition with Burt Danson."

"I'm sorry. I almost forgot," Devon announced then smiled timidly at her friend. "Good luck with the acting audition."

"I'm up against Jamie Smyth, goddess of Fairview Glen," Ivy remarked dramatically then rolled her eyes. "I'll need all the luck I can get."

"Call me tonight and let me know how it went," Devon announced then got out of the jeep.

Devon remained standing in the parking lot staring at the creepy museum even after her friend's jeep pulled away. She gathered her courage and approached the front entrance. Devon stood before the large, double doors with stained glass windows and knocked several times, but there was no response. One of the men on the scaffolding, Karl Price, appeared to be watching her.

"Devon? Is that you?"

She glanced alongside the building at the construction worker. "Karl?" she announced with surprise. "I didn't know you were working for Larry's Construction."

He jumped off the scaffolding near her. "Yeah, I started a couple of months ago."

Karl was only a year or two older than she was and a year younger than Devon's brother. By almost any woman's standards, Karl was a handsome man and possibly a fine catch if good looks were all a woman needed. Having a decent paying job would only add to his stud status. His dark hair was the perfect length, reaching partway down to his collar, and he had the most captivating blue eyes. He stood a respectable six-foot with just enough muscle to gain attention. Pure eye candy. His loose morals and shoddy intellect was another story. Devon could admire his shoulders all day but become bored the moment he opened his mouth.

"What brings you here?" He eyed her, not used to seeing her so neatly dressed, and grinned. "I don't remember seeing you this dressed up before."

"I have a job interview."

"Oh? Your old man setting you free from the ranch, huh?"

"Something like that," she muttered, although it was a sore subject.

"The boss is probably in the basement," he informed her. "He must have a workshop down there. I hardly ever see the guy." His mood immediately turned enthusiastic. "Hey, why don't we go out for drinks tonight? I broke up with Jamie, so I'm available. It'll be fun. I'll pick you up at seven."

Devon stared at him a moment in mild disbelief. As if his being available was all a woman needed to jump into his arms. Was he asking her out or summoning her to his side? He always did have an inflated ego.

"I'm sorry," she replied while shifting uncomfortably. "I'm helping my father at the ranch tonight."

She didn't know why she lied as if attempting to spare his feelings. A simple, 'I'm not interested in going out with you' would have been acceptable, considering how poorly he'd treated women over the years.

"Yeah, I understand," he replied with some disappointment then managed a smile. "We can go out some other time."

Devon managed a tiny smile and immediately regretted not setting him straight right away. Now there would be another awkward moment later on.

"I, uh, better get to my interview before I'm late," she announced, even though she had intentionally arrived fifteen minutes early.

Chapter Five

Devon entered the museum and passed through the small lobby area. She then paused and stared at the never-ending walkway of partially finished displays. Although far from complete, the background for the sets was realistic and almost creepy. She wandered through the maze of displays and winding walkways. A majority of each set was mostly contained on one side of the walkway, alternating which side, but the walkway itself was built through the display, so visitors would be entrenched in the scene on both sides. The walkway material itself changed with each set to maintain a particular feel. The walkway could be fake gravel, stone, brick, fake ground, or even just concrete depending on the time period and relevance to the display itself.

Judging by the sheer number of empty displays, it would be some time before the museum would be opening. She wasn't sure how long she walked the never-ending walkway in and out of displays, but she didn't seem to be getting anywhere fast. She finally reached what looked like a dungeon entrance with an open, wrought iron door, fake torches on either side of the opening, and block stone steps leading down to the basement. The sign read 'dungeon'. That was unsettling. Fake torches lining the stairs were the only source of light, although the stone steps were oddly illuminated to keep anyone from tripping. If the owner was going for creepy, he succeeded. She was nearly paralyzed with fear about continuing down the steps, and the museum wasn't even complete yet.

If someone chose to avoid the dungeon, the winding walkway curved and continued back through the museum to the front past more displays. Unfortunately, Devon's business was down a level in the basement or as it was apparently called the 'dungeon'. Devon felt slightly apprehensive, and she didn't even know why. She proceeded down the broad, stone steps to the bottom. The stone dungeon atmosphere gave way to the beginning of the first of many displays, which were all obviously horror sets. A chill swept through her as she easily recognized most of the sets without their respective monsters. Being immersed within the horror displays was chilling even with the lights on. Devon was both impressed and frightened. She walked through several displays with a strange uneasiness and nervously rubbed her chilled arms while carefully studying each one.

She paused within an elaborate church scene that contained a large, marble altar. There were amazingly realistic silk flower arrangements and unlit, electronic candles displayed upon the altar and around the set. A stained glass window with a false light behind it gave a mysterious glow to the display. As she continued through the 'dungeon', she lost track of how many displays she'd passed through. Each one was more terrifying than the last. There was the mad doctor's lab, a vampire display, a phantom's lair, two cemeteries, the church display, the mummy's tomb, and several others she couldn't even comprehend.

The one that frightened her most was the dungeon's very own torture chamber. If they chose to do so, visitors would pass through an open, iron door and enter the massive room containing torture devices. Since the room was sectioned off, visitors could opt out of the torture chamber part of the tour. Devon couldn't resist poking her head inside to take a peek. Even though there weren't any wax victims, the chilling devices were enough to send terror through her. There were shackles on the walls, a stretching rack, an iron maiden, a guillotine, and various other equipment she couldn't even guess their painful purpose.

Devon continued on the main walkway toward the very back of the dungeon before finally reaching a door marked 'morgue employees only'. She somehow assumed that was the room she was looking for. Devon knocked on the door. There was no response, but she heard music coming from inside. Devon slowly opened the door and saw an elaborate workshop with several life-like wax men and women crowding the room. Some were dressed in expensive costumes, while others were unclothed, revealing doll-like bodies covered in wax.

The cluttered workshop was filled with wax body parts, looking more like a psychopath's paradise than a workshop. She finally encountered her first live person. A man in a white lab coat sat at the counter with his back to her while holding a paint pen in his hand. She watched while he applied the final touches on a wax head resting on the counter before him.

"Try not to blink," Brant announced then immediately groaned. "Damn it, you moved."

Brant turned on the swivel chair and reached for a rag. He saw Devon and jerked nervously in his chair, accidentally striking the wax head with his elbow. As the wax head teetered, he frantically scrambled to catch it before it fell. He steadied the wax head then stood and faced Devon with a nervous smile. Brant Sheffield was a moderately handsome man in his early thirties with short, dark hair and possibly the darkest eyes she'd ever seen. He was built athletic yet not excessively tall and looked a little like a science teacher in his white lab coat speckled with paint. His reaction to her presence screamed introvert, and his inability to make eye contact revealed his lack of confidence.

"I didn't mean to startle you," Devon announced then pointed beyond the room. "I knocked, but I guess you didn't hear me."

"It's not your fault," he announced then grinned nervously and indicated the workshop. "I'm not used to things moving down here."

"I'm Devon Vincent," she announced while attempting a cheerful tone. "I'm here for a job interview."

She was about to add that she was, in fact, early, but when she glanced at her watch, she realized she was now five minutes late. Wandering through the museum displays must have taken longer than she'd thought.

Brant wiped his hands on a stained rag then approached her with some hesitation, almost as if he thought she might bite, and shook her hand.

"Brant Sheffield. It's a pleasure to meet you," he announced then immediately fumbled over himself while finally making eye contact.

He seemed uncertain how long to hold her hand, which made her somewhat tense. He remained moderately nervous and finally released her hand as if embarrassed that he held it too long.

"Tyler was supposed to be here to interview you, but he was called away early this morning," he explained. "You're Ross' friend, right?"

"Yes," she announced then offered a devious smile, "but don't hold that against me."

Brant chuckled softly and seemed to relax just enough to make her less uncomfortable. He then returned to his wax head, dipped the rag in turpentine, and wiped away the excess paint.

"What do you think of the museum so far?" he asked without looking at her. "I know it's far from finished, but the sets are nearly complete."

"The sets are amazing," she announced. "I thought they were very--" Devon hesitated then held her breath a moment. She exhaled and chuckled almost nervously. "Honestly, your dungeon is pretty terrifying. I nearly turned around when I reached the torture chamber."

He cast a quick glance at her and chuckled almost evilly in his throat. "I'll take that as a compliment." He resumed his work. "I'm terrible with interviews," he informed her and again seemed to be avoiding eye contact with her by working on his creation. "If you're as reliable as Ross says you are, and you don't mind working long hours until we're back on schedule, you can get started tonight, if you're available."

Devon stared at his back with noted surprise then hid her smile. "Yes, of course."

Brant searched for his misplaced paint pen. "Fine. Uh, come back around six o'clock. I'll get you started," he informed her as he found his paint pen. "Ross will be in then." He finally looked back at her, cast a glance at her attire, and appeared almost humored. "You may want to wear old clothes. Paint seems to get on everything around here."

As she eyed his white lab coat covered in paint spatters, she realized he wasn't kidding.

Chapter Six

Devon left the building and walked across the large porch. She had nearly an hour to wait for her brother to pick her up. She hadn't anticipated the interview only lasting two minutes. Calling her brother on his cell phone to pick her up early wasn't really an option since he was running errands. Also, cell phone reception was spotty in the areas outside town. She stared at the vast fields of corn surrounding the museum. It was as if there wasn't another soul alive in the world. She could see a glimpse of the funeral home in the distance from her elevated position on the porch.

Rather than wait an hour in the museum parking lot and risk another conversation with Karl, she decided to walk to the funeral home and see what her friend, Tony O'Brien, was doing. Or in the mortician's case, *whom* he was doing. Devon walked along the back road and took the leisurely walk to the funeral home nearly half a mile away. It was actually further than it looked. She reached the elegant funeral home, which was also Tony's residence, and approached the massive building.

The funeral home was old and lavish with stained glass windows on the first and second floor. A brand new, black hearse was parked in the carport attached to the home. The funeral home consisted of three stories. The entire first floor was devoted to the funeral home business while the second and third floors were Tony's living quarters. Tony bought the business after the old funeral director retired. Despite his young age, Tony had already been operating the funeral home for two years. She tried the front door since it was unlocked most times. Devon entered the foyer, which was filled with flowers.

The funeral home was inviting yet creepy at the same time. To either side of the foyer were sliding, wooden doors leading to a right and left front parlor. If there would be a viewing, they would happen in the two front rooms. Both doors stood open. Devon peered into each room, but neither had been set up for a viewing. She was relieved for that. She hated visiting the funeral home when Tony had *company*.

"Hello?" she called out in the deathly silent home.

There was no response, which immediately set her on edge. Of course, who was she expecting to respond? If Tony were in the back prepping a body, he probably wouldn't hear her. She walked along the quiet corridor and passed several other rooms with the doors open. There was the casket display room with nearly a dozen caskets on display. Most were open, lending a creepy sort of appeal. On the other side was Tony's neat and tidy office, where he greeted loved ones and discussed business. Devon approached the kitchen and was about to push open the door when it suddenly opened, startling her. Tony cried out when he saw her, and she jumped back and did the same.

Tony clutched his chest and stared at her while attempting to catch his breath. Tony wasn't what most women would consider handsome, but he was possibly the sweetest man Devon had ever met. He was tall and lanky, standing well over six-foot-two with dark hair, green eyes, and straight, white teeth.

"Damn it, Devon," he cried out. "Couldn't you have at least announced yourself? Things aren't supposed to move around here."

"I did call out," she protested, although she probably could have called a second time. "And you nearly had me for a client as well."

"Well, now that we've jump started each other's hearts," he announced. "What brings you here? It's not even lunchtime."

"I had a job interview at the museum next door," she informed him. "It took a whole two minutes. I didn't feel like waiting for Martin there, so I thought I'd drop by and give you a fright."

"Ross said he'd got you an interview at the museum," Tony remarked and grinned. "I didn't realize that was today. I was just taking a break while Mr. Malone is on the machine."

Devon knew what that meant. It meant Tony was replacing his client's blood with embalming fluid. She'd seen the process before out of curiosity and didn't care to watch again.

"Did you want some tea or coffee while you wait for Martin?"

"I thought you'd never ask," she teased. "Could I use your phone to call Martin and tell him I'm here? Cell phone service sucks out here."

"You can use the kitchen phone," he replied. "You're not the first person to complain about cell service. I thought when they built the resort, it would mean better service out here."

"No, they put the towers on the other side of the resort closer to the highway," Devon replied. "You know, along with restaurants, gas stations, and shops. They had to make sure that building that monstrosity of a resort just ruined the view but didn't give our town any added revenue."

"Ironic," Tony teased. "The old folks in town didn't want the resort because they feared it would ruin their quiet, little town. Now they're pissed because no one comes to their quiet, little town."

"What's wrong with wanting it both ways?" Devon teased then offered a playful smile.

Tony led her to the kitchen while laughing.

§

A black blazer pulled into the funeral home parking lot and approached Devon near the front door. She hurried off the patio, climbed into the passenger side, and smiled at her brother. Her brother, Martin, was a handsome man in his late twenties. He kept his dark hair neatly trimmed and his commanding blue eyes were enough to lure in the ladies. He stood over six-feet-tall and had just enough muscle mass to be very popular with women. His high paying gig at the nearby resort gave him financial freedom as well.

Where women were concerned, her brother was still testing the waters, so Devon knew it'd be a long time before he brought anyone home to meet the family. Devon admired her brother for getting out there and storming the dating scene. One of them had to be out there working on producing grandchildren for their parents. Devon wasn't in much of a hurry.

Martin eyed her and grinned. "Judging by that smile, I'd say the interview went well."

"I got the job," she announced proudly.

"That's great," he remarked cheerfully then smiled slyly. "Dad's going to be pissed." He added a throaty chuckle. "What's your boss like?"

"He's a little strange," she casually replied. "Nervous type."

"The Norman Bates, psycho killer, nervous type?" Martin suddenly asked while raising demanding brows. "I hope you're not going to be working alone with some pervert."

"Please, Martin," she announced with a groan. "Give the overly protective brother business a break."

"I'm allowed to worry. Men are pigs," he boldly informed her then hesitated and considered the comment. "I should know; I'm one of them."

She playfully slapped his arm as he laughed. "I'm starving," Devon announced. "I was so upset about the interview; I didn't eat this morning. Let's go to the diner for some breakfast."

Martin made a face. "Why don't we go to the resort and have breakfast at one of their restaurants?"

"That's fifteen minutes away," Devon protested. "The diner is right in town."

"Yeah, I know, but Marlene is working this morning," he remarked.

"So?" Devon squawked. "What does that matter? You like Marlene."

"Well, I'm not sure Marlene likes me right now," he informed her then grimaced. "We sort of went out last weekend."

"You took Marlene out?" Devon asked with surprise then raised her brows. "Or you *did* Marlene?"

"Uh, possibly the second one."

Devon rolled her eyes then glared at him. "I thought you said you wouldn't go out with her. You know she has a temper." She then considered the comment and cringed. "Not to mention her brother's temper."

"I know," Martin groaned and allowed his head to fall back against the seat. "I was weak." He turned his head and eyed her while cringing. "I was having a dry spell and gave in to the temptation." He managed a tiny smile. "I'm only human, Devon."

Devon rolled her eyes. "How many times can you use that excuse? It's starting to wear thin," she remarked then shook her head. "So now we can't go to the diner whenever Marlene's working in fear of gourmet condiments on our burgers."

"Just until she finds a new man to piss her off," Martin replied. "Two weeks tops."

Devon shook her head. "Drive, lover boy," she scoffed. "I'm starving." She then eyed him as he put the car into gear. "Oh, and try not to sleep with our waitress at the restaurant."

Martin grinned slyly. "I'll try, but I won't make any promises."

Chapter Seven

Devon's family owned a cattle ranch that had been in her family for generations. The old, large plantation style farmhouse had been restored to its original grandeur, which contained two floors, many windows, and multiple balconies. The ranch had several large barns nestled on more than two hundred acres of land. In addition to several other outer buildings, there was a long cabin of sorts, which was the bunkhouse for the ranch hands. A dozen horses and a few head of cattle grazed within a paddock near the barn. The larger herd was still out in the lush pasture further from the house.

Devon, now changed into jeans and an old shirt, left the house and headed for the paddock. She approached the tall, wooden fence and was immediately greeted by an excited black and white pinto gelding. Devon climbed onto the fence and affectionately patted the horse.

"Hey, boy," she announced cheerfully. "Did you miss me?"

The horse snickered lowly as if answering her. An older cowboy rode up to the fence and stopped his horse near her. Devon's father, Jack, was tall and built solid like her brother. Years of working the ranch had made him strong with an impressive build. There was no doubt that Martin got his good looks from their father. Although his dark hair was grey on the sides and starting to thin, he was still a handsome man. Her father leaned forward in the saddle and grinned at her while tilting the brim of his cowboy hat.

"I've missed you too," she informed the horse while playing with its nose. "No ride tonight though. I have a new job, and I can't be late."

"Do you honestly think he understands what you're saying?" her father teased.

"Every word," she announced in a moderately cold tone without looking at him.

"Martin said you got the job at the museum," he announced and put on a false smile. "I'm glad you found something to keep you busy."

Devon frowned and barely glanced at her father. "Yes, it should keep me far away from the wranglers," she scoffed and climbed off the fence.

Her father immediately frowned at the subject. "We discussed why you can't work the cattle," her father announced firmly.

"Yes, I know," she remarked in a snarky tone. "They're men, and I'm just a girl. I belong barefoot and pregnant in the kitchen like a good, little housewife."

Devon turned and headed back toward the house without giving him a second glance.

"Devon," he called after her. "That's not fair."

She ignored him and continued toward the porch. Martin approached from the house wearing dress pants, a neatly ironed shirt, and a jacket. He looked like the handsome devil he was. Devon looked him over and smiled her approval.

"Hmm. Dressed to kill," she announced cheerfully. "Someone's anticipating a good evening."

"If I'm lucky--right through to a good morning," Martin teased.

"You're such a dog."

Martin nodded to their father who dismounted his horse and headed into the barn. "Piss off the old man again?" he asked.

"As usual."

"So now probably isn't a good time to tell him I won't be helping out this weekend, huh? Good to know." He cast a look at her. "Ivy's on the phone," Martin informed her. "She says it's important. Sounded upset."

"Oh, no," Devon moaned as her expression dropped. "The audition."

"If you need a ride to Ivy's house, the bus leaves in fifteen minutes," Martin informed her.

§

Devon sat on the porch railing and watched Ivy where she sat slumped on the wooden swing looking sedate. Ivy's house was close to town, although still surrounded by cornfields. It was possibly the same cornfield that surrounded the museum and funeral home. Devon had never explored the farmland surrounding her friend's home, so she wasn't sure what property it touched.

"I know Jamie got the job," Ivy moaned. "She was so giggly and flirtatious coming out of the conference room at the hotel." She frowned and gently rocked the swing with her foot. "Do you have any idea what that job would mean?"

"Long hours surrounded by exceptionally large egos?" Devon teased.

"You're funny," Ivy snarled.

"I'll be honest, Ivy," she remarked. "I don't know much about this acting job or why every woman in town is fawning over it."

"Burt Danson, an actual producer from Hollywood, is holding auditions for a long-term role in a soap opera," Ivy informed her. "They're going to be filming a few episodes at the resorts, and they want some local talent to play the part."

"Again," Devon announced. "I don't understand the attraction. It's a part-time gig. A few weeks and it's back to Ivy, bank teller."

"You understand nothing about the industry," Ivy announced with a groan.

Devon raised a skeptical brow. "And you do?"

Ivy rolled her eyes and shook her head at her friend's lack of interest. "If it goes well, the part could turn into a permanent role. It's a way into the industry." She leaned back on the porch swing and groaned. "My first real chance to be someone and that bitch Jamie is going to snatch that job out from under me."

"You don't know she got the job," Devon reminded her. "I mean, she's not exactly talented. You can act circles around her. You were always the lead in the school plays."

"Not always," Ivy scoffed. "Jamie had her share." She groaned with irritation. "I wish she'd fall off the face of the earth."

"No, we're not going back into that dark hole," Devon announced. "I can't go through that voodoo curse book again."

"I'll behave," Ivy muttered.

"Speaking of Jamie--"

Ivy groaned.

"I ran into Karl at the museum today," she announced boldly. "He said he broke it off with her."

Ivy snorted a laugh. "I overheard Jamie telling Paula she'd dumped him."

"Paula Jarred?" she gasped with surprise. "I didn't even know those two were on speaking terms anymore. I thought they had some falling out a few years back after graduation."

"They aren't friends. I think Jamie was just trying to get under Paula's skin," Ivy reported.

"When did you see those two together?" Devon finally asked.

"At the audition. I can't believe Paula, of all people, was auditioning for that acting job," Ivy muttered and shook her head. "I mean, really? The role isn't the part of a hooker. She has zero chance of getting that part."

"Hmm?" Devon remarked while sinking into thought. "So she's actually willing to give up her full-time job as town lush?"

Ivy laughed for the first time and sat up straight on the swing. "Her brother will give her a run for that title." She then eyed her friend. "Did you eat before you came over?"

"No," Devon replied and sighed with defeat. "I wanted to get out of there and avoid another confrontation with my father."

"You should stay for dinner," Ivy announced. "I'll be able to get you to the museum in time."

"I am hungry," Devon replied.

Ivy stared at her friend and sighed. "Don't let your father get to you, Devon," she announced. "He's stubborn and set in his caveman ways."

"It just pisses me off that if I want to work, I have to find a job in town," Devon practically lashed out. "I grew up around the cattle and the wranglers. I can do the job better than most of the men. I should be able to work the ranch."

"I think some of your dad's problems come from Martin refusing to work the ranch," Ivy informed her. "His own son wouldn't do it, so he doesn't want his daughter filling that spot."

"No, that's not it," Devon snapped. "It's because of Jamie's perverted brother, Joe."

"Because *he* harassed *you?*" Ivy suddenly demanded. "That seems like a stupid reason to disqualify you from working the cattle."

"My father liked Joe," Devon remarked. "He was going to replace the foreman one day. Then I report him for what he did, he fires him, and I'm forbidden from working the ranch. You know, because the guys might realize I'm a girl and get all hot and bothered."

"Your father's concerned for your safety," Ivy announced. "I don't think he's worried about the boys getting a hard-on around his daughter and acting out their uncontrollable desire."

"It's actually the same difference," Devon remarked. "He's not so much worried about me. He doesn't want to risk losing more hard working perverts. Keeping me away from them is his best solution to avoiding a future problem."

"You've never had a problem with them before," Ivy announced. "You're not exactly a china doll. I've seen you handle those guys on their own level. I don't understand the problem."

"I've given up trying to understand it myself," she muttered.

"You can handle a little harmless flirting from the guys. What Joe did was reprehensible on every level," Ivy announced. "He should have been fired. Your father should realize the difference."

"You can't explain anything to my father," she remarked. "He thinks I should get married, pop out a few kids, and be a housewife." Devon shifted uncomfortably. "Not that I knock my mother for the life she chose, but I don't want to spend the rest of my life being maid and cook to everyone else."

Ivy drew a deep breath and sighed. "Sadly, that's the reality for most women in this town," she remarked. "If I don't get that part in the soap opera, I know I'm going to end up working at the bank the rest of my life. I can get a head start waiting on others before moving on to waiting on a husband and kids." Ivy sneered at the thought. "I have to get out of this one-horse town before that happens."

"You and me both," Devon muttered.

Chapter Eight

That evening, Devon walked through the museum dungeon and past the phantom display on her way to the workshop. She paused to study the partially finished exhibit. She found it surprising that the phantom was already finished and set in place since she didn't recall seeing the menacing, disfigured killer even started. The life-like wax phantom was seated before the old pipe organ, which was possibly an antique they'd purchased along the way. She nervously approached the display with a curious look and walked around the side of the phantom with its back to her.

The phantom was dressed mostly in black, including black boots and fedora boldly tilted on its head. The purple cape with black liner was elegantly positioned over its shoulder, giving the phantom an almost regal appearance. According to legend, the phantom was more or less a refined killer, suavely stalking its prey. As she got closer, she looked at the phantom's profile and the white mask covering nearly three-quarters of its face. It was a terrifying image. Devon was curious if Brant had made his face disfigured beneath the mask. She wasn't sure why, but she felt curious enough to take a peek. Devon hesitated and reached for the mask just to see if it could be removed and what lie beneath.

The phantom suddenly turned and lunged for her. Devon jumped backward with a loud, startled scream. The phantom removed the white mask, revealing the man beneath it. Her friend, Ross, laughed at her expense. Devon's expression dropped as she stared at her friend in the costume. She angrily slapped him on the shoulder, causing him to yelp.

"Damn it," she cried out in a shrill tone. "You scared me!"

"That was the whole idea," Ross teased while adding an evil chuckle.

Ross Conners was a tall, slightly round man just a year older than Devon. With his dark, moderately wavy hair, he had the look of a practical joker. He wasn't the most handsome man, but he had enough personality to make friends with nearly everyone. He definitely gave the impression of a big kid, especially with his lack of maturity and non-existence seriousness. Ross looked past Devon, fidgeted slightly, and offered a nervous smile.

"Uh, hey, Mr. Brook."

Devon turned to see Tyler Brook standing not far from the scene. Brant's business partner, Tyler, was a serious, sophisticated looking man in his late forties. His sandy brown hair was kept businessman short, he was meticulously clean-shaven, and he wore an expensive suit. Tyler was by no means unattractive, but he had a definite snob appeal about him. Brant, dressed in his finest paint speckled lab coat, stood a few feet behind his business partner and wiped his hands on a dirty rag.

Tyler, seeming more like a high school principal, glared his disapproval over Ross' behavior. "Are you finished fooling around?"

"Yes, sir," Ross announced with his head lowered like a whipped dog.

"Then remove that costume before you ruin it and put it back in the wardrobe closet," Tyler ordered. "There's plenty of work to be done."

Ross removed the cloak, flashed a tiny smirk at Devon, and hurried away. Despite being yelled at, his sly grin revealed it had been worth it to see the look on Devon's face.

Tyler turned toward Devon and smiled more cheerfully. "I hope Ross didn't give you too much of a scare," he announced then sighed shamefully. "He can be a bit over-the-top."

"I'm used to it," she replied while hiding her smile. "We've been friends a long time."

"Sorry I missed our interview this morning," he announced then nodded to Brant. "You've already met my business partner, Brant."

"Yes."

"Brant's more of the artist than I am, so he'll be instructing you on what he wants you to do," Tyler announced then fidgeted and looked at his watch with disappointment. "I don't mean to be rude, but I must return to the city tonight."

"I understand," she replied. "It was a pleasure meeting you, Mr. Brook."

"It's Tyler," he informed her and smiled pleasantly. "Despite what Ross says, we aren't formal around here." He then looked at Brant. "Did you mention our field trip on Thursday?"

"No, I was getting to that," Brant replied.

"Good," Tyler announced then smiled at Devon. "I'll see you Thursday morning."

She watched as Tyler hurried off to his important business in the city. Brant's eyes followed him until he was gone and showed little emotion. He briefly glanced back at Devon then turned and walked away from the phantom display.

"I'll get you started in the back," Brant announced as he walked away.

Devon realized she was supposed to be following him and hurried after him. She caught up to him and walked alongside him, although he didn't look at her.

"What field trip on Thursday?" Devon asked now curious.

"Tyler has been tirelessly seeking props and furniture for the displays," Brant informed her. "He found an old wax museum a few hours from here and arranged to buy most of their inventory, including some wax people. We're renting a moving truck to bring whatever we find back with us. We'll need you and Ross to assist with the move." He finally glanced at her and managed a smile. "Don't worry; we have movers for the heavy lifting. We're mostly responsible for crating the wax figures, so they aren't destroyed before we get them back here. Even if they're only in semi-decent shape, refurbishing them will save us a lot of time and work on creating all new wax figures. The process is a long undertaking, and he's anxious to get the museum up and running on schedule."

"Hmm, sounds like fun," she announced cheerfully while observing Brant's profile.

Brant gave her a humored look and flashed a smile. It was the first time she'd actually seen him smile since he seemed reluctant to look at her. She hadn't realized how handsome he actually was. In her opinion, he needed to smile more often.

"I'm glad you think so," he announced as if holding back some secret as to why she shouldn't be excited about their field trip. "You'll be in charge of bubble wrap."

"Bubble wrap?" She raised a skeptical brow. It didn't sound like much of a challenge. "What exactly does that entail?" she asked not sure she understood her bizarre assignment.

"Just the way it sounds," he replied simply. "Your job is to keep Ross away from the bubble wrap. It's to be used for packing; not popping."

Devon hid her smile and held back her laugh. She wasn't sure if he meant it to sound as funny as it did, but she knew Ross too well.

Chapter Nine

Devon sat on a stool beside Brant before the counter within the moderately cluttered workshop. There were several wax heads lined along the table waiting for their hair, eyes, and makeup. Devon had been slightly distracted at first, eyeing the horde of wax men and women standing and crouching in odd positions not far from the counter. Every single one seemed to be staring at her. Although there were plenty of normal looking wax men and women, some of the others were slightly creepy, possibly for the horror displays.

She found herself staring at some poor, unfortunate wax man with anguish on his face where he lay on the floor with his arms stretched above his head. What was particularly disturbing was that he had no lower half to his body. Brant implanted strands of hair onto the female wax head before them. It was a slow process involving one strand of hair at a time with the use of something resembling a large needle on a pen. He handed her the pointy instrument and watched while she mimicked what he'd done. Judging by how long the process took, Devon realized it would probably take all day just to insert the hair onto one head.

"Why don't you use wigs?" she asked.

"We do on the minor characters," he replied, "but I like our 'stars' to look as realistic as possible. Doing a wax head right is an art form and it takes days even weeks to do it properly. It's not a sprint; it's a marathon."

She again eyed the partial wax man on the floor and shifted uncomfortably. "I have to ask," she finally announced. "Why is there only a top half to that wax man?"

Brant didn't even bother looking since he obviously knew which unfortunate soul she referenced. "Oh, that's just Oscar."

"Oscar?" she asked then shook her head as if he were not just toying with her for the fun of it.

"Yeah," Brant replied. "Oscar's going on the rack next week. I need to add some guts and torn flesh before he's complete." He gave a casual nod across the room. "His bottom half is over there."

Devon stared at Brant's profile a moment while considering the 'rack' comment. She glanced across the room and finally saw Oscar's bottom half, which contained part of his spine, torn flesh, and some intestines. She nearly gasped at the sight. Oscar was the stretching rack victim! Devon cringed and returned her attention to her work.

"What did poor Oscar do to deserve the rack?" she remarked in as serious a tone as she could manage.

Brant cast a look at her and immediately hid his smile. "He was my last assistant, but it didn't work out," he teased.

It was Devon's turn to look at Brant, but he had already resumed his work while grinning, obviously pleased with himself. She was almost relieved to discover Brant actually had a sense of humor. Ross poked his head into the workshop and looked around.

"Is he gone?"

"Yes, he's gone," Brant announced with a moderately disgusted sigh as his good mood vanished.

Ross was relieved and entered the workshop. He approached the counter, leaned on Devon's shoulder, and watched with childlike fascination as she worked.

"He was in a foul mood tonight," Ross huffed then cast a look at Brant and appeared sympathetic. "Don't let him get to you, Brant."

"He hasn't," Brant replied then eyed Ross. "Just make sure you have that display finished before you leave tonight. I don't want to hear him complain again."

"Consider it done," Ross announced cheerfully. "Just keep the troll off my back."

Devon refrained from commenting as the two men complained about Tyler. Obviously, neither man cared much for him.

§

Devon pushed a handcart containing a wax woman wearing a dress from the late 1700's across Dr. Frankenstein's lab. She paused and looked at the detailed lab display. It looked like a real tower laboratory complete with fake stone walls and floors. There were electronic machines, a false skylight, and a slanted table with a sheet covered monster strapped to it. The eerie silence was broken by low moaning. Lightning suddenly flashed beyond the fake skylight, and a large bolt of electric current sizzled and flashed between two circuits. Devon looked around with surprise. The monster suddenly moved beneath the sheet and pulled against the straps. Devon gasped with surprise when she saw the covered creature move. Ross jumped out from behind the table and laughed.

"Cool, huh?"

Devon glanced at the display and marveled at the details. "It's fabulously creepy."

"This place is going to be freakin' awesome." Ross then eyed the wax woman on the handcart. "Hey, this looks great," he announced. "You do this one?"

"Just the makeup, and it only took me four hours," Devon announced proudly while mocking herself.

Ross chuckled and leaned on her shoulder. "It takes time even after you've mastered it," he informed her. "As Brant likes to say, it's not a sprint; it's a marathon."

"Yes, he's already used that line on me," she remarked with a laugh. "Brant makes it look so easy."

"Yeah, he's into his art," Ross announced. "He's a real workaholic. It's a good thing too since his business partner is a slave driver."

"Sounds like their partnership isn't exactly fifty-fifty," she remarked.

"I love Brant to death, but he's a bit of a pushover," Ross informed her. "He needs to stand up to Tyler. Thankfully, Tyler doesn't spend a lot of time here. He's into his fancy parties with his wealthy friends. We shouldn't see much of him."

Chapter Ten

The rental truck was already parked outside the old, dilapidated wax museum located on some back road in a rural town that didn't even show up on GPS. Tyler's expensive, black BMW pulled into the cracked parking lot that contained nearly as much grass as macadam. The wax museum itself appeared to have been out of business for years. The sign was almost faded beyond recognition, and the stone siding was falling off in chunks. Tyler and Brant got out of the front of the car while Ross and Devon got out of the back. Ross and Devon exchanged wide-eyed looks. They followed their bosses with less enthusiasm toward the creepy building.

"I'm suddenly very afraid," Ross announced and linked onto Devon's arm for protection.

She pulled her arm away from him and managed a smile, but she feared he wasn't joking.

"Where the hell did Tyler find this place?" Ross muttered to Devon.

"I don't even know how he found the town," Devon responded.

They followed their bosses into the building and were nearly floored by the condition of the interior. If they had paid admission to a haunted house, Devon would have been impressed. As it was, she was skeptical. The old displays were covered with years of dust and cobwebs. To their dismay, the wax figures were still within their respective scenes. It was a creepy undertaking to pack them up, especially in their current condition. Thankfully, the wax men and woman were intact. Once they were disrobed and the cobwebs sucked from their hair, they would be salvageable. It would be a lot of work but still less than creating them from scratch.

Two burly moving men appeared in the hallway rolling two, six by three crates strapped to an appliance dolly. They stopped a few feet from Tyler and indicated the crates.

"We have the first six already on the truck," the first man announced.

"That was fast," Brant remarked with surprise. "What time did you guys arrive that you were able to pack so many already?"

"They were already in the crates when we got here," the mover informed him.

"The owner said he'd try to pack some up for us," Tyler remarked then nodded with approval. "That only leaves twenty. Makes our job easier." Tyler turned to Ross and Devon. "Why don't the two of you start crating up the rest of our lovelies while Brant and I see what else we can salvage from the displays?"

Ross immediately pointed to the first display containing an old-fashioned, horse-drawn hearse with glass sides for viewing the casket inside. Old, dusty silk flowers garnished the casket encased in the hearse.

"Can we have that?" he eagerly asked.

Devon nodded with approval and grinned. "That is pretty cool."

"I suppose that would be an interesting addition to the dungeon displays," Tyler replied.

Ross excitedly clapped his hands together then held them in the air. "Yes."

"As long as it's not completely rotted," Tyler warned him. "I don't want to waste too much time on that thing if it's just going to fall apart while we move it."

Ross nodded in agreement. They watched Tyler and Brant walk through the museum while checking out the other displays. Ross immediately ran into the old cemetery display and checked out the old-fashioned hearse with childlike enthusiasm. Devon joined him and helped check for rot and decay.

"Wax museums are creepy by themselves," she informed Ross then looked around. "This one is in a whole other realm of creepy."

As she looked around the old museum, she heard a loud creak. When she looked to where Ross had been standing, he was gone.

"Ross?"

She glanced beneath the hearse but he wasn't there. She straightened and saw Ross inside the back behind the glass with the casket. His face was pressed against the glass while he pawed at her like a demented zombie. She rolled her eyes.

"Enough goofing around before you break it," she scolded.

Ross climbed out of the back, creating the most hideous creaking sound from the old display. Devon approached the wax horse hitched to the hearse. She admired the leather harness and the dirty but elegant plume attached to the top of the bridle between the horse's ears. She studied the black horse caked with dirt and cobwebs. The horse was almost a requirement for the rest of the display. Once cleaned, the set would look amazing. She ran her hand along the horse's realistic coat and approached the head to take a better look at the decorative bridle. Being into horses, she was completely captivated by saddles, bridles, and other leather rigging.

"Must have been quite the undertaking making a wax horse," Devon announced to Ross, who was somewhere behind her. "It's so realistic."

"I should probably--" Ross began as she reached the front of the horse.

Devon checked out the horse's bridle and immediately saw a large portion of the shoulder had pulled away revealing actual bone. Devon cried out, jumped backward, and tripped over a fake tombstone. She stared at the horse while screaming and attempted to get her footing within the fake moss. Ross grabbed her under the arm and pulled her to her feet. She backed into Ross and stared at the horse while panting with horror.

"They, uh, use stuffed horses," Ross remarked delicately.

She looked back at him with horror clearly on her face. "Oh, shit," she cried out while attempting to turn her fear into anger. "That's disgusting!"

"I'm not a fan of taxidermy myself," Ross replied then shook his head. "But that's how they do it."

Devon eyed the horse then looked back at Ross and shook her head. "Uh, uh. No way," she cried out. "There's no way we're displaying that poor, dead creature. I'm already freaked out!"

Tyler and Brant ran toward the display and stared at them.

"We heard screaming," Brant announced and looked around. "Is everyone okay?"

Ross picked fake moss from Devon's hair and managed a smile. "Uh, yeah," he announced. "We're fine. Just Devon's first time seeing a horse, uh, well, in that condition."

"Well, a word of warning," Tyler announced. "If you see any wax rats, don't touch them. They're not wax, and they will bite." He eyed the display and sank into thought. "We're going to need a flatbed cart to move that horse, I'm afraid. Looks pretty heavy. Maybe the movers have one."

Tyler headed for the front door to chase after the two moving men. Devon vigorously shook her head.

"No way," she practically cried out as anxiety filled her. She looked back at the horse and immediately looked away. "I'm not getting near that thing. I can't even look at it without wanting to throw up."

Ross leaned closer to her ear and whispered, "Not your call, Devon. Play it cool."

"No, absolutely not," she cried out, catching Brant's attention.

Brant walked onto the display and joined them several feet from the horse. He stared at Devon with a curious look.

"What's going on?" Brant asked.

"She's a little freaked by the horsey," Ross remarked. "She'll be fine."

"No, I won't," Devon snapped at Ross then pulled away and hurried from the scene. "I don't want to be anywhere near that. It's not right."

Brant and Ross hurried after her. Ross immediately attempted to smooth things over with Brant.

"I'll talk to her," he announced. "She'll be fine, I promise."

Brant ignored him and stopped Devon near the door. "What's wrong, Devon?"

She stared at him with surprise. "What's wrong? There's a dead horse on display! How could someone do that?"

"We'll work through it, Brant," Ross insisted. "She'll be fine. Just let me take her outside for a few minutes for some fresh air."

She glared at Ross while enraged. "Stop saying I'll be fine!"

Tyler entered the museum while beaming with delight. "We're in luck," he announced cheerfully. "They have a flatbed cart. I'm pretty sure it'll take four of us to load it though."

"We're not taking the horse," Brant informed Tyler, surprising him.

"What?" Tyler asked. "Why not? We don't have one to use with the hearse."

Brant straightened proudly. "Because it's a taxidermy horse, and it's already falling apart," he announced. "I can't fix taxidermy, and I don't trust that it was done properly. Who knows what sort of vile little creatures are infesting that thing. As a former scientist, I don't want to run that risk."

Tyler stared at Brant a moment then shrugged. "Fine," he announced with little hesitation. "I'm sure you'll think of some way to display the hearse without the horse. Come on. We have a lot of work to do."

Tyler continued through the museum. Brant remained behind and looked at Devon while offering a tiny, reassuring smile.

"Better?" he asked.

Devon insecurely rubbed her arms and managed a smile. "Yes, thank you." She fidgeted slightly. "I know I've already caused you enough grief, but could I ask for another favor? A big one."

Ross stood alongside Devon in the rear parking lot not far from the back door. They watched the stuffed horse burn among several old crates and boxes. Devon insecurely rubbed her arms but smiled with relief.

"Rest in peace, big fella."

Ross placed his arm around her shoulder and pulled her against him. He ran his knuckles across the top of her head, rumpling her hair while she squirmed to free herself from his clutches.

"You are one freaky, psycho chick," he informed her then kissed the top of her head. "But I love you anyway."

Chapter Eleven

An older, red sports car pulled into the driveway of a charming, smaller two-story home within the quiet town. Twenty-three-year-old Jamie Smyth parked the car and headed into the house. She was still the same beautiful young woman from her teenage years but now a few years older. Her blonde hair was a little shorter, her makeup a little lighter, and her clothes not quite as revealing but twice as expensive. Jamie entered the house and headed for the stairs without greeting her mother, who was sitting in the living room. Dorothy looked up from her newspaper and immediately gave her daughter a disapproving, raised brow.

"Not even going to say hello?" Dorothy remarked in an almost scolding tone.

Dorothy hadn't changed much in seven years. Her hair was still worn up in the same granny bun, although it contained more gray than it had. Jamie frowned while throwing her head back. She then turned and headed back into the living room where her mother sat in her usual chair closest to the light. Jamie smirked with something resembling loathe.

"Hello, mother," she announced in an insincere polite tone.

Dorothy didn't let her daughter's tone or lack of interest interrupt her evening. "How was work?" she asked while setting her newspaper aside.

"Sucked," Jamie huffed.

"Jamie," she scoffed while looking above her reading glasses at her. "Don't talk like that. It's not becoming of a young woman."

Jamie groaned at the comment.

Dorothy looked across the room and smiled cheerfully. "Chelsea, Jamie's home," she announced.

Jamie glanced across the room to the tall-backed wheelchair in its usual place near the large, bay window. Chelsea sat partially reclined in her wheelchair and stared at nothing with the same blank expression she'd maintained for the last seven years. Jamie fidgeted and appeared uncomfortable while catching an eyeful of her sister. Chelsea looked more like a child's doll than a young woman. Her once long, blonde hair was cut shoulder length and lacked its radiant shine from her teenage years. Her mother used excessive amounts of makeup on her face to hide the fact that she was flaccid and nearly void of life. She wore a gaudy flower print dress with lace trim resembling old-fashioned doilies around the neckline and sleeves. Her ensemble was completed with a large, fake pearl necklace.

Jamie folded her arms across her chest and looked back at her mother. "She doesn't care, mom," she scoffed. "She doesn't even know I'm here. Hell, she doesn't even know she's here."

Her mother frowned and glared at Jamie. "The doctors said it's possible she hears and understands everything we're saying," Dorothy insisted. "Until someone proves otherwise, we'll speak to her as if she understands us."

"Then do her a favor and don't let her see herself in a mirror," Jamie scoffed while raising a cocky brow, "because that dress is hideous."

Jamie turned and headed up the stairs. Dorothy watched her disappear then shook her head and returned her attention to her newspaper.

"Your sister hasn't changed much," Dorothy informed Chelsea. "Still charming as always."

§

Jamie entered her bedroom and immediately shut and locked the door. She tossed her purse onto a nearby chair and flopped onto the bed with her cell phone already to her ear. She groaned when voicemail picked up.

"Hey, it's me," she announced into her cell phone. "Give me a call. I can almost guarantee I got that acting job."

She disconnected the call then turned on the television by the remote control. There was a soft tap against the window, startling her. Jamie looked at the window with some surprise then saw who it was and frowned. She jumped off the bed and pulled the curtain the rest of the way back to reveal Karl in the window. He motioned for her to open the window. She groaned in disgust and opened it. Karl immediately climbed through the window and entered her room.

"Took you long enough to get upstairs," he bluntly informed her. "I must have been standing on that trellis for ten minutes."

Jamie folded her arms across her chest and glared at him. "We're not dating anymore, Karl," she launched hotly. "You don't get to sneak through my window like that."

Karl grinned then walked past her and flopped onto her bed, making himself comfortable. "And yet here I am," he announced.

"Get out, Karl," she ordered while pointing to the window.

He folded his hands across his abdomen and smiled innocently. "I came to talk, and I'm pretty sure you can't make me leave."

"No, but I can scream or call the police on your ass," she snapped.

"Then I get to tell your mother how I routinely snuck through your window for our nightly romps," he replied while grinning.

Jamie sneered at him. She didn't seem to care for that option. "What do you want, Karl?"

He sat up on the edge of the bed and attempted to pull her against him by grabbing her around the hips while also helping himself to a handful of her buttocks. She forcibly removed his hands from her backside and took a step away from him.

"That's not happening," she informed him. "We broke up. That means you don't get to put your hands on me anymore." She again folded her arms across her chest and glared at him. "If you're finished begging me to take you back, I'd like you to leave now."

Karl stood and waved her off. "Maybe it's for the best," he announced while heading toward the window. "Devon Vincent started working at the museum, and she's always had a thing for me. I wouldn't mind banging her. There's a real chance she's an actual virgin. If I'm dating you, I can't pop her cherry."

He was about to slip out the window when Jamie groaned with disgust and grabbed his arm, stopping him. As he turned, she grabbed him by the back of the neck and kissed him passionately. Her free hand grabbed his crotch with a little added vigor. He yelped slightly then pulled her roughly into his arms and practically yanked her pants down before tackling her to the bed.

Chapter Twelve

It was Friday morning. Devon entered the museum workshop a few minutes early for her shift but was surprised when she didn't find anyone working. She wasn't that early, and Brant was always there, it seemed. She looked around feeling slightly discouraged then saw a note on the counter. Devon picked up the note.

"Follow the werewolf," she read aloud then set the note down and groaned. "Great."

She looked around the workshop then noticed cut out paw prints on the floor. They headed out of the workshop. Another one of Ross' games. She cautiously followed the paw prints from the workshop, passed several displays, and headed into the graveyard scene. The frighteningly realistic set was dimly lit with tombstones, fake grass, and a massive crypt in the background. She heard a crack of thunder as the dark sky lit up. It was immediately followed by low moans. Devon jumped nervously and looked around with concern. She was almost certain Ross intended to scare her again, so she braced herself and anticipated something jumping out at her from behind the tombstones. The ground beneath her feet broke open, and zombies rose from the fake ground. Devon jumped with surprise then let out a startled scream. She immediately relaxed and rolled her eyes.

"Ross," she scoffed under her breath.

A zombie suddenly lunged at her from behind the tree. Devon screamed louder this time and jumped backward. Although she immediately recognized Ross beneath the horror makeup and torn clothing, she couldn't help but take another step away. A decayed hand fell upon her shoulder. Devon screamed and spun around. Brant smiled while holding the fake hand and waved it at her. Ross grabbed her from behind while groaning loudly and bit her neck. She screamed again, having felt his teeth against her skin, and pulled away from him. She turned and playfully beat him with her palms.

"You jerk!"

Brant removed a remote control from his lab coat pocket, stopping the sounds and movements with the push of a button. He replaced the remote control to his pocket and smiled with embarrassment.

"Sorry," Brant announced timidly. "I couldn't resist playing along."

"You're just as bad as he is," she announced while shaking her head.

"I'm teaching him well," Ross teased. "Besides, you have a beautiful scream."

"Thanks," she muttered. "I think."

"Okay," Brant announced while hiding his smile. "Playtime is over. Back to work."

Ross gave his best zombie moan and shuffled his way back to the workshop. Devon rolled her eyes and shook her head then realized Brant was staring at her with a strange smile.

"I really am sorry," he remarked although his smile told a different story.

"Remember that when I return the favor one day," she announced then rubbed her neck and frowned. "That bastard actually bit me."

§

Devon sat before the counter in the workshop and carefully painted a wax woman's face with the paint pens while Brant stared over her shoulder, critiquing her work. She felt she was getting the hang of makeup, which was particularly amusing since she didn't wear any herself. She found Brant hovering over her a little intimidating at first, but he wore some expensive cologne that she found very pleasing.

"Much better," Brant announced cheerfully. "After lunch, I'll show you the horror makeup. Blood, puss, and all that good stuff. I'd like to finish Oscar and get him situated on his rack."

Devon held back her laugh and avoided looking at Brant. "You really get into this, don't you?"

"A lot better than my former job."

She became curious and eyed him. "What did you do before you got into horror wax?"

"I was a scientist," he replied with little enthusiasm. "I worked in a lab with my parents. Nice, sterile, cold environment."

"Definitely a big change for you."

"Working with my parents wasn't a good idea," he informed her. "Tyler got me into wax, so to speak. He had a museum a few years back, but everything was destroyed in a fire. When he found this place, he decided to rebuild his wax museum. That's when he rescued me from my parents. Not much warmth in my family."

"I can't say I have that problem," she remarked then laughed. "Almost the opposite. My brother is completely smothering." She then considered the comment and made a face. "My father, on the other hand, could learn to step back a little."

"Is he smothering the same as your brother?" Brant asked.

"No, not the same as my brother," she replied with some irritation. "My father is smothering because he doesn't think women should have jobs outside the house and raising a family."

"Really? Not in my family," Brant informed her. "My sister is expected to achieve just as much as I do." He seemed to reconsider that comment. "Actually, they expect more from her, since she has a higher IQ. No free passes in my family."

"Is she a scientist too?"

"Yes, it was expected of us," he replied with a defeated sigh then shook his head. "I can't tell you how disappointed they are with me." There was a hint of a smirk on his face. "When I quit the lab and invested in this place a year ago, you would think the world had ended." He suddenly laughed while sitting down alongside her. "On the bright side, it's turned their matchmaking down a notch or two. Since they can't brag about my profession anymore, they don't bring as many future brides home to meet me."

She turned on her rolling chair and stared at him with surprise. "They're pushing you to get married?" she gasped.

"Every chance they get," he remarked.

Devon immediately frowned, knowing how that felt. "My father thinks I should be married, barefoot, and pregnant too," she informed him. "I get so angry with him."

"In my family, it's my mother pushing for grandchildren," he remarked with little emotion. "I'm afraid my sister and I have been very disappointing in that respect too." He drew a deep breath then sighed. "I'd love to give you some inspirational talk about dealing with your father, but I can't even stand up to my own family, so I'm the last one to give out any advice."

She studied him a moment and marveled at the transformation in just a few days. He was finally comfortable enough to look her in the eyes and not act so nervous around her. He must have figured out she wasn't going to bite him. For a brief moment, she stared back at him. Her thoughts immediately strayed to how handsome he looked in his lab coat. She could definitely see the scientist from his past. Perhaps a little geeky in the nerdy genius sort of way, but she definitely classified him as datable.

It had been a while since she'd been interested in dating anyone. She'd always been attracted to cowboys, but her father's ranch hands always seemed to crush her fantasies with their drifter lifestyle talk. Devon snapped out of her trance and realized she and Brant had been staring into each other's eyes a little too long without anyone speaking.

"Hey, hey," Ross cried out from the doorway. "Lunch has arrived!"

Both jumped as if they'd been caught doing something they shouldn't have been doing. They turned on their stools and saw Ross enter the workshop holding up two paper bags. Tony followed him into the room.

"Tony," Devon announced with enthusiasm, surprised to see him. "What are you doing here?"

"I'm the official delivery boy," Tony teased.

"A mortician that delivers," Brant remarked with a hint of humor then grimaced at the comment. "Sounds a little creepy to me."

"What's this?" Tony announced while eyeing Brant with surprise. "Dr. Sheffield acquired a sense of humor? Will the wonders never cease?"

"I'm training him well," Ross teased. "He's a work in progress."

"Don't train him too well," Tony remarked and indicated the paper bags. "I'm not springing for lunch every day."

Ross grabbed his sandwich from the bag. "I'll pay you back one day."

"I hear that every other day," Tony remarked with a defeated sigh. "I doubt I'll ever see a cent of that money." Tony approached the small refrigerator, looked inside, and then eyed the guys. "What? No beverage?" he demanded as he straightened. "Who was in charge of drinks? Come on, guys. I bring food. You can't expect me to spring for everything."

"There's more soda upstairs," Brant informed him. "No one died."

"I'll get the soda," Devon offered.

Chapter Thirteen

Devon entered the kitchen through the door marked 'private'. It was a shortcut from the workshop to the kitchen. There was also a rear entrance to the museum basement, which allowed for deliveries, particularly of bigger items. The construction workers from outside were sitting around the kitchen table having their lunch. Karl helped himself to a soda from the refrigerator then noticed Devon as she entered.

"I heard you got the job," Karl teased.

"Yeah," she replied while hiding her smile. "Working with Ross is like working in a cartoon strip."

Devon opened the refrigerator and removed four cans of soda.

Karl hovered over her while uncomfortably close, giving the appearance of a hungry wolf. "We should go out tonight and celebrate your new job," he informed her as if it were already decided. "We'll go to the new nightclub at the resorts. I hear it's wild on Friday nights."

Devon fidgeted and wondered how many times she'd have to turn Karl down before he took the hint. "I can't," she informed him. "I have plans with Ivy."

"We'll all go together," he insisted while grinning. "I'll find her a date."

Devon could only imagine which of his crazy friends he would pick for Ivy. "We've already made other plans," she replied in a firm tone.

The four construction workers at the table snickered lowly, possibly enjoying seeing their co-worker shot down. Karl appeared irritated by their mocking snickers. He placed his hand on the counter on either side of Devon, trapping her against the counter.

"I don't think you get it, Devon," he announced while grinning slyly. "I'm giving you a-once-in-a-lifetime opportunity to go out with the most popular man in town. Since you're not my usual type, I'd think you'd jump at the offer."

She wondered if he even heard himself when he spoke. Perhaps he felt he was paying her a compliment or doing her a favor.

"Ego check, Karl," she snapped hotly. "I'm not interested in you, and I never will be. Peddle your once-in-a-lifetime opportunity to someone else."

The guys burst out laughing, which only irritated Karl further. He grabbed her arm forcing the soda cans to fall to the floor. For a brief moment, she froze. The incident in the barn with Joe came flooding back in a horrible tidal wave of fear.

"You're being rude," he snarled.

As she stared into his eyes, mildly panic-stricken, something inside her suddenly snapped. Devon yanked her arm free from Karl and violently shoved him back a step. The other workers stared in silence, no longer finding the situation funny.

"Keep your fucking hands off me, Price," she shouted in anger.

"What's going on here?" Brant suddenly demanded, surprising everyone.

Karl looked at Brant within the kitchen doorway and attempted a casual smile. The four construction workers collected their lunches, leaped up from their chairs, and practically bolted from the kitchen.

"Devon and I were just talking," Karl informed him while attempting to laugh it off.

"And if this conversation ever comes up again, you'll be doing it with a broken nose," Devon lashed out in anger at the egotistical man.

Brant looked from Devon to Karl with a stern glare. "I don't know what you said to her, but I suggest you get out of my museum."

"You can't be serious," Karl announced with a nervous laugh.

"Would you like me to call Larry and have him remove you?" Brant demanded.

Karl became irritated then turned and pointed a warning finger at Devon's face. "If I lose my job over this, you'll be sorry."

Brant suddenly grabbed Karl's wrist, twisted his arm behind his back, and slammed him face first onto the kitchen table. The table squeaked as it moved from the force. Brant leaned over Karl's shoulder while keeping him painfully pinned to the table.

"Don't threaten my employees," Brant growled into his ear. "If you so much as look at her wrong, we'll finish this conversation in the emergency room."

Brant released Karl's wrist and took a step back. Karl immediately straightened and spun to face Brant. A tense moment passed, as it appeared Karl would retaliate since he had the size advantage. The moment was short-lived, and he seemed to think better of it.

"Now get out," Brant snarled.

Karl gave Brant a dirty look and hurried from the kitchen. Brant shook his head with irritation then looked at

Devon, who could do little more than stare at her boss with her mouth hanging open.

"Are you okay?" Brant asked.

"What the hell was that?" she practically gasped, unable to believe what she'd just witnessed.

"What was what?" he asked with surprise.

"You took Karl down like a deranged ninja," she announced while staring at him.

"That was a basic self-defense move," he informed her. "If I went ninja on him, they'd be scraping him off my kitchen floor."

"You can do that?" she gasped.

"I was the rich, geeky kid in school," he casually replied while sighing. "If my father hadn't made me take karate, I'd probably still be trying to escape my gym locker." He tilted his head while staring at her. "Are you okay?"

"Yeah, I'm fine," she replied then picked up the discarded soda cans.

She attempted to hold the cans, but she was shaking too badly. Brant took the cans from her and set them on the counter.

"It's okay," he announced gently while staring into her eyes. "He's gone."

"I know," she replied while placing a trembling hand to her forehead. "It's just--" She groaned and shook her head. "I used to handle that sort of thing better. After a similar incident with one of my father's ranch hands, I just feel like everything inside freezes. It's like I lost the ability to defend myself."

"I thought you handled yourself rather well," Brant remarked. He offered a tiny smile then casually shrugged. "You really didn't need me interfering. I just have a short fuse and an explosive temper."

"I don't always feel as if I'm in control of my life anymore." She folded her arms insecurely across her chest and fidgeted. "Pretty stupid, huh?"

"No, it makes sense," he informed her and leaned against the counter. "Broken trust; decreased confidence; anger with no outlet. It's as if you've already met my mother."

Devon eyed him a moment then felt herself relax and smile. Both laughed. Brant collected the cans of soda and indicated the basement door.

"Come on. We should get back downstairs," he announced with an odd seriousness. "Before Ross eats both our lunches."

Chapter Fourteen

It was late afternoon by the time Ross and Devon were finally able to set up the wax figures in the phantom display. The display was coming together nicely and was close to being finished. The phantom was seated before his pipe organ in a menacing pose while a woman lay unconscious on a fainting couch. Devon added some final touches to the unconscious wax woman then frowned and pulled a cobweb from her blonde hair.

"Those thirty wax figures we got from that closed museum were a godsend," Devon announced then shook her head. "But they're still dusty as hell."

"You should do what I did," Ross announced while sitting on the bench alongside the phantom and pretended to play the organ. "Take their wigs outside and beat them against the side of the building."

Devon eyed the wax woman a moment then uncertainly tugged on her scalp. With some effort, the blonde wig lifted, almost startling her. There was a residue left around her waxy, bald head, which was a mild glue meant to hold the wig in place. Devon sighed with relief then laughed nervously.

"I thought I was going to rip the whole face off for a minute there," she announced. "Brant's better creations have hair implanted right into the wax."

Ross stood and turned to face her. He held his hand up. She tossed him the wig, which he immediately beat against the fake wall. Devon cringed as she watched the dirt fly from it.

"I can't believe how realistic some of those wigs are," she announced. "Especially considering how old they must be."

"A little glue to hold them in place, and they're nearly real," Ross replied and tossed the wig back to her. "I don't know why Brant wastes so much time implanting hair into his favorites."

She caught the wig and replaced it on the woman's head. It would need more glue to secure it, but at least it wasn't dusty. A flap of wax stuck up at the edge of the wig. Devon pushed it back down and secured the wig over it.

"I should get the glue," Devon remarked.

"I'll take care of it later," Ross informed her with little care. "I have plenty of other things that need a little glue."

Brant entered the display dressed in a stylish, black tuxedo while struggling with the tie. He barely even noticed them, since he was having such difficulty with his own wardrobe.

Ross looked up and whistled then chuckled. "Someone's got a hot date tonight."

"I wish," Brant muttered and nearly gave up on his tie, throwing his hands down with frustration. "Another tiring formal party at my parents' house in the city. The world would undoubtedly end if I didn't attend."

Without prompting, Devon approached and helped him with the tie. He watched in near surprise as she skillfully fixed it.

"Ah, just tell them to blow off," Ross announced with noted irritation. "If I had parents like yours, I'd disown them."

"Sometimes I'd like to," Brant replied then sighed. "But they're my parents, and I was taught to respect my parents." He remarked then frowned. "Even if they are irritating as hell."

Devon straightened and smoothed the tie while grinning proudly at her handy work. He eyed the tie then looked at her and laughed.

"How did you get so good at that?" he asked.

"It's the same knot I use on my horse's saddle girth," she replied then flashed a smile.

"Huh," he remarked with some surprise then fidgeted and looked at his watch. "I have to leave in half an hour," Brant informed them. "If you could clean up what you're working on, you'll be able to leave early."

"We're almost finished with this display," Ross informed him. "It'll just be another hour. We'll lock up on our way out."

"Tyler won't like that," Brant announced with a sigh. "It'll have to wait until Monday."

"The entire weekend off?" Ross questioned. "What's the occasion?"

"I'm required to spend the weekend at my parents' house," Brant informed him then rolled his eyes. "Believe me; I'd rather be working. I wouldn't doubt my mother finally found a suitable host to carry her grandchildren."

"Honestly, Brant, you need a life," Ross informed him. "I'm sure if you tried hard enough, you'd be able to find one or two illegitimate rug rats of yours running around out there."

Brant seemed to tense then chuckled. "I highly doubt it, Ross," he remarked. "My life hasn't been nearly that interesting."

"Man, if I had your money--" Ross began.

"You'd buy a decent car," Devon scoffed without hesitation. "That clunker of yours has been dying a slow death for years."

Ross glared at her, obviously offended that she'd trash his treasured car. "Hey, sister," he snapped, "you don't even own a car."

"I'd love to stay and debate this all night with you," Brant announced then muttered, "trust me, I would, but I have to go next door and get my weekend bag. See you on Monday."

As they watched him leave the phantom display, Ross shook his head shamefully then cast a stern look at Devon and folded his arms across his chest.

"What's wrong with my car?" he demanded with annoyance.

She groaned, shook her head, and walked away from the set. Ross hurried after her.

"Seriously," he announced. "It's a classic."

"It's a multi-colored beast held together with Bondo and duct tape," she snapped back as they left the display.

The wig on the unconscious wax woman shifted, and the waxy flap again popped open. Beyond the wax were strands of jet-black hair.

Chapter Fifteen

It was early evening and the diner located in the center of town was busy with its usual Friday night dinner crowd. The diner was a 1970's throwback with tables, booths, and counter seating. Jamie approached the small counter separating the kitchen from the diner and clipped her new order to the revolving wheel. Another waitress, Marlene Preston, deposited a pile of dirty dishes into a tub just near the kitchen door. Marlene impatiently glared at her young, blonde co-worker.

"You could tend to your tables *without* young, good-looking men too, you know," Marlene scoffed with annoyance.

"I was getting there," Jamie protested, although her tone conveyed she did not intend to do so. "Don't worry about my tables." She gave her co-worker a quick once-over, conveying her superiority over the woman. "When I'm famous, you'll show a little more respect."

"You didn't get that acting job yet," Marlene snapped. "So stop acting all high and mighty."

"Burt Danson was very impressed with me," Jamie informed her proudly while adding a sly grin. "You're just jealous."

Jamie spun on her heels and walked away with an added swagger to her walk. Marlene watched her and rolled her eyes. Marlene was an attractive woman in her late twenties and possibly had been one of the more popular women in town before Jamie came of age. Her hair was jet-black and as smooth as silk. Her creamy white complexion and full lips made her almost impossible to ignore. Add her curvaceous body, and she was a vision of beauty. There may have been a time when she had the same insufferable attitude as Jamie, but maturity seemed to tone that down. The phone rang not far from where Marlene stood. She snatched the phone from the hook with some hostility.

"Fairview Diner," she announced with a huff. She listened to the caller on the other end then frowned. "One moment."

Marlene looked across the diner and saw Jamie flirting with a young, handsome customer who wasn't even in her section.

"Jamie--"

Jamie turned. Marlene held the phone in the air with an impatient look on her face. Jamie immediately turned giddy and rushed to the phone. Marlene approached the nearby counter and poured some coffee to those seated at the counter even though most had full cups. It was obvious she was attempting to listen to Jamie's conversation. Despite Jamie's initial enthusiasm with the call, she appeared slightly flustered.

"Uh, yeah. I can meet you," Jamie announced into the phone then paused and cast a look around the diner. "I'll be there. Thank you."

Jamie hung up the phone and stood unusually still and silent a moment as if contemplating her next move.

Marlene appeared suspicious of the look on the girl's face and approached.

"Something wrong?" Marlene asked while tilting her head.

"No," she replied a little too quickly then looked toward the kitchen beyond the counter. "Matt, I'm taking the rest of the evening off. My mother needs help with Chelsea."

The cook waved her off almost as if used to the routine. Jamie removed her apron while Marlene glared at her.

"That wasn't your mother on the phone," Marlene snarled.

Jamie glared back at her co-worker. "Tell Matt that, and I'll tell him about the missing money from the register."

Marlene stared at her with wide, horror-filled eyes. "You took the money from the register, you little bitch," she practically cried out.

Jamie smirked slyly. "You can't prove I took it," she mocked, "but I can certainly make you look guilty. Don't fuck with me, Marlene. I have important things to do tonight, and I won't let you ruin it for me."

Marlene could only stare at her without comment. Jamie smiled mockingly and rushed out of the diner with a plan in mind. Marlene folded her arms across her chest and watched Jamie disappear.

"I'm going to get that bitch."

§

Nearly an hour later, Jamie got out of her old, red sports car and stared at the abandoned farmhouse located on the far end of town. She had changed into a low-cut, red dress that clung to every curve of her body. Her hair was styled with the greatest care, and her makeup was flawless if not a little thick. It was a little before seven o'clock that evening, and the sun was already hiding behind some trees, casting a shadow on the farmhouse. Jamie approached the dilapidated house and eyed the old, broken window in the front room. A dim light could be seen through the separation of the tattered curtains.

She nervously walked onto the porch, the sound of her high heels clomping against the rotted boards. She hesitated, appeared to reconsider her meeting, and then forced herself to knock on the door. It creaked open, causing her to shiver at the sound. It was uncertain if someone opened it or if it moved just from her knocking. She nervously pushed the door open and peered inside. The dimly lit hallway appeared vacant. Jamie slowly entered the foyer of the dilapidated farmhouse and looked around the hallway. She grimaced at the state of the building. The interior walls were cracked, lacked paint, and were falling apart. The floorboards appeared slightly rotted, and the stairs had seen better days. Jamie nervously looked around waiting for someone to greet her.

"Hello?"

There was no response. She approached the living room containing the light and glanced over the room. Several pigeons flew past her, headed up the stairway, and flew out a broken window. Jamie jumped with surprise then held her chest while panting. A shadow loomed over her from behind. Jamie recovered from the pigeon parade and turned back toward the hallway. A man wearing the phantom costume stood directly before her, his white mask covering most of his face except a small portion of his left cheek, mouth, and chin. Jamie let out a scream and jumped back just as a large dagger was thrust downward for her. The knife sliced her lower arm, but she had managed to avoid being stabbed in the chest.

She cried out with horror and pain but barely took time to clutch her bleeding forearm before bolting down the hall and away from her attacker. Unfortunately, she ran in the opposite direction of the front door. The phantom chased after her, his purple and black cloak gracefully flowing behind him. Jamie ran into the old kitchen and immediately bolted for the door. She attempted to open it and realized too late that it had been boarded from the outside. As she turned, the phantom was already behind her and thrust his knife for her. She leaped out of his path, and the knife struck the single pane window on the kitchen door, easily shattering the glass.

By the time he freed his dagger, Jamie was already running across the kitchen and back for the hallway. The phantom chased after her, making up time in his elegant, shiny black boots matched against her clumsy, excessively high heels. She was nearly upon the closed front door when the phantom grabbed her around the waist and tackled her to the floor. She screamed as she fell backward onto the floor with her attacker landing on top. Jamie was slightly winded. She looked up as he hovered over her with the knife prepared to plunge into her chest. Jamie screamed and thrust her high heel sharply into his calf. He cried out with surprise allowing her precious seconds to plan her escape. He had pulled back just far enough for her to knee him in the groin, causing him to fall off her and drop the dagger.

Jamie rolled across the floor and away from him then sprang to her feet. She saw the discarded knife near his hand and lunged for it. As she dropped to her knees to grab the knife, the phantom snatched it, and with a backward swing, stabbed her in the midsection. Jamie cried out with horror and agony while looking into the phantom's eyes. His teeth gritted as he gave the knife a sharp twist inside her. She gasped, spit up blood, and slid off the knife.

The phantom moved to his knees over her where she writhed in agony and attempted to scream. He clutched the bloody knife in his black-gloved hand while holding it over her body. He grunted with rage and stabbed her in the chest. Jamie's body jerked slightly as blood spilled from her chest and mouth. Before she gasped her last breath, he pulled the knife free and violently stabbed her several times in the abdomen. When he finally pulled the dagger free after the last thrust, she wheezed then became still. The phantom moved off her, straightened proudly while panting slightly, and then grinned with satisfaction.

Chapter Sixteen

It was early Saturday morning, and although she hadn't gotten much sleep, Devon was up early, as was mostly everyone on her father's ranch. Devon had decided to go for a long ride around the two-hundred-acre ranch. It had actually been a while since she'd been out for such a long ride. After her run-in with Joe a month ago, she was told to avoid the ranch hands. Devon rode her black and white pinto horse at a leisurely canter across the countryside and slowed when she happened upon some of the wranglers hanging out with the herd of heifers. She debated socializing with the guys but, ultimately, didn't feel like hearing about it from her father if she did. She was about to continue with her ride when two of the ranch hands galloped across the pasture to greet her.

She stopped her horse and decided it was only polite to say hello since they made the effort. Devon couldn't help but wonder if they were mad at her for getting Joe fired. Maybe that was why her father was upset. Perhaps firing Joe got the other wranglers wound up. What if they shared hostility toward her regarding Joe? She was now anxious to meet with the guys, particularly alone. She hadn't considered how they might feel toward her at that moment. Worst case scenario, she knew she had the faster horse and could outrun them.

The two wranglers, Peter and Ryan, stopped their horses before her, pushed their hats back on their heads and leaned on the saddle horns with matching grins on their youthful faces. Both men were in their mid to late twenties and shared the same boyish good looks.

"Morning, ma'am," both men cheerfully announced almost in unison.

"I'm a ma'am now?" she teased, although the greeting did concern her.

Were the men already on edge around her, fearing anything they said and did would now be grounds for dismissal? It made her uncomfortable, but she decided not to make a big deal about it. Both men laughed at the comment.

"Where have you been?" Pete practically demanded. "It hasn't been the same around here without you."

Devon was slightly surprised to hear him say that. Hadn't they heard why Joe had been fired?

"Martin said you got into a fight with your father," Ryan remarked. "We feared you packed up and moved to the city."

"That would never happen," she remarked then eyed the men almost suspiciously. "Martin didn't tell you what my father and I fought about?"

"He seemed unclear himself," Pete replied then made a slight face. "Something about Joe, I suspect, but Martin was sort of rambling at the time."

She shifted uncomfortably in the saddle and decided to tackle the subject head-on. "You heard what happened with Joe, didn't you?"

"Just the meat and taters of it," Ryan remarked then shook his head. "Must've been pretty bad for you to go to your father." He shifted uncomfortably on his horse. "I mean, the rest of us have been playfully disrespectful to you at times, and it's never been a problem."

"Joe was a pig," Pete scoffed with irritation. "Always making lewd comments about other guy's girls. I'm too much of a gentleman to repeat some of the things he said about you behind your back. Probably shouldn't have told your father either." He shifted and gave her a nervous look. "I thought maybe that's why you weren't coming around anymore. Something I said may have set him off, and he told you to stay away from us."

Devon stared at the men a moment and wondered if the guys told her father things that upset him more than what she'd told him. Perhaps that was part of the reason he didn't want her hanging around the guys.

"After what happened with Joe, he told me to stay away from the wranglers," she replied with honesty. "I just assumed it had to do with Joe's advance and that we shouldn't mix girls with the guys."

"Well, your father isn't from our generation," Ryan announced. "He doesn't understand friendships between guys and gals. We can say stupid things, but that doesn't mean we're looking to bed a woman."

"So you guys aren't mad that I got Joe fired?" she finally asked while feeling a nervous pang.

"Mad?" Pete practically cried out. "Mad at Joe. If we'd caught him coming on to you, he'd be hanging from the nearest tree."

"By his nuggets, no less," Ryan added.

"I've personally seen you handle the guys without anger or complaint," Pete announced. "I've seen the guys get a little friendly with an innocent hug, and I've seen you deal with them. It's always been 'problem solved'. Joe must have crossed one hell of a line for you to report him to your father. Knowing him the way we do, it doesn't come as much of a surprise. We told him to mind his manners around you, but he didn't listen. I'm sure he got exactly what he deserved."

"I'm glad I came out here today," she remarked and felt herself relax. "I've been fretting that you and the other wranglers blamed me for Joe. Especially with my father ordering me to stay away from you guys."

"I'm sure he's just being overly protective of his little girl," Pete replied. "I'm sure I would too. Honestly, Devon, you're safer with us than anywhere around here for miles. We're practically family, and the guys miss you something terrible."

"Well, we don't miss you on poker night," Ryan announced and smirked. "With the way you cheat at cards and all."

Devon playfully glared at him. "I never cheated at cards," she announced. "You guys are just terrible poker players."

"Hang out with us a while," Pete announced cheerfully. "We need some stimulating conversation around here. I can't handle any more boring conversations with some of these guys."

"Okay," she replied cheerfully. "Just for a little while. I don't want my father catching me. I don't feel like getting into another fight with him right now."

Devon spent the rest of the day with the ranch hands tending to the herd, keeping strays from wandering off, and having a good time doing it. She couldn't deny she missed being a wrangler.

Chapter Seventeen

The tavern was moderately crowded as it usually was on a Saturday night. Devon and Ivy entered, paused by the main door, and looked around. There were already several drunken men hanging around the bar while trashy looking women made their plays. They spotted Ross and Tony in the back playing pool. Ross' laugh was unmistakable and traveled despite the crowded room and loud music. Ross saw them and signaled to a table near the jukebox. Devon and Ivy approached the table and sat down. Ivy looked around the room with disappointment.

"One of these days, I'd like to head to the resort clubs and have some real fun," Ivy announced with a huff. "I'm getting bored with drunken farm boys."

"So you'd prefer drunken businessmen for a change of pace?" Devon teased.

"At least the music would be better," Ivy remarked while listening to the same country songs blaring from the prehistoric jukebox. As she scanned the bar with a bored sigh, her eyes suddenly lit up. "There he is! I can't believe he's here!"

"Who?" Devon asked while looking around the crowd for whatever handsome devil Ivy had her eyes on.

"Burt Danson," Ivy gasped while grabbing Devon's arm. "He's the one who'll be hiring the actress for the soap opera. We have to go over there and socialize."

Devon again scanned the room until she found the man in question. Burt Danson was a heavyset man in his forties with slicked back hair dyed excessively dark. He wore a flashy gold watch and a thick gold chain. He was quite possibly the least attractive man Devon had seen in a long time. He sat at the bar alongside Paula Jarred. Paula was now a bleached blonde, who dressed the part of a low budget porn star. Excessive substance abuse had physically taken its toll on her. A thick layer of makeup was all that kept her from looking like death warmed over.

"Paula," Ivy scoffed while glaring through narrow eyes. "She's making moves on Burt."

"*Apparently*," a woman announced from nearby, "she had the same idea we had."

Devon and Ivy turned to see Tamara Little standing near their table. Tamara maintained her attractive appearance over the last seven years. Her strawberry blonde hair seemed a little more strawberry than blonde, suggesting she may have changed hair color. Tamara placed her drink on their table and collapsed in the vacant chair between them.

Tamara's eyes remain fixed on Paula. "That girl has no shame," she scoffed. "She'll sleep her way right into that job."

"You know about her auditioning for the soap role?" Ivy asked with surprise.

"Of course," Tamara replied while sneering. "I was there when she slinked in. She looked like an overpriced streetwalker."

"You auditioned for the job too?"

Tamara gave Ivy a humored look but withheld her laugh. "Nearly every woman under thirty in this town applied for that job," she informed her.

All three looked back at Paula as she clung to Burt's shoulder with her breasts pressed against his arm. They appeared to be having an intimate conversation. Burt seemed to be enjoying the flirtatious company as well.

"But ultimately, it's not who you know," Tamara informed them while indicating the couple, "it's who you blow."

"It's hard to believe you two were once friends," Devon remarked.

"That was a long time ago," Tamara remarked. "It was nothing for her to get me into trouble. I despise the bitch."

"We can't let her sleep her way into the job," Ivy informed Tamara. "We need to do something."

"Like what?" Tamara remarked while snorting a laugh. "You see her crawling all over him. He's under the hypnotic spell of her slutty wiles."

"We should invite him over," Ivy suggested.

"Ivy," Devon groaned, attempting to nix the idea. She knew her friend was fiercely competitive and it wouldn't end well.

"It's worth a shot," Tamara agreed. "Two on one. We might get him away from her."

"I'm sure two on one is exactly what he has in mind," Devon muttered.

Neither woman heard her or at least they didn't acknowledge the comment. Devon groaned as the two women headed toward the bar to steal Burt away from Paula.

Several minutes later, Paula watched and silently seethed as Burt joined Tamara, Ivy, and Devon at their table. She glared at her brother, who was slumped on the bar alongside her, and slapped his arm startling him.

"What are you hitting me for?" he demanded in a slightly drunken tone.

Joe was possibly good-looking at one time, but he lacked personal hygiene possibly since he'd lost his job a month ago. His dirty blonde hair was more dirty than blonde and hadn't been properly combed in days. His facial stubble didn't know if it wanted to be a beard, and his clothes were dirty and wrinkled, possibly suggesting he had slept in them more than one night.

"Those bitches stole my ticket out of this hellhole," she exclaimed to her brother. "Go over there and do something!"

Joe glanced across the tavern as if he hadn't even been paying attention to what had happened over the last twenty minutes. He snorted a laugh and minded his beer.

"No way," he announced and took a large swallow of beer. "I don't get involved in catfights, and I want nothing to do with Devon Vincent."

"Why not?" Paula demanded in a near temper tantrum. "She's the bitch who got you fired."

"She's also the bitch with an influential father roughly the size of a brick shithouse," Joe informed her. "I touch her; he kills me. If he doesn't, her hot-headed brother does. Notice the pattern? Both stories end up with me dead. No girl is worth dying for."

"You're pathetic," Paula scoffed and leaned heavily on the bar. "I'm going to get even with them if it's the last thing I do."

Joe eyed his sister then motioned to the bartender. "Stan, we need a few shots over here."

Stan laughed and poured them each a shot from a special, unmarked bottle. The contents of the shot glass were clear, indicating it might be homemade moonshine. Paula frowned and accepted the drink. Joe smiled and extended his shot glass to her. They clinked glasses then drank them down and slammed the glasses on the bar. Joe lit a cigarette and took a drag from it before Paula snatched it from him for herself. Joe frowned and lit another cigarette for himself.

"I don't know why you're getting all bent out of shape about this acting job," Joe remarked and eyed his sister. "You said Jamie auditioned for it."

"So?" Paula demanded.

"So," he announced and attempted to straighten, although he was limited by his unsteadiness. "There's nothing you're willing to do for this job that Jamie hasn't already done. You know how she is when she wants something. She always gets what she wants no matter who she has to maim along the way."

Paula shifted uncomfortably. "I wish you wouldn't say things like that," she muttered and took a long drag from the cigarette then blew smoke out above her head. She glared at her brother. "Just once, I'd like to even the score with Jamie. Getting that role on the soap opera instead of her would do it."

Joe groaned and guzzled several swallows of beer before looking at her. "The only way to beat Jamie is to *off* Jamie," he remarked.

Paula frowned and indicated the shot glass to the bartender. "Not really my thing."

"Then stop fighting that blonde demon," Joe announced firmly.

She shook her head and sighed. "You don't know how close to a demon Jamie actually is," Paula huffed.

"Actually, I do," Joe remarked nearly sedate and eyed his sister. "You don't want to cross her or you'll end up dead too."

Paula shot a surprised look at her brother as her eyes widened. "I told you to keep quiet about that stuff," she gasped in a loud whisper. "If anyone ever finds out about that--"

"Relax," Joe snorted and took a large swallow of beer. "No one will hear it from me."

Chapter Eighteen

Devon sat at the table wishing she were anywhere but there as her friend and Tamara entertained Burt. Burt ate up the attention and laid on the charm. Devon couldn't even stomach listening to the man speak. Her initial take on the slimy producer was a self-absorbed narcissist who intended to use his position to take advantage of as many women as possible. She didn't understand how Ivy didn't see it. What concerned her more was that maybe Ivy knew and was playing the game anyway.

Tony and Ross had returned to the table from their friendly game of pool, eyed Devon demandingly, and indicated those sitting at *their* table taking *their* seats. Devon frowned and shrugged. Both men rolled their eyes and headed for the bar. Devon attempted to focus her attention anywhere but on the two women flirting with the unattractive man. She caught a glimpse of Paula sitting alongside Joe while casting hostile looks at their table. Devon eyed Joe, felt immediately repulsed, and looked away.

She wished the man would fall off the face of the earth. She knew he secretly blamed her for her father firing him. It would be humorous if it weren't so gut-wrenching. How was it possible that Joe kissed and groped her while he had her cornered in the horse barn, yet he thought she was responsible for him losing his job? Devon still blamed herself for how poorly she handled the incident. She'd been raised around ranch hands and skillfully handled their harmless flirting amazingly well.

When Joe cornered her, she froze. His hands were on her, and she couldn't keep him from pawing her, something none of the guys had ever done before. Despite that she secretly wanted to kill him, she felt helpless to stop him. If her brother hadn't come to the barn looking for her, she wasn't sure what would have happened. She was so upset; she couldn't even tell Martin what happened in the barn. Later, she gave the tamed down version to her father and brother, which cost Joe his job.

Even though her father had done the right thing, she ultimately resented him because of his reaction. He seemed more upset by having to fire one of his best wranglers than by the incident itself. Insisting she stay away from the ranch hands after that left her feeling he blamed her for Joe's inability to control his sexual desires. He wanted her to avoid the ranch hands, and she was no longer allowed to work the cattle.

Devon snapped out of her own thoughts when she heard Ivy giggling like a schoolgirl over something the slimy producer had said. She couldn't believe Ivy's flirtatious behavior around a man she obviously didn't find the least bit attractive. How far did her friend intend to take the flirting for some stupid job? Burt leaned on the table and cast his beady eyes upon Devon.

"I don't believe you auditioned for the soap role," Burt announced while mastering the quick once-over in an almost casual manner.

"I'm not an actress," Devon bluntly informed him without interest.

He waved her off. "There's nothing to it," Burt announced. "You memorize a few lines while pretending to be someone else. You're an attractive girl. You should audition. I'll have my secretary set it up."

Devon managed a smile although it possibly came off as more of a sneer. "No, thank you," she replied. "I'm not interested in an acting career." She eyed her friend and raised her brow. "Or any of the ass kissing that goes with it."

Ivy became uncomfortable and immediately shifted. She wasn't nearly as flirty after the comment. Burt was only momentarily set back but resumed his sleazy charm without hesitation. He placed his hands on each woman's thighs and shifted looks between them.

"What do you say we go back to my suite at the resort?" he announced while grinning. "There's a sunken hot tub in the living room and champagne chilling in the frig. We can discuss the soap opera role and have a few laughs."

Ivy shifted uncomfortably and cast a look at Devon. "I can't," she announced. "I have to give Devon a ride home tonight."

He shrugged then grinned. "Devon can join us," Burt announced. "The more the merrier."

"No," Devon sharply corrected while raising her brows demandingly as she glared at him. "Devon can't join you. She's not into sleazy perverts."

Ivy immediately shifted in her chair but didn't defend Burt from the accusation. Burt put on a false smile, but he was obviously annoyed with Devon for calling him out. He looked at Ivy.

"Friends like that one will only hold you back," he announced while sneering. "I'm sure she can find another ride home. Are you joining Tammy and I in my suite or not?"

Ivy removed his hand from her thigh and stared into his eyes. "She's not holding me back," Ivy remarked, although not nearly as boldly as she could have. "She's saving me from myself."

Without further comment, Ivy stood and approached Tony at the bar. She said something to him, and he joined her for a slow song on the dance floor. Burt shook his head with a look of annoyance then glanced at Tamara and resumed his sleazy smile.

"I guess it's just you and me, Tammy," he announced and placed his arm around her while leaning closer.

Tamara stared at him a moment and practically shivered from what she must have seen in his eyes. She pushed him away from her and raised a cocky brow in response.

"It's Tamara," she snarled and moved her chair away from him.

She casually leaned on the table with her head propped on her fist and avoided looking at him. She suddenly seemed bored. Burt stared at her with surprise then glared at Devon.

"Well, my dear," he scoffed. "I think you've missed your calling as a cut-throat talent agent."

Burt stood and left the table. He headed back to the bar and joined Paula and her brother. Tamara cast a quick glance at the bar and watched the scene unfold. He placed his arm around Paula's waist, whispered something in her ear, and she was immediately crawling all over him once again as if nothing had ever happened. Tamara straightened, drew a deep breath, and eyed Devon.

"I wish we were friends years ago," Tamara announced bluntly.

Devon couldn't help but laugh. "Why? You need someone to hold you back in life?"

"No, I could have used someone like you to save me from me a long time ago," she replied.

Ivy returned to the table with Tony and Ross in tow. They no sooner sat down when they saw Paula leaving the tavern with Burt. The sleazy couple couldn't seem to keep their hands off each other. It was close to repulsive. All five watched their lusty exit.

Ross shook his head. "Guess we know who got that job."

"Don't be so certain," Tamara announced. "Jamie's full of surprises herself. She's not going to let Paula beat her at her own game."

Chapter Nineteen

Loud moans were heard from the black, luxury sedan parked off to the side of the moderately dark, tavern parking lot. The music from the tavern mostly drown out the sounds of pleasure coming from the back seat, although the rocking car could be seen several yards away. Two country boys headed from their pickup truck toward the tavern and passed by the car with the front windows open, allowing the female moans and male grunts to be heard clearly. Both men in their mid-twenties peeked into the back of the car as they passed then exchanged grins and laughed.

Paula straddled Burt while facing him as she bounced up and down with purpose on his lap. He groaned loudly while clutching an exposed breast in each hand leaving her shirt bunched up beneath her arms. With the familiar grunt followed by a loud groan, Paula leaned forward and kissed him passionately. As she pulled back and met his gaze, he grinned while pleasantly exhausted.

"I think I'll be seeing more of you at the resort over the next few months," Burt announced then chuckled.

Paula grinned taking his meaning and pulled her shirt back down as she climbed off him. "I look forward to that."

"Just between us until it's official," he warned her while pulling up his pants and zipping them.

"I know," she replied but maintained her beaming grin of delight.

§

Paula entered the bar only twenty minutes after she had left and wore a devious grin on her face. The five at the table near the jukebox exchanged bewildered looks. Ross glanced at his watch.

"Wow," Ross announced as his eyes widened dramatically. "That's got to be a record."

"Wouldn't be the first time Paula got it on with some guy in the parking lot," Tamara informed them while casually sipping her drink. She then considered the comment. "Or the men's bathroom."

Tony and Ross gave Tamara a surprised look.

"Why the men's bathroom?" Tony practically gasped while making a face.

"Less traffic than the women's bathroom," Tamara replied.

"Hell," Ross cried out. "That place is so disgusting; I don't even want to take a piss in there."

They watched as Paula joined her brother at the bar. She leaned on his shoulder and said something in his ear. He laughed at whatever she had said. Paula eyed the three women then approached their table. All three women ignored her as she leaned on their table. Tony and Ross couldn't help but stare at her, obviously still caught up on the men's room comment.

"I've got this job in the bag," Paula announced while grinning deviously.

Tamara cast a look at her and raised a cocky brow. "Don't you mean in the sack?"

"Say what you want, but I intend to be rich this time next year," Paula boldly announced while straightening as she flaunted her cleavage.

"Men will tell all sorts of lies to get a woman into their bed," Devon informed her.

"Or the back seat of their car," Ross muttered.

"They'll even promise jobs they don't intend to give them," Devon continued.

Paula eyed Devon and snorted a humored laugh. "Oh, the town virgin is suddenly an authority on men?" She smirked mockingly at Devon. "What do *you* know about men?"

Ross casually leaned back in his chair and raised an arrogant brow. "Enough to have two male friends who are fiercely loyal to her," he remarked.

Paula appeared humored and cast a look at Ross, mocking him. "Oh, really? The town idiot and the dead fuck?"

Both men immediately squirmed in their seats. Tony avoided looking at Paula and appeared embarrassed. Ross didn't look away from her and maintained a serious expression.

"I may be a dead fuck, but I know I never slept with a freaky chick like you," Ross announced in a loud, brazen tone.

It was difficult to embarrass Ross since he enjoyed embarrassing himself and usually found a way to take everyone else with him. Paula was moderately stunned by the reversal of insults. When she couldn't come up with a counter-response, she sneered and stormed away from the table. All eyes were suddenly on Tony, who immediately shifted uncomfortably.

"You slept with Paula?" Ross cried out in a hushed tone. "What were you thinking?"

Tony shrugged with embarrassment while avoiding eye contact. "I had too much to drink," he groaned. "I wasn't thinking."

"It's back," Tamara scoffed, causing the others to look up.

Paula approached their table while staring at the bar then pointed and smiled deviously. "Hey, Devon, isn't that your new boss?"

All five looked at the bar. Brant sat in a secluded corner of the bar with his head in his hands while huddled over his drink. Devon and Ross exchanged surprised looks. Brant was supposed to be gone all weekend. What was he doing at the bar?

"Hmm. I think I'm going to seduce your new boss," Paula announced while tossing her hair over her shoulder. "He looks pitiful enough to be a quick lay. Then every time you see him at work, you can think about him grunting like a pig while fucking me."

"I think I'm going to blow chunks," Ross suddenly announced while placing his hand over his mouth and pretended to dry heave.

Devon and Ivy watched Paula leave the table and approach Brant at the bar where she squeezed in next to him. Devon wasn't sure why the thought bothered her as much as it did, but it would be a horrible image burned into her mind forever. Paula leaned on Brant's shoulder and said something to him. Brant looked at Paula and responded although they couldn't hear the conversation through the crowd.

"That woman has no shame," Tamara muttered, having taken a moment to watch the display.

"She attempted to seduce my father once," Ivy remarked under her breath and finally looked away. "Just to see if she could."

"She got mine," Tamara hissed.

Devon couldn't keep from glancing at the bar. Brant drained the contents of his glass and pushed it across the bar. Devon watched with a frown, wondering if he could be so easily seduced by the town slut. He seemed drunk enough, and she did manage to corrupt Tony. Paula pressed her breasts against his arm and rested her hand on his shoulder while speaking softly to him. Brant pulled away from her and, judging by his expression, said something unfriendly. Devon stood, prepared to intervene. Ivy pulled her back to her seat.

"He's a big boy," Ivy announced. "He can take care of himself."

They watched as Brant stood, tossed some bills across the bar, and left the tavern. Paula looked at the bartender. They exchanged devious grins. Paula hurried out the door after Brant. Devon sprang to her feet and ran from the bar after Paula with Ross only a few steps behind her. As Devon ran outside, she saw Brant's car speeding away from the building. Paula was already heading back for the door and smiled smugly at Devon.

"Your boss is a real stud," she teased.

"You're such a bitch," Devon snarled. "You had to embarrass him, didn't you?"

Paula laughed mockingly as she passed. Devon made a fist and was about to swing when Ross caught her wrist and pulled her against him. Paula hadn't even been aware how close she was to being sucker punched. Ross didn't release her until Paula had disappeared inside.

"What's wrong with you?" Ross demanded while staring into her eyes.

"What's wrong with me?" she cried out. "What's wrong with you? How could you just let that bitch treat that poor man that way?"

"Brant's a big boy. He can fight his own battles," Ross informed her then glared demandingly. "Besides; did you want me to hit a woman?"

"No, of course not," she snapped, "but you shouldn't have stopped me."

"Let it go, Devon," Ross announced firmly. "She's not worth it."

Devon groaned and headed inside.

Chapter Twenty

Ivy's jeep pulled up to her small, suburban home. Devon got out of the driver's seat and helped her drunken friend to the front door. Ivy laughed uncontrollably as she staggered into the house. Her mother was waiting up for her, as she usually did on nights they went to the tavern. Ivy's mother shook her head in disappointment then helped her to her room. Devon found Ivy's relationship with her mother moderately humorous. Of course, since Martin spent many overnights elsewhere, that gave Devon plenty of leeway with her evenings out.

Devon returned to Ivy's jeep to drive herself home, as she did many evenings. Even though she didn't have a car, she was often the designated driver, since she didn't drink much. Devon drove along the back road that led past the museum. To her surprise, the lights were on. The jeep slowed, entered the parking lot, and parked near the main entrance. Devon got out of Ivy's jeep and approached the front doors. She knocked, but there was no response. She turned the knob, and to her surprise, the door was unlocked.

It seemed odd that Brant would leave the door unlocked if he wasn't within earshot of the door. Devon walked across the lobby and passed through the first floor displays. Several displays now contained the recently refurbished wax people. Devon recognized a few new ones that hadn't been in place when she and Ross left on Friday evening. Brant had been busy, it would seem. He couldn't possibly have just gotten back from his parents' house. As she passed, she took a little extra time to marvel at the newly added wax people.

Although Devon wore soft-soled boots, she could still hear the gentle clomping of her shoes in the frighteningly silent museum. With minimal lighting, the displays were even creepier than usual. She paused before an amazing display depicting Cleopatra. The wax woman had been Cleopatra at the old, dilapidated museum as well. She cleaned up nicely. Devon was actually surprised he was able to get all the dirt from her excessively shiny, black hair. She couldn't resist and walked into the display. Devon approached the wax woman and studied her hair in particular, although the lighting was dim.

Some of the wax figures they'd rescued from the old museum were of poor quality, but Cleopatra was in amazingly great shape. The eyes, in particular, were quite realistic. In the dim lighting, her eyes appeared almost teal in color. Devon wasn't a history genius, but she was pretty sure Cleopatra didn't have teal eyes. It didn't matter since the visitors wouldn't get close enough to notice her eye color anyway.

Devon heard a clunk from deeper within the museum. She jumped with surprise and scanned the creepy surrounding area. She suddenly realized she didn't want to be alone in the museum. It was almost frightening, even though she knew everything was fake. She left the display and continued along the walkway toward the back. She finally reached the dungeon entrance and headed down the stone stairs.

As she passed the horror displays, she eyed each one. A few of the horror sets also contained wax figures, which was even more surprising. The wax men and women depicted frozen looks of horror in their final fatal moments of existence. Each wax man and woman seemed to stare at her as she walked through, almost as if they were begging to be rescued by the non-existent monster not yet within the display. Devon shivered as she passed. If she found the displays creepy now, what would she think in a month from now when all the horror displays were completed? It was a chilling thought.

Devon approached the partially open workshop door, which had a light on. She peered inside and saw Brant slumped over the counter with his head in his hands. There was a wax head and paint pens on the counter before him. He'd obviously been through a lot that night, and Paula had clearly gotten to him with her persistent advances. Devon felt sorry for him and wanted to console him. She figured he could probably use a friend right about now.

She then noticed that there were more paint pens scattered haphazardly across the floor. She wasn't sure what they were doing there. Were they defective? Devon was about to announce herself when Brant suddenly cast everything from the counter. Objects flew to the floor with a loud crash, startling her. Brant suddenly sprang to his feet with a sharpened putty knife in his hand and plunged it into the nearest wax woman's head. Devon placed her hand over her mouth, held back her horrified gasp, and darted away from the doorway.

Everyone had left the tavern for the night. It was nearly three o'clock in the morning when Paula shook her brother where he lay slumped on the bar. He was out cold and wasn't about to go anywhere anymore tonight. Paula shook her head and stumbled from her bar stool. She could barely stand on her own but the walk home in the cool, night air would clear her head. She drunkenly waved to the bartender, who was cleaning glasses.

"Night, Stan."

"You need a ride home?" he asked.

"No, I'll walk," she informed him. "The fresh air will do me some good."

Stan gave a slight wave as Paula left the tavern. She entered the parking lot and walked toward the dark, back road. She staggered and stumbled her way along the road while humming a tune. Her house was about a quarter of a mile from the tavern at the end of a private, wooded lane. Paula swung her house keys while staggering and giggling the entire way. She turned down the private, wooded lane, which seemed even darker due to the trees. A twig snapped within the dark woods. Paula stopped and looked into the woods. There was no one there. She passed it off and continued along the lane toward her house in the near distance.

Rustling was heard within the woods. Paula stopped and scanned the woods surrounding her driveway. She squinted, attempting to focus in her drunken condition. Although the woods were mostly dark, she didn't see anything moving. She heard the sound again and looked back. A deer appeared from the woods, stared at her a moment, and then continued across the dirt driveway. Paula laughed while placing a hand on her chest.

"Someone's jumpy tonight," she muttered then continued toward the house.

Her family home had seen better days. It was in need of new siding, a coat of paint, gutters, and a new porch roof. In addition to the creepy, dark house, which she'd again forgotten to leave a light on for herself, there were several beater cars scattered along what constituted a front yard. The front yard hadn't been mowed in years, allowing tall weeds to grow between the junk cars. Joe's fascination with classic cars led to the junkyard that was once the front lawn, but it was his lack of mechanical skills that kept them there.

As she passed the collection of beater cars, she heard a loud clunk from one of them. Paula turned toward the cars and immediately scanned the area. There was a loud wail followed by excessive hissing as two cats ran across the driveway and darted under the front porch.

"Damned cats," she muttered and continued toward the house.

Another cat sat in the driveway and casually washed its paws. She smiled and bent down to pet the cat, nearly falling in the process. The cat suddenly hissed at her and puffed twice its normal size. Paula straightened with surprise and struck something behind her. She spun around with a startled gasp and saw the phantom standing directly behind her. He placed his gloved hand over her mouth, spun her around, and pulled her against him while she attempted a muffled scream. She weakly thrashed against his hold, but she was too drunk to effectively defend herself.

He dragged her toward one of the beater cars, opened the mostly rusted back door, and tossed her into the back seat. She attempted to gather her wits and reached for the opposite door as he jumped into the back seat with her. The door wouldn't open and the handle came off in her hand. She screamed and turned onto her back to face her attacker. The phantom was already on top of her. He clutched her throat with one hand and squeezed until she could no longer scream. Paula gasped, attempting to catch her breath while struggling to loosen the grip on her throat. She could barely move her legs, unsuccessfully trying to toss him off balance.

When he revealed the large dagger in his right hand, her eyes widened in horror, and she managed a weak, muffled gasp. He thrust downward with the knife and struck her in the chest, easily penetrating her bone with the sturdy blade. He ripped the knife free with some difficulty while keeping his hand on her mouth to muffle her screams. She stared at him while enduring the pain as she faded fast from the blow. The phantom sneered and thrust the knife a second and third time into her chest while staring into her eyes. She stared back but no longer moved. He removed his hand from her mouth, allowing her involuntary breath to escape.

The phantom wiped the blood from the knife on the back of the front seat, moved off her, and climbed out of the car. He casually shut the door and replaced the knife to his sheath. He looked down and saw a small kitten purring as it rubbed against his black boot. He reached down, affectionately scratched the kitten's head while it purred, and then straightened. He turned and walked away.

Chapter Twenty-one

Three o'clock Monday morning. The museum was mostly dark and peaceful. Two outside lights remained on; one in the front and one in the back as a security measure. Someone slipped through the shadows and approached the back basement door. A crowbar was used to pry open the less secured door, allowing the intruder to slip into the dungeon. The intruder set the gas can he'd been carrying on the floor. He shut the door behind him then turned and shined his flashlight around the dark workshop. The light fell upon a policeman.

"Holy hell," Karl exclaimed while jumping back in alarm.

When the officer didn't move, Karl took a closer look at the policeman in the uniform from the 1920's and realized it was just a wax figure dressed the role. It was probably Ross' idea to stake a wax cop at the back door in the event of a break-in, which obviously worked. Karl smirked and shook his head at his own paranoia. He was about to pick up the gas can when he heard a clunk from within the lower level of the museum.

With all the lights off, there couldn't be anyone else inside. He reconsidered picking up the gas can and opted to check out the sound first. Karl used his flashlight to hurry across the cluttered workshop and approached the interior door. He doused the light and slipped along the walkway. There were a few security lights on, which barely provided enough light to keep from running into objects and only allowed him to see the walkway before him. The displays cast creepy shadows, sending a chill through him.

After walking through three displays without hearing any further sounds, it was apparent he was alone. He turned on the flashlight and looked around, no longer concerned with giving away his location. He shined the light on the vampire display and saw a wax woman lying on the fake grass. He held his breath at how realistic she looked then was about to turn when he saw a flashlight not far from the wax woman. The flashlight puzzled him. He scanned the display with his own flashlight.

A large blur suddenly came at him. Before he could cry out, he was tackled to the floor. Karl was momentarily winded from the hard tackle. Despite having lost his breath, he recovered quickly and raised the flashlight to strike the attacker on top of him. In that brief flash, he saw his attacker's face and appeared surprised. Karl was punched several times in the face by the intruder's gloved hand, nearly knocking him unconscious. The gloved hands clutched his throat and squeezed. Karl attempted to fight off the killer, but he wasn't strong enough. His eyes momentarily bulged while staring at his attacker as he gasped for air. His eyes eventually rolled back, and Karl became still. He was then grabbed under his arms and dragged across the display.

Chapter Twenty-two

Later Monday morning. It was a dreary day outside, and the forecast was calling for heavy thunderstorms throughout most of the day. The rain seemed to be holding off, but the skies were dark and threatening. Devon and Martin entered the diner and looked around for a vacant booth, although there were plenty of empty tables. Martin immediately fidgeted when he saw Marlene was working that morning.

"This is a bad idea," he muttered to his sister. "Too soon."

Devon gave him a playful shove toward one of the few vacant booths. "Take your spittle eggs like a man," she huffed.

They sat at the booth near the window. When Marlene approached, Martin shifted uncomfortably in his seat, uncertain what to expect.

Marlene smiled almost cheerfully while eying Martin. "Hi, Martin," she announced in a strangely pleasant tone, surprising both.

It was obvious it was going to be a sneak attack on the waitress' part. Devon somehow felt nervous for her brother and waited for the bomb to drop. She'd heard about Marlene's Jekyll and Hyde personality but had never actually witnessed it.

"Uh, good morning, Marlene," he responded while attempting to sound as pleasant as possible. "Uh, how are you?"

She frowned at the question, causing both to tense and await the explosion that was sure to follow. With Martin's womanizing ways, he was bound to cross the wrong woman eventually.

"I'd be better if Jamie had shown up for work this morning," Marlene scoffed with annoyance. "She left me stranded by myself with the breakfast crowd." She shook her head. "Usually, she only does that sort of thing on Sunday mornings when she's hungover. The nerve of her. After having the entire weekend off, you'd think she'd have the decency to show up this morning."

Devon and Martin were surprised that her hostility hadn't been directed at him. Both relaxed, although remaining untrusting.

"Don't be too harsh on Jamie," Martin replied, showing surprising compassion. "She has to help take care of her sister. That's a lot of responsibility."

"It's a tragedy," Marlene remarked while frowning then shook her head. "They should've left the poor girl go." Marlene stared out the window, and her expression immediately saddened. "See what I mean?" She gave a nod out the window.

Martin and Devon looked out the window. Dorothy pushed the reclining wheelchair along the sidewalk with the young woman immobile within it. Chelsea wore a big, gaudy bow in her dull, blonde hair. Her once beautiful face was flaccid and heavily painted with makeup. Her eyes remained open with her usual fixed gaze. Devon looked down at her menu and felt both saddened and sickened by the tragedy that had befallen the girl only two years older than herself. Marlene continued to stare out the window and shook her head.

"Poor Chelsea," Marlene announced with a sad sigh. "She was going to graduate just a few weeks before the accident. Had a scholarship and everything." She attempted to wipe the image from her mind. "Seven years she's been stuck in that chair without a spark of brain activity." She shook her head. "Poor girl. So much nicer than her sister."

"Jamie's a spoiled, miserable girl," Devon huffed without looking up from her menu.

"You wouldn't get much of an argument from anyone on that one," Marlene remarked. "You went to school with her, didn't you?"

"Don't remind me," Devon scoffed. "She and her friends thought they owned the place."

"Didn't she get expelled for lewd conduct with one of her teachers?" Marlene asked.

"No," Devon snapped and eyed Marlene. "She was the victim, as usual. The teacher was fired though."

"That girl has nine lives, I swear," Marlene muttered while making a face. "Around here too. I don't know how she still has a job. If I pulled half the shit she did, I'd have been fired by now."

Marlene and Devon again looked out the window and watched Dorothy and Chelsea until they were gone. Martin studied the menu, no longer interested. Marlene managed a cheerful smile despite her foul mood regarding Jamie's disappearing act.

"Can I get you some coffee and tea to start?" she asked while eying both.

They nodded in response. Marlene left the table to get their beverages. Devon set her menu aside and sank into her own world.

Martin finally relaxed. "I really dodged a bullet on that one, huh?" he remarked with a nervous chuckle. When

Devon didn't respond, he eyed her and appeared curious. "Is something wrong?"

"Hmm?" she announced while looking up. "Uh, no. Everything's fine."

"Why don't you come to the city with me one of these weekends?" Martin suggested. "I'll take you to my hunting grounds. It's a place called the Ruby Club. Strictly highbrow people in this place. It's where I meet all my best dates."

"Is that where you met your latest conquest, Suki?" she announced while grinning.

Martin frowned at the comment and sat back in his chair. "She stood me up."

"I don't think I've ever met any of your girlfriends," Devon informed him.

"When I find the right one, I'll bring her home," he announced then grinned. "No telling what excitement today may bring."

"The weatherman says thunderstorms with gusty winds," Devon teased.

"You're so negative."

"I have reason to be."

"What's wrong?"

She shifted uncomfortably. "I didn't tell anyone, but I went to the museum late Saturday night," she informed her brother. "I saw Brant trash the workshop and brutalize a wax woman."

"Brutalize?"

"He stabbed it in the head with a sharpened putty knife," Devon informed him and cringed. "It was very scary."

"Maybe you shouldn't go back there," Martin announced while shifting uncomfortably.

"I can't just call off."

"Sure you can," Martin replied then grinned. "It's easy. I do it all the time."

Ross slid into the booth alongside Devon, startling her. When she jumped, he chuckled evilly.

"I wish you'd stop doing that," she groaned.

Martin hid his smile because he'd obviously seen Ross approaching since he was facing the door.

"Mind if I join you for breakfast?" Ross announced cheerfully.

"Depends," Martin remarked. "Are you mooching off us?"

"There's a strong likelihood," Ross casually replied without emotion.

Marlene showed up with two cups of coffee and a cup of tea for Devon. As she walked away, Ross leered after her.

"It's like she's a mind reader or something," Ross remarked.

"Considering she didn't take our order, I assume she's getting our usual," Martin announced then shook his head. "I hate being thought of as predictable."

"You and me both," Ross muttered while sipping his coffee.

As if on cue, both noticed the scrapes on Ross' knuckles.

"What happened to you?" Devon announced while indicating his knuckles.

She knew they didn't look that way Saturday night when she'd left Ross and Tony at the tavern. He eyed his knuckles then chuckled in a jovial manner.

"Oh, that," Ross announced and met her gaze. "Well, you know how I sometimes drink too much and say what I'm thinking?"

Devon rolled her eyes. "This can't be good," she muttered.

"Actually, I think you'd be proud of me," he remarked while grinning. "I got into it with Joe after you took Ivy home Saturday night."

"Joe?" Martin suddenly asked with surprise. "Former ranch hand Joe?"

"Yeah, that's the one," Ross announced cheerfully. "I defended your sister's honor and gave him quite the shiner as a token of my affection." Ross made a fist and slow punched in the air.

Martin shifted in his seat while frowning. "What did the jerk say about Devon?" he practically demanded.

"He didn't say much of anything," Ross reported. "It was just payback for groping her in the barn."

Devon suddenly stiffened and avoided looking at her brother. Martin stared at Ross and appeared ready to explode. He leaned forward on the table and glared at Devon.

"What does he mean; Joe groped you?" Martin suddenly demanded. "You said he backed you into the corner and kissed you. I never heard groped."

Devon met her brother's gaze and immediately shifted in her seat. "I didn't say anything because you were already borderline when I told you he kissed me."

Martin strummed his fingers on the table and silently seethed a moment. He drew a deep breath, leaned back in his seat, and finally met her gaze.

"Since Ross already punched him, and Dad fired him, I'm willing to let it go," Martin remarked, although his eyes still looked devil red. He finally relaxed and stared into her eyes. "Please tell me dad doesn't know. He'd kill him for sure. Even now a month later."

"No, dad doesn't know," she practically gasped and stared at him with a horrified look. "I definitely wasn't going to tell dad. He knows all the good spots to bury a body."

Martin sighed with relief and gently rubbed his temples. "Okay," he announced and nodded. "Let's just avoid talking about Joe for a while."

Devon finally relaxed and nodded. "Agreed." She then glared at Ross and smacked him on the shoulder.

He yelped in surprise. "Don't be mad at me," Ross cried out. "You two talk about everything. How was I supposed to know you hadn't told him?"

"Because, you idiot," she snarled. "Joe came out of it without any broken bones."

Chapter Twenty-three

Martin's black blazer pulled up to the front steps of the museum in the pouring rain. They were lucky to leave the diner and reach his truck just before it started to downpour. The rain didn't appear to be letting up. Since Devon was going to be soaked regardless, she jumped out of the blazer and darted for the porch. She entered the museum and wondered if any part of her wasn't soaked from her short sprint. She removed her wet jacket and hung it on a large rack just inside the lobby. As she ran her fingers through her wet hair, she wondered how bad it looked and wished she'd gone with a ponytail that morning. Devon turned to see Brant standing only a couple of feet away with a cup of coffee in one hand and a towel in the other. He offered Devon the towel, which she gladly accepted and dried her hair.

"Beautiful day, isn't it?" he teased.

"This is just the beginning," she informed him. "There's a massive thunderstorm coming this way. There will be some flooded roadways tonight."

Brant frowned and looked toward the lobby window at the black skies beyond the glass. "I hope the power holds out," he announced then made a face. "I'm afraid we won't get much done if it doesn't. We need a new generator. The old one died during the last power outage." He drew a deep breath then managed a smile and handed her the cup of coffee. "It'll just be the two of us today, so we'll see how much we can get done before we lose power. Ross is running some errands."

"We had breakfast this morning at the diner," she remarked then cast a look at him. "He mentioned he was running for more paint pens, although I thought we had plenty on Friday."

"Yeah, we did, but I used them rather aggressively yesterday. Would you like to see what I'd finished over the weekend?" Brant asked while grinning.

Devon fidgeted slightly while staring at him. It seemed like a good time to ask him about the weekend he didn't spend at his parents' house.

"I thought you were going to be gone all weekend," she remarked.

"I had a disagreement with my mother," he informed her while frowning. "I'm lucky I made it through dinner on Friday night." His grin then returned. "I got a lot of work finished though. Not a bad tradeoff."

She didn't have the heart to mention seeing him at the tavern on Saturday, and she certainly wasn't going to bring up what she witnessed at the museum in the early morning hours.

The vampire display was eerie with its crypt and tombs surrounding the cemetery setting, which was dimly lit with fake torches. Naturally, it was a nighttime setting, since vampires preferred it that way. Devon lingered around the set and took in all the amazing details while Brant eagerly awaited her reaction. A lavishly dressed male and female vampire attacked a cemetery full of men with swords and stakes. It was a gruesome scene depicting men with torn, bloodied throats.

Devon recognized one of the wax men as a reconstruct from the old museum. She remembered uncrating him. She couldn't be sure, but she swore he was supposed to be Teddy Roosevelt, even though Ross had heavily debated that theory with her. So Teddy Roosevelt was now a vampire-hunting villager. It was slightly amusing. Once Brant turned on the special effects, the vampires moaned and hissed. Teddy Roosevelt stood with his sword prepared to decapitate the vampire attacking his friend.

Despite the noise and movement within the set, Devon took time to study Teddy's eyes. Whoever had created the wax figures from the old museum certainly had access to the most realistic looking glass eyes. The eyes Brant provided looked good, but not nearly as good as the reconstructs.

"Honestly, though," Brant announced. "He looks like Teddy Roosevelt, right?"

Devon looked at him with surprise then laughed. "That's exactly what I'd been telling Ross when we uncrated him," she announced. "He argued with me half the day over it."

"Yeah, me too," Brant replied. "I think Ross needs glasses."

They were about to continue across the loud, animated display when she paused to look at the other villager victims. Despite the dirty blonde hair, one of the men looked a little like Karl. It was uncanny how so many of the wax men and woman looked like famous people or people she knew.

In the next scene over, there appeared to be a man plunging a stake into an open casket. Devon heard the bone-chilling pounding of the stake supposedly entering the vampire's body. The vampire flew up within the coffin with the stake in its chest and his long fingers clutching the wooden projectile. Devon jumped with surprise then placed her hand on her chest. She wasn't expecting the hydraulic actions of the vampire, and it seemed unfair that Brant refused to share that information ahead of time with them. She was almost certain it was because he enjoyed scaring her. As she studied the vampire with the stake through his heart, there was enough gory detail to make her cringe. Brant did fine work on the stake through the heart and the gruesome corresponding wound.

"What do you think?" Brant asked cheerfully.

"It's very, uh, realistic," she informed him then shivered at the gruesome detail. "I'm guessing our younger visitors will have nightmares."

"I can live with that," Brant teased with a pleased look on his face.

She couldn't stop thinking about what she'd seen on Saturday night within the workshop. After casting several looks at Brant, she finally turned to face him.

"I wasn't doing much over the weekend," Devon informed him. "You could've called. I would have gladly come in."

Brant fidgeted slightly and managed a tiny smile. "I wouldn't have been very good company," he muttered while running his fingers through his hair.

Devon returned her attention back to the violent, loud display. Brant turned off the scene with the remote control from his pocket and left the room. Devon looked around, realized he'd left, and hurried after him.

Devon and Brant sat at the counter in the workshop that afternoon and worked on a full-sized zombie laid out before them. The zombie required a lot of decay on his exposed fleshy parts, so they tag teamed the job. Brant seemed less enthusiastic than usual with his work and was forced to correct half of what he did. He used enough turpentine to fill the room with fumes, making Devon slightly lightheaded. She eyed him several times while working on the zombie's lower leg.

"Would you like to talk about the party?" she finally asked.

"I wouldn't want to bore you," he muttered with little enthusiasm.

She looked back down and concentrated on her work. "Sorry, I didn't mean to pry."

"It's not prying," he quickly chirped then looked up and fidgeted. "I don't mind really." He drew a deep breath, tossed down his rag, and stared at the wax zombie before him. "My mother's always playing matchmaker. She thinks she has to bring women to the house in hopes I'll find a suitable mother for my children. Needless to say, it didn't start off very promising and gradually got worse." He groaned and shook his head. "This one was so much like my mother; it was almost frightening."

Brant collapsed into his chair, snatched a paint pen, and worked on the zombie's hand.

"So my weekend sucked," he announced with a sigh then eyed her. "How was yours?"

"Uneventful," Devon replied. "As usual, Ivy got drunk, and I had to drive her home." She hesitated and considered her next comment carefully. "I, uh, saw you at the tavern on Saturday."

He looked at her with surprise then managed a humored smile. "Then you knew I wasn't gone the whole weekend." He casually shrugged. "I needed a few drinks after my Friday night fiasco. If I lived closer to my parents, I'd be an alcoholic by now."

She was too embarrassed to look at him. "I wasn't sure I should mention seeing you at the tavern," Devon remarked.

He finally looked at her and appeared surprised. "Why not?"

"Because you were sort of *busy* at the time," she announced timidly.

He stared at her a moment as if attempting to figure out what she meant. He then realized what she'd witnessed.

"Yeah, busy," Brant scoffed. "Busy eluding some trashy woman."

"Paula," she informed him. "She attempted to seduce you, because she knew you were my boss and wanted to piss me off."

Brant hesitated a moment then glanced at her. "Why would you be pissed off by that?" he asked.

Devon stared at him and realized she didn't have a good answer. "Well," she fumbled. "You know; because you're my boss, and it would be awkward."

He returned to his zombie hand and nodded. "Yeah, I guess it would." Brant then considered something else. "Pretty sad that the only offer I'd had in months was part of a revenge scheme."

"I'm sorry," Devon suddenly announced while turning toward him. "I didn't mean to make you feel bad. Obviously, Paula could never hope to attract someone like you if you weren't totally wasted."

Brant cast a glance at her and laughed. "It's okay," he remarked. "You don't have to spare my feelings but thanks anyway. I'll survive."

Their eyes briefly met. Devon couldn't help but stare into his eyes. It was true; he was a handsome man by any standards. The lights flickered and went out. Devon gasped with surprise and looked around the excessively dark

125

room. Since there were no windows, it was nearly pitch black.

"Guess that's lunch," Brant announced with a sigh. "Don't move. There's a flashlight somewhere around here."

She heard his chair roll across the floor as he had so many times before. A loud crash followed.

"Brant?"

"That works better when I can actually see," he groaned, obviously in some pain. A small light brightened the area surrounding him. "It's not much, but it'll be bright enough to get us up the stairs to the kitchen. I have some kerosene lamps."

Chapter Twenty-four

Devon and Brant sat at the small kitchen table while laughing over several glasses of wine as the storm raged outside. They'd already had too much to drink, although neither seemed to notice or care. The kerosene lamp did an excellent job of lighting most of the kitchen even if neither could see straight. Devon had never seen the sky look so black before, and the rain poured down like a waterfall outside the window. Despite calling it a lunch break, with the power out, it was more of a permanent break. It didn't seem as if they would be getting any work done, so they were in no hurry and possibly in no condition to return to the dungeon.

Brant refilled each of their glasses despite that they were both feeling a little too good already. Devon was enjoying their executive lunch and her mildly drunken state. She was having a good time talking with Brant, especially after the wine loosened him enough to speak his mind. Unfortunately, the wine also loosened her enough to entertain misguided thoughts regarding her handsome boss.

"There's always a party with Ross around, I'm afraid," Devon informed Brant while giggling.

"I've enjoyed working with him," Brant replied honestly. "Try working in a lab some time. What a bunch of stiffs. Everyone is so serious."

"I couldn't even imagine. I suppose I've been exposed to Ross for too long," Devon remarked then carefully considered her next question, but large quantities of wine allowed her to ask it anyway. "Tyler doesn't really have much of a sense of humor, does he?"

He chuckled at the question, finding it amusing. "Tyler is a businessman. He's only in it for the money," Brant announced then sighed. "I suppose that's why he makes a good partner. Someone has to run operations and deal with the public. I'm not exactly comfortable socializing with investor types. Or any type for that matter."

"Neither am I, but you don't have much choice in this town," Devon replied while sipping her wine. "Everyone pretty much knows everyone else's business. You have to know who your allies are."

"I don't think I have many of those," Brant informed her. "I've only ever been accepted among other scientists. We talk the same language, I suppose."

"I grew up around cowboys. You can just imagine the language I've learned," she teased and giggled. It was at that moment she realized she'd had too much to drink and attempted to sound less giddy. "After the incident last month, my father insisted if I wanted to work, I had to find a job in town away from horses and cattle." She made a face. "Honestly, he'd prefer it if I just got married and played mommy to his grandchildren. He doesn't really care for the idea of me working in the real world."

"Guess we have something in common then," he informed her. "I wasn't able to express myself growing up. My father molded me into his little protégé. This museum represents an entire fortune spent on a dream to find out who I really am. So far, it's been the best time of my life.

Whether it turns into something I can make a living doing is another story."

"Judging by your work, you're a true artist, Brant," she informed him. "It takes a lot of passion and commitment to be an artist."

Brant smirked and looked away. "I must be the exception," he remarked timidly. "Passion has never been my strong point."

Devon placed her hand on his forcing him to look back at her as she stared into his eyes.

"I disagree."

Brant gently cupped her hand and caressed it. She couldn't deny his touch sent a tingling sensation through her body. Or was that just the wine? He pulled his hand away, smiled with some embarrassment, and replaced the cork to the third bottle of wine.

"I think you've had too much wine," he remarked then chuckled while muttering, "Me too."

She was actually enjoying her moderately drunk condition. Devon leaned back in her chair and smiled warmly while studying the handsome man. Brant was, without a doubt, the smartest man she'd ever known, and it was quite the turn-on. Her thoughts were actually starting to scare her. They heard a loud crack of thunder and simultaneously jumped. Devon was jolted back to reality and attempted to push any lustful thoughts from her mind. Both looked out the kitchen window.

"It doesn't appear as if we'll accomplish much this afternoon," he announced with a defeated sigh. "You may as well leave early, although I hate the thought of sending you out in this storm."

"I'll wait it out," she replied. She couldn't admit she was having too much fun drinking with her boss. "Martin is at work, so I don't have a ride anyway."

"I'd give you a ride, but my car is at my house next door," he announced then chuckled. "I fear we'd both drown before we reached it."

She laughed at the comment and smiled in response. "I'm sure we can find something to do until the power comes back on," Devon boldly announced then immediately realized what she said and how he might take it the wrong way.

He eyed her a moment in silence, almost confirming that he'd taken it the wrong way. His eyes then lit up at the thoughts racing through his mind.

"Raid the wardrobe closet, dress like pirates, and have pretend sword fights?" he suggested almost without hesitation then grinned teasingly.

It took a moment for his words to register. Devon was slightly stunned by the mischievous comment. Even though she knew he meant it to sound like a joke, she actually wondered if he was being serious. She fidgeted slightly and leaned forward in her chair, nearly collapsing on the table, and met his gaze.

"I have a confession to make," Devon announced while hiding her devious, drunken smile. "I've tried on half the clothes in that wardrobe closet already."

Brant stared at her a moment with a stunned expression then chuckled. "Me too." His look then turned serious despite his buzzed state. "Not the dresses, of course. I don't have the legs for them."

Devon suddenly burst out laughing and placed her hand on his lower arm while nearly falling across the table.

Chapter Twenty-five

Devon and Brant laughed while she clung to his arm as they headed down the stone dungeon steps into the basement. Brant carried a battery-operated lantern while Devon clutched a large flashlight. They decided to take the longer route rather than the kitchen shortcut to the workshop. In their drunken condition, they had the strange desire to explore the displays in the dark in an attempt to scare themselves silly.

"Ross can never know about this," Brant warned her with a stern look while partially holding her up. "He screws around enough when he thinks I'm not watching. He can't know I actually condone this sort of bad behavior."

She laughed almost uncontrollably, giddy from too much wine. "Trust me; I'm not telling Ross you and I played plundering pirates during a power outage." Her eyes widened dramatically as her look turned serious. "He's been trying to get me into those shackles in the torture chamber for days. I swear; he's hell-bent on playing out some depraved sexual fantasy in that torture chamber."

Brant chuckled, humored by the confession. "I suppose I'm a hopeless romantic," he announced while grinning. "Mine involves the altar in the church scene."

He suddenly stopped on the steps, apparently realizing he'd spoken aloud. Devon also stopped and looked at him with surprise. His eyes widened as he stared at her.

"I am so sorry," he practically gasped. "I shouldn't have said that aloud. That was so inappropriate."

As she stared into his eyes, she was almost speechless. "That's my fantasy too," she gasped enthusiastically as she fell against him, knocking him against the wall.

Devon stared into his eyes while grinning uncontrollably at the sexual fantasies racing through her mind. She groaned softly as her free hand traveled his chest.

"That would be so much fun," she announced with her mouth close to his.

Brant stared into her eyes unable to speak as their mouths practically touched. He was slightly stunned while she barely controlled her grin.

"So, uh, you want to do that instead of the plundering pirate thing?" he announced timidly almost unable to get the words out and allowed his lips to brush past hers.

Devon turned enthusiastic and practically crawled up his body. "Yes, let's do that instead."

He held her hand to his chest to keep it from caressing him then brushed his lips past hers. She shut her eyes and groaned in anticipation of his kiss.

Brant drew a deep breath and resisted kissing her. "I think you had too much to drink," he gently insisted.

Her eyes opened, and she immediately met his gaze while maintaining her grin. "I'm fine," she giggled.

"You know," he announced and affectionately caressed her hand. "The full effect will be lost without the candles and the backlight from the stained glass window." He gently cleared his throat. "Why don't we do the pirate thing first and save the other thing for when the power is restored?"

She stared at him a moment, considered the comment, and then nodded. "You're probably right." Devon moved away from him and headed down the stone steps as if the entire conversation had been forgotten already.

Brant groaned softly, ran his fingers through his hair, and followed with less enthusiasm. "Chivalry sucks," he muttered.

As they neared the bottom, they heard what sounded like running water and looked at each other with confusion. Both hurried down the rest of the stairs and saw a foot of water covering the basement floor. Brant and Devon stood at the bottom of the steps and stared at the flooded basement.

"I don't believe this!"

Brant stepped into the water, hurried along the water covered walkway, and entered the first display. Devon hurried behind him and saw Dr. Frankenstein's lab under a foot of water. The sets were already saturated.

"It's ruined," he cried out. "All that work straight to hell!"

Devon remained silent while standing in the water a few feet behind him. She didn't know what she could possibly say to comfort him. She did find it a little surprising that the water was practically clear enough to see the floor. She somehow thought the water would be murky. Of course, she doubted Brant would care to hear that at the moment.

"This can't be happening!" Brant announced as he turned in the water to face Devon with a look of defeat on his face.

"We'll call someone to pump out the basement," she gently informed him while attempting to clear her head. "It may be okay. I'm sure we can fix it."

"Nice try," he announced with a groan. "I'd better cut the circuit, just in case the power comes back on." He ran his fingers through his hair and sighed. "Wouldn't want to be electrocuted."

Brant trudged through the water and headed past the displays on his lengthy journey to the workshop. Devon looked around, gasped softly, and hurried after him. As they entered the graveyard display, Devon and Brant watched wax zombies float face first in the water past them. Both stopped, unable to take their eyes off the worst affected display since there had been a lot of activity located on the ground. Brant stared at the zombies and headstones floating in a layer of fake moss.

"Lovely," he scoffed showing no emotion. "I'm ruined."

The wax zombies gently floated around the room with their tattered clothing drifting behind them. A female zombie bumped into their legs. Devon looked at the blonde zombie face down in the water and noted the alluring red dress. She didn't remember a zombie wearing a dress like that. She pulled away from Brant and turned the wax woman over. Devon stared at Jamie Smyth floating in the water, her dead eyes staring back. Devon then saw the bruises on her neck and the gruesome, excessively clean stab wounds to her chest and abdomen. She then realized that Jamie had been murdered! Devon let out a shrill scream and jumped backward into Brant.

"Oh, my God," Devon cried out unable to take her eyes off the dead woman. "Jamie!"

Jamie's corpse once more bumped against her legs, causing Devon to scream again. Brant gathered Devon in his arms and physically pulled her away from the floating dead woman while staring with his own look of horror. He turned, forcing her through the water back toward the steps. They crashed into a floating wax zombie and fell together into the water. Devon splashed in the foot deep water attempting to get her feet under her. She stared at the male zombie and screamed hysterically while pushing it away even though it was just wax. Brant pulled her to her feet and hurried her from the display.

Chapter Twenty-six

Brant stood in the museum kitchen with the phone to his ear while nodding at what the person on the other end was saying. Devon had her arms folded across her soaked body and trembled from the chill and her shock. She purposely stood only inches away from Brant, hoping she'd feel secure, but it wasn't working.

"Thank you, Deputy Havens," he responded then hung up the phone and turned toward Devon. "The police are on their way."

Devon continued to shiver while staring at him with fear in her eyes. "She was murdered, wasn't she?" she asked with a quiver in her voice, although she already knew the answer by the gruesomeness of her injuries.

Each time she shut her eyes, she could see the deep stab wounds in Jamie's chest and torso, the blood washed away from soaking in the water. Brant gently pulled her into his arms and attempted to comfort her. She immediately clung to him despite their wet bodies.

"The police can handle it," he announced in a comforting tone while gently rubbing her shoulders, which was possibly his own coping mechanism. "You'll be more comfortable next door at my house. You can change into some dry clothes."

She mechanically nodded without moving from his arms. He attempted to pull away, but she didn't release him. Brant hesitated then resumed holding her.

§

There was a fire burning in the living room fireplace within Brant's house, which gave off enough light to brighten the entire room. The home was older, but it contained beautifully detailed woodwork and a large, marble fireplace. Brant, already changed into dry clothes, kneeled before the fireplace while poking the fire to keep it burning. Devon approached from the hallway wearing one of Brant's shirts and a pair of his shorts. She continued to rub her chilled arms as she approached the fireplace. She kneeled beside him and shivered. Brant glanced at her as she stared at the fire and didn't look away. He set the poker aside and touched her shoulder.

"Are you okay?"

"I'll be fine," she whispered and stared without emotion at the flames.

Brant moved back a few feet, removed a tea mug from the coffee table, and extended it to her.

"Drink this," he announced reassuringly. "You'll feel better."

Devon moved closer to him, accepted the mug, and sipped the contents. She immediately made a face from the warmed alcohol mixed with cider. Brant sat on the floor and rested against the sofa. Devon immediately moved across the floor and sat surprisingly close to him. Brant uncertainly placed his arm around her shoulder and held her against him. She set her cup on the table and clung to him with her head to his chest. She didn't care that he was her boss or that she barely knew him; she just wanted him to hold her. He circled his arms around her and held her close, perhaps for his own security as well as hers. Through the pouring rain just outside the large, bay window, they could see the red and blue flashing lights of the approaching police vehicle. He affectionately kissed the top of her head.

"I'll deal with the unpleasantness next door," he gently informed her. "You just stay here. If they want to talk to you, I'll bring them over."

Devon didn't want to release him, but she knew someone had to greet the police at the museum. She wasn't sure how long he was gone before she moved to the sofa, collected into a small ball, and shivered with the tea mug in her hand.

§

Nearly two hours later, Sheriff Carter stood by the fireplace in Brant's home while writing on his notepad in chilling silence. Devon and Brant now sat on the sofa huddled together while the sheriff questioned them. Devon appeared completely relaxed now and possibly drunk after drinking the entire contents of her mug as well as Brant's that he'd left behind when he went next door. Brant remained tense regarding the sheriff's line of questioning while Devon clung to him happily clueless.

"I understand Karl had been working on the museum last week," Sheriff Carter announced. "When was he here last?"

"Friday afternoon," Brant informed him then fidgeted. "I'd dismissed the construction company for improper conduct."

Sheriff Carter eyed Devon as if reading between the lines then looked back at Brant. "There have been complaints about Larry's Construction in the past," the sheriff remarked then wrote something in his notebook. "The outer museum basement door appears to have been forced open. It's not noticeable at a glance, but there are fresh notches in the wood."

"We used that entrance last Thursday for our delivery," Brant informed him. "I'm positive I locked it when we were finished, although I'm not sure what I did with the keys."

"Was there anyone here Friday evening?" Sheriff Carter asked. "That's the night she'd disappeared."

Brant only briefly considered the question. "No. Ross, Devon, and I left about five o'clock on Friday," he announced. "I went to a dinner party at my parents' house in the city and didn't get home until early Saturday morning."

"What about your partner, Tyler?"

"He was either at his beach house or in the city, as he is most weekends," Brant replied.

"Anyone else at the museum on Friday?" Sheriff Carter asked.

"Just the construction crew and the four of us," he replied then hesitated. "And Tony."

Carter raised a curious brow. "Tony O'Brien?"

"Yes," Brant announced. "He brings lunch on Fridays. He's Ross' friend."

"Once they're finished pumping the water from the basement, we'll conduct a more thorough search," Sheriff Carter informed him.

"Thank you, Sheriff."

Brant freed himself from Devon's grip and walked Sheriff Carter to the front door. Only a moment passed when Devon heard a familiar voice from the front door. Ross entered the living room and hurried for Devon as she sprang up from the sofa.

"Devon, are you all right?" he practically gasped.

Devon staggered toward Ross and drunkenly fell into his arms. "Oh, Ross. I'm so glad to see you," she cried out and hugged him.

Ross held her to keep her from falling. He stared at her with some surprise then cast a look at Brant, who stood nearby.

"Is she drunk?" he asked with surprise.

"Maybe a little," Brant replied.

Chapter Twenty-seven

It was late Monday afternoon, and the storm had finally passed, although there were plenty of flooded roadways, downed trees, and power outages. The small town was particularly hit hard, especially along the back roads. The resort area seemed less affected by the aftermath of the storm since most of the power lines were underground and there were few older trees with weak limbs. A few smaller branches scattered about parking lots was the extent of the damage to the newly developed resort area.

Tamara walked across the mostly filled hotel parking lot toward her lightly used, powder blue compact car. She was dressed in her black housekeeping uniform and comfortable shoes looking exhausted from her morning working the seven to three shift at the hotel. She pressed the button on her keychain, electronically unlocking her car door as she approached. Tamara got into the car, sat behind the wheel a moment, and then looked at herself in the rearview mirror. Although only twenty-three, she looked much older. She frowned, started the car, and pulled out of the parking lot while avoiding larger puddles.

The light blue car drove away from the resort area and headed for town along the back road, which was the quickest route to her apartment on the other side of town. There were several tree limbs down, and the back road was covered in puddles and debris. As she drove down the lightly traveled road, Jamie's red sports car appeared behind her. Tamara glanced into her rearview mirror and immediately recognized the car.

"Great," Tamara scoffed. "Probably wants to gloat about getting the job."

Jamie's sports car picked up speed while entering the oncoming lane and drove alongside Tamara's car. She glanced to her left, half-expecting to see Jamie gloating, when the sports car picked up speed and swerved in front of her. Tamara cried out with surprise and turned the wheel to avoid hitting the sports car. Her car ran off the road, hit the gravel, and struck an embankment. Tamara was thrown against the seatbelt, which held her in place upon impact. She clung to the wheel a moment while panting from the near collision. The sports car stopped on the street and backed up until it was on the road a few yards in front of Tamara's disabled car. Tamara sneered and sprang from her car.

"What the hell is wrong with you?" she cried out demandingly while flinging her arms around wildly at her former friend. "You could have killed me, you stupid bitch!"

The car suddenly rocketed backward in reverse. Tamara saw the car coming and attempted to jump out of the way. She was nearly clipped by the sports car while leaping over the hood of her own car. She slid off the car hood and fell onto the gravel before it. Jamie's car pulled alongside her. Tamara slowly picked herself up from the gravel while gingerly rubbing her shoulder. She looked at the car with anger and was about to scream at Jamie when she saw the phantom lunging for her. Tamara let out a startled scream as a stun gun was thrust against her midsection. She jerked and jolted before falling to the ground.

§

Tamara opened her eyes and stared at the old, partially rotted ceiling above her. Within the dimly lit room, she could make out a cobweb-covered chandelier. She groaned softly and looked around while attempting to sit up. Her arms were immobile, stretched out on either side of the dining room table, and somehow tied to it. Her ankles were tied together and to the table as well. Tamara gasped and immediately fought her bindings, but she couldn't free herself. A tear in the old, heavy curtains allowed the setting sun to shine partially through, indicating she'd been out for several hours. A strange scraping sound alarmed her.

"Help," she cried out, although it was possible no one would hear her.

The scraping sound got louder and seemed to be coming from behind her head. It was the only area she couldn't see from her tied position on the table.

"Please, let me go," she sobbed. "Why are you doing this?"

The scraping sound stopped. Tamara nervously looked to her right and saw the phantom standing over her where she was tied to the table. Tamara screamed when she saw him. He raised an ax above his head. She continued to scream while fighting the ropes holding her to the table. The ax came down and struck her in the abdomen. Tamara cried out then gasped as her body jerked, and she spit up blood. The ax was pulled from her body and thrust downward again. She managed a faint whimper then became motionless. The ax was pulled from her body and struck her again and again, sending blood flying across the room. When the phantom had cast his final blow, he left the ax in her torn abdomen and walked away. Blood seeped through the splintered table and dripped into a puddle on the floor below.

Chapter Twenty-eight

It was a little before noon on Tuesday. Ross, Devon, and Martin appeared uncomfortable as they sat in the front, left parlor of the funeral home. Voices were heard within the right side parlor across the hall from them. Tony was comforting his grieving client. Dorothy Smyth sobbed into her handkerchief as she stepped out of the front parlor and walked along the hallway with Tony by her side.

"You've been so kind in my time of need, Tony. Jamie would appreciate you taking care of her like this," Dorothy announced while fighting her tears. "You'll make all the arrangements?"

"I'll take care of everything, Mrs. Smyth," Tony informed her while gently touching her elbow. "Why don't you go home and rest?"

Dorothy nodded. "Chelsea's waiting for me at Dr. Sherman's office," she announced. "Gina was good enough to keep an eye on her for me while I took care of Jamie's final arrangements."

Tony offered a pleasant smile and escorted her to the front door. He shut the door then glanced into the left, front parlor and saw his friends. He entered the parlor and closed the double, sliding doors behind him, allowing them some privacy in case someone else showed up unexpectedly. All three were silent while staring at their friend.

"Sorry I'm running a little late for lunch," Tony informed them while nervously running his fingers through his hair. "Prepping Jamie isn't going to be easy. It's been a while since I've had a client younger than me. And considering the circumstances--"

Tony hesitated and didn't finish the thought although they knew what he wanted to say. Prepping someone who'd been brutally murdered couldn't be easy, particularly someone so young, and from their small town where everyone knew everyone else.

"Emotionally, I'm wiped out," Tony announced gently while fidgeting.

"Take your time," Ross announced, possibly being serious for the first time in his life. "It's been a difficult couple of days for all of us."

Tony eyed Martin and seemed a little surprised to see him. "Didn't expect to see you here, Martin," Tony remarked and offered a tiny smile. "I thought you were allergic to funeral homes?"

"I avoid them when I can," he replied then tensed. "After yesterday, I didn't think I should leave Devon alone."

"It was nice of Brant to give us the day off," Devon remarked.

"I think he was pretty shaken himself," Ross informed her.

"When I went to the morgue to pick up the, uh, Jamie's remains, Sheriff Carter was there. He shared some news about the murder," Tony announced, fumbling for something to say.

All three suddenly perked up, giving him their full attention.

"What did he say?" Devon asked.

"Jamie was killed Friday evening sometime between six-thirty and nine at night," Tony informed them. "According to Marlene, Jamie received a phone call at the diner from some man, and she left in a hurry. Marlene suspected it may have been Burt Danson, the producer. Dorothy said Jamie came home, changed into a slinky dress, and left without a word a little after six-thirty. She assumed she was going to meet some friends at a dance club at the resort area. When she didn't come home that night, Dorothy didn't think much of it."

"Jamie applied for the same acting job as Ivy had," Devon reminded them. "Maybe Burt had something to do with her murder."

"Sheriff Carter was on his way to the resorts to question Burt Danson," Tony replied then hesitated and looked around. "Where's Ivy? She'd be interested to hear this."

"Late as usual," Ross remarked.

"Tamara also auditioned for the acting job," Devon informed them. "Even though we don't really know anything for sure, we should warn her about Burt as well. Just in case."

"Paula too," Ross interjected.

"Screw Paula," Devon scoffed.

"That's an interesting theory about this Burt guy," Martin announced and seemed curious. "I mean, if she was going to meet him, it's pretty clear he was somehow involved."

"Better than Carter's original theory," Ross interjected and raised his brows. "He was working the jilted lover theory. Honestly, I don't think Karl was too broken up over Jamie dumping him."

"I heard they haven't been able to find Karl to question him," Martin added then eyed Ross. "I don't think you should discount him so quickly. Maybe he'll give a confession to her murder, and it'll be over with." He then considered something else. "What about your boss, Brant?

He could've killed Jamie and still made it in time for his parents' dinner party. If there really was a party."

Devon and Ross both glared at Martin.

"Brant wouldn't harm a fly," Devon insisted.

"Not according to what you'd told me the other day," Martin scoffed.

Ross turned his head and stared at her demandingly. "What happened the other day?"

"After Paula made a pass at him in the bar, he trashed the workshop," Martin informed Ross. "Devon saw him butcher a wax woman."

"He was just venting," she insisted. "Besides, he'd never even met Jamie."

"That you know," Martin remarked. "Jamie could have stopped by to visit Karl at the museum. The construction company was working there for months."

"If Brant were a killer, he'd have whacked Tyler by now," Ross informed Martin.

"I don't trust that man," Martin remarked while shaking his head. "Sexual frustration can motivate a man to kill a woman."

"Hey, I'm sexually frustrated, and I've never thought about killing women," Ross boldly announced.

"Excluding Martin, I'd say we're all pretty much sexually frustrated," Tony teased with a slightly embarrassed laugh.

"I'm not sexually frustrated," Devon corrected.

"No, you're just sexually frigid," Ross announced while chuckling.

Martin glared at Ross.

Ross caught his glare then fidgeted. "I was just kidding." He glanced at his watch and attempted to change the subject. "Where the hell is Ivy?"

vy's jeep pulled up to the old farmhouse in the middle of the vast farmland around quarter after twelve. She uncertainly got out of the jeep and stared at the creepy, abandoned building while clutching her large handbag securely against her side.

"Is this some sort of joke?" she remarked under her breath while staring at the old farmhouse. "Why would he want to meet here?"

She strummed her fingers on the car door, drew a deep breath, and then shut the door with determination. She straightened proudly, smoothed her form-fitting, flattering dress, and approached the house. She stepped onto the porch and nearly changed her mind when the floorboard creaked beneath her. She forced herself to approach the already partially open door and pushed it open the rest of the way. She peered into the creepy hallway and looked around.

"Burt?" she called out while scanning the area and clutching her large bag.

When there was no response, she looked back at her jeep and again considered leaving. She groaned and removed a small tube of mace from her bag before entering the house. She nervously closed the door behind her and again stared at the dilapidated interior. She took several steps into the hall then peered into the sitting room on the left. There were several pieces of old furniture, but not a living soul. She approached the sliding doors on the right and attempted to open them. They didn't budge.

"Burt?" she again called out.

When there was no response, she shook her head and turned back to the front door. There was a loud creak from upstairs. Ivy paused and looked up the half-rotted steps and insecurely clung to her shoulder bag in one hand and the mace in the other. She drew a deep breath and approached the stairs. Within the dust, she could see fresh shoe prints, obviously from a man, heading up and down the steps. Ivy hesitated then nervously walked up the rickety steps, careful to mind the rotted boards. She reached the top while keeping her mace aimed and her finger on the button. She scanned the open bedroom doors to the right side of the hall. A shadow moved within one of the rooms.

"Burt?" she announced while trembling and waited for him to respond.

When there still wasn't a response, she slowly headed toward the bedroom and peered inside. Her brows immediately knitted with a curious look. She hurried into the room, disappearing inside. A second passed. Ivy suddenly cried out.

Chapter Twenty-nine

The police cruiser pulled behind Tamara's stranded car a little after noon. Sheriff Carter and Deputy Havens got out and approached the abandoned car. They separated and walked on either side of the car. Deputy Havens was forced to walk on the bank partway then had to return to the back of the car. He approached Sheriff Carter as he stood by the driver's side. Carter opened the car door, peered inside, but found nothing. He then straightened and looked around the back road.

"Guess she ran off the road," Deputy Havens remarked while indicating the condition of the car. "With all the downed branches and puddles, I'm not surprised."

"Yeah, it would look that way," Sheriff Carter replied, although his expression conveyed he wasn't completely satisfied. "Her mother said she called the hotel this morning, but Tamara didn't report for her shift. She suddenly doesn't show up for work after her car breaks down?" The sheriff shook his head. "I find that a little hard to swallow." He eyed his deputy. "I'll drop you off in town, so you can start asking questions. See if anyone's seen her. I need to get to the resort and track down Burt Danson."

Deputy Havens peeked inside the car. "I don't see a purse or car keys," he remarked then straightened with a glimmer of hope in his eyes. "It's still possible she was picked up by a friend."

"Then let's check with all her friends," Sheriff Carter announced. "There's something strange happening in my town. If some psycho has his sights on young women in this town, he's going to meet the business end of my Magnum."

§

Devon and Ross walked along the sidewalk in town after their shortened lunch with Tony, who had too much work to do. It was a beautiful day, although the town seemed quieter than usual. It was obvious the residents were concerned over what had happened in their sleepy, little town. There were several other residents enjoying a walk through town on the bright, sunny day, but there was limited conversation among them.

"I'm glad Martin was called away after lunch. I have to watch everything I say to you," Ross remarked. "You'd think with all the women he's bedded, he'd be a little more open-minded."

"I think it's guys like him he's trying to protect me from," Devon teased.

They paused on the sidewalk outside the bank where Ivy worked. Devon stared at the building while deep in thought then looked at Ross.

"I'm going to find out why Ivy stood us up for lunch," Devon informed him. "I'll only be a minute."

"I'll time you," Ross announced and gleefully set his watch.

Devon smiled at the challenge and hurried inside. Not surprising, the bank was nearly empty as it usually was around lunchtime. There were only two tellers working and only one customer at the counter. Devon approached the vacant teller.

"Hello, Devon," the young woman announced cheerfully. "If you're looking for Ivy, she left for the afternoon."

Devon stared at her with surprise and immediately felt anxious. "She has?" she questioned with surprise. "Did something happen?"

"No," the teller replied. "She received a phone call and had to leave early."

"Was it her mother?"

"No, it was a guy."

The words chilled her. "Thanks," Devon announced although she was concerned by the revelation. "I'll check her house to make sure everything's all right."

Devon hurried from the bank as her heart pounded and her anxiety rose. She approached Ross on the sidewalk and stopped before him.

He stopped the counter on his watch and grinned. "Under a minute. A new record."

Devon grabbed his arm without comment and dragged him along the sidewalk.

"Owe, that hurts," he whined and attempted to pull his arm free. "What's the hurry?"

"Ivy left work early," Devon announced and shook her head with concern. "I have a bad feeling she's doing something stupid."

"So? Why is it she does something stupid, and I'm the one getting his arm twisted off?" Ross demanded. "How's that fair?" He attempted to stop her, but she continued to pull him along.

"She left after receiving a phone call from a man," she remarked without slowing her pace as they headed for Ross' car.

"Just like Jamie?" Ross nearly gasped.

"We'll stop by her house and see if she's there," Devon announced. "If not, maybe her mother knows where she went and who she was meeting."

"You think she intended to meet Burt Danson?" Ross cried out softly. "Jamie was possibly meeting him when she was--"

"I know," Devon announced. "So we should hurry."

§

Ross' old mustang was more Bondo than car anymore. The engine sounded as if it had actual horses running through it. The part black, Bondo red, and baby shit green car pulled up to Ivy's house. The beast came to a grinding stop and rattled before shutting down. The doors creaked, sounding like fingernails on a chalkboard when they opened. Ross and Devon jumped from the car and hurried up the steps to the quiet, little house. Devon knocked on the door with urgency. Ivy's mother, Candice, opened the door and stared at them with some surprise. Perhaps it was the loud car that startled her.

"Devon, I didn't expect to see you today," she announced then turned sympathetic, having heard about her ordeal. "How are you feeling, dear?"

"I'm fine, Mrs. Jennings," she announced although she was preoccupied with more important concerns. "Is Ivy home?"

"No, she's not," Candice announced with little concern. "She came home, changed, and then left maybe half an hour ago."

"Did she say where she was going?" Devon immediately chimed in.

Candice stared at Devon, obviously surprised by the urgency in her tone. "No, but by the way she was dressed, I assumed she was meeting a guy." She eyed both. "Is something wrong?"

Devon and Ross exchanged concerned looks then returned their attention to Ivy's mother.

"I don't want to alarm you," Devon announced while fidgeting, "but we need to find Ivy. Did she say anything at all about her phone call? It's important we know where she went."

"What's this about?" Candice nearly gasped alarmed by Devon's concern.

"The night Jamie was murdered, she got a phone call at the diner believed to be from Burt Danson," Devon explained.

"Or someone pretending to be Burt Danson," Ross added.

"We think someone may have lured Jamie to her death with that phone call," Devon informed her as delicately as possible. "When they told us at the bank Ivy received a phone call from a man and took off--"

"We really need to find her," Ross interjected.

Candice placed her hand over her mouth while staring at them. She immediately replayed in her mind her last conversation with Ivy.

"She said something about having to meet someone," Candice fumbled over her own thoughts. "I think, uh, I think she may have mentioned a farmhouse. It was an old farmhouse because she said something about how she thought it had been torn down."

Ross and Devon exchanged looks and immediately came to the same conclusion.

"Baxter's old farm!"

"Miller's farm!"

They stared at each other with surprise. Candice appeared horrified.

"We'll take two cars and split up," Candice announced then darted back inside to snatch her car keys.

She returned to the porch only a second later then hurried Devon and Ross into the driveway. Ross indicated Candice to Devon.

"You go with Mrs. Jennings to Baxter's old farm," he announced. "I'll check out Miller's farm."

Devon nodded and climbed into Candice's car. Ross jumped into his beast and turned the key. The engine grinded, revved, sputtered, and then thumped before shutting off. Steam came from the hood. Ross jumped out of his car and ran for Candice's car, jumping into the back seat.

"Change of plans," he announced. "We'll go together. Safety in numbers."

"Piece of shit car," Devon scoffed.

"Hey, that's a classic car," Ross protested. "It just needs a little love." He then frowned. "But we don't have time for that much love."

Chapter Thirty

Mrs. Jennings pressed her foot on the accelerator and drove at high speeds along the back road. Devon clung to the passenger side door while Ross tumbled across the back seat. Ross pulled himself back into a sitting position and clung to the front seats.

"Does anyone even know where we're going?" Ross asked.

Mrs. Jennings didn't respond. She suddenly screamed and swerved to miss a squirrel in the road. Ross tumbled across the back seat once more.

"Wait," Devon cried out. "What's that road?"

Mrs. Jennings slammed on the brakes, and the car slid to a grinding halt. Ross flew into the front seats then struck the back seat.

"I was safer on the floor," he muttered while rubbing his sore neck.

An old, overgrown dirt road was seen beyond an open cattle gate. All three stared out the side window. It was possibly the first time anyone had seen the old, rusted gate open.

"That's the old Farley farm," Ivy's mother announced. "I'd forgotten it existed."

"It went up for auction last month, didn't it?" Devon asked.

"So?" Ross demanded.

"That gate's been closed forever," Devon explained. "Now it's open. Let's have a look that way."

The car shot backward and then spun onto the dirt road. Dirt flew behind the car as it jetted down the bumpy road. Ross peeked up unsteadily from the floor of the back seat. Devon glanced at Mrs. Jennings with alarm.

"Could you slow down?" Devon asked. "The element of surprise has a certain charm."

Mrs. Jennings immediately slowed down and attempted to calm herself.

§

Ivy's jeep was parked before the old farmhouse, but there was no sign of Ivy. Mrs. Jennings' car pulled alongside the jeep. The car no sooner stopped when Candice sprang from the driver's seat and ran for her daughter's jeep. Devon and Ross chased after her. They looked inside the jeep through the open windows then straightened and looked toward the old farmhouse. Devon hurried to the old house and ran onto the partially rotted porch. Candice attempted to follow, but Ross caught her arm and stopped her.

"You should wait out here," he announced then hurried after Devon.

Ross stepped onto the porch as Devon pushed open the slightly creaking door.

"Devon, don't go in without me," Ross whispered, but she ignored him and entered the house.

He groaned and attempted to walk on the less rotted boards that creaked and groaned beneath his feet. He ended up running across the porch as if running over hot coals. Ross entered the farmhouse hallway and immediately looked up the creepy steps that were partially rotted and missing. He grimaced then placed his hand on Devon's arm.

"I should probably go first," he announced then hesitated and pushed Devon along the hallway while hiding behind her.

Devon was too nervous even to realize Ross was using her as a shield. She peered into the first room they reached, which would have been the old sitting room. There were a few pieces of old furniture that were probably home to a dozen or more rats. The furniture was mostly chewed through with stuffing scattered around the floor. Devon was about to turn toward the room across the hall when she spotted something in the far corner of the room. She uncertainly entered the sitting room and approached what looked suspiciously like a body on the floor with a sheet covering it. Ross saw what she was staring at and clutched her arm.

"Maybe we should call Sheriff Carter," Ross suggested in a whisper.

Devon ignored him and continued her slow approach toward the sheet covered object. She reached out with a trembling hand and had to focus so she wouldn't react to Ross squeezing her arm, nearly cutting off her circulation. She grasped a corner of the sheet and pulled it off while jumping back a step and colliding with Ross. Ross cried out, causing Devon to scream as well. Both stared at the old grandfather clock lying on the floor. Devon and Ross finally exhaled and managed a tiny, nervous laugh. They practically hugged each other then returned to the hallway. Devon indicated the room with the closed door on the other side of the hall, which logically would have been the dining room. Devon attempted to open the door, but it wouldn't budge. She eyed Ross suspiciously.

"Why would the door be locked?"

"It's probably just stuck," he informed her. "It's a sliding door. I wouldn't doubt the wood is just warped or rotted."

Ross gently pushed her aside and pulled on the sliding door. Something snapped, and the door slid open with a thunderous crack, nearly falling off its track. They peered into the room and immediately focused their attention on the old dining room table. The old table contained a large pool of partially dried blood in the center. The wood was freshly splintered in the middle of the table caused by either a sword or ax. Blood had seeped through the cracks and collected into a pool on the floor beneath the table. Ross and Devon stared with shock at the large amount of blood that also streaked over the side of the table, as if something or someone had been pulled from it. Apart from blood spatters, there wasn't any other trace of blood on the floor. Whatever had been killed was placed on a tarp or blanket to keep from leaving a trail of blood.

"Ivy," Devon gasped with horror and cast a frightened look at Ross.

Ross couldn't take his eyes off the blood and appeared unable to speak.

"How in the world did you guys find me?" a female voice asked from behind them.

Ross and Devon screamed in unison while spinning around. They stared at Ivy, who stood in the hallway clutching her large purse. Ivy screamed when they screamed.

"What's going on?" Candice cried out from the front door.

Ross, Devon, and Ivy all screamed and spun toward the door. When they screamed, Candice screamed. Everyone took deep breaths and attempted to calm down. Ivy's mother ran toward the dining room and hugged her daughter.

"Oh, Ivy. I was so worried!"

She returned the hug and sighed. "Well, you can relax," Ivy huffed and pulled away while frowning. "The bastard never showed."

"Who?" her mother demanded.

"Burt Danson," she replied and made a face. "Apparently, he's been playing the casting couch game with his potential actresses."

"I can't believe you'd come out here by yourself to meet that snake," Devon suddenly cried out. "And after Jamie was murdered. What if he's the one who killed her?"

"I know it was stupid."

"Aren't we all forgetting something rather important?" Ross remarked while raising his brows.

Once they looked at him, he indicated the large pool of dried blood on the dining room table as if he were giving away a new car. Candice and Ivy saw the blood and cried out with horror.

"Holy hell," Ivy cried out. "What happened?"

"We thought you were killed," Devon informed her.

"Come on, let's get out of here," Ross announced and grabbed Ivy's arm. "We'll call Sheriff Carter from Ivy's house."

Ross practically pulled Ivy from the house. As they hurried off the porch, something sharp stuck Ross in the side. He cried out and looked at Ivy's large bag. A tiny kitten climbed his shirt.

"What the hell--?" he cried out and removed the kitten and its sharp claws from his side.

He stared at the kitten with surprise then looked back at Ivy. She grimaced slightly and opened her bag.

"Just put it back with the others," she announced.

Ross looked into her bag and saw three more kittens and their momma cat. Ross groaned and returned the kitten to her bag. As they headed toward the car and jeep, Ross hesitated and stared at the barn.

"Hey," he announced with surprise. "I think there's someone in the barn."

The three women turned toward the barn with surprise but didn't see anything except darkness beyond the partially open doors.

Candice grabbed Ivy's arm and tugged on her. "I don't care what's in there," she cried out. "Let's get out of here."

Devon followed Ivy to her jeep while Ross jumped into the back seat. Devon paused by the jeep door and looked back at the barn. The barn door gently swayed in the breeze, and she swore she saw something move within the darkness.

"He's right," Devon remarked nervously. "There's someone in the barn."

"Do you suppose it's Burt?" Ivy asked.

"I don't want to stick around to find out," her mother announced from her own car door. "Let's get out of here."

"We should check," Devon insisted without taking her eyes off the partially open barn door.

"You are not going into that barn," Ivy's mother cried out.

"We won't," Devon announced and glanced at the frantic woman. "We'll just drive up to it, give the doors a gentle nudge, and see who runs out."

"You're insane," Candice exploded then drew a deep breath and attempted to remain calm. "Just keep the car doors locked."

Candice jumped into her car while the others got into Ivy's jeep. Ivy started her jeep then drove toward the barn, gently pushing the big doors inward with the front bumper. The headlights from the jeep lit up the interior of the old barn. They saw Paula Jarred hanging by her neck from the barn rafters while her chalky white body swayed in the breeze. Her midsection was completely hollowed from a large slice starting at her sternum running down to her groin. Her insides lay in a heap on the dirt floor beneath her feet. Devon, Ivy, and Ross all screamed when they saw the savagely murdered woman.

Ivy continued to scream as she threw the shifter into reverse and floored the pedal. The jeep flew backward from the barn. There was a sudden jolt and a distinct crash. Ross was cast across the back seat. All three sat immobile a moment. Ivy and Devon uncertainly looked behind them. Ross pulled himself onto the seat and looked out the rear window. The front of Mrs. Jennings' car was smashed. Ross nervously waved at her from the back seat of the jeep.

Chapter Thirty-one

Later that afternoon, Devon sat silently in the sheriff's office while watching him casually route through papers on his moderately cluttered desk. Although a lot of people in town thought he was just a dumb, hick cop, Devon knew he was a problem solver. He always seemed to be jotting notes in his little notebook. She was pretty sure he was taking names to kick some asses in the future. His large frame and muscle mass was enough to intimidate even if others didn't think he was exceptionally bright. He finally leaned on his desk and met her gaze.

"Do you have a ride home?"

"Well, I came here with Ivy, so I assume she's taking me and Ross home," Devon replied then eyed him when he didn't initially respond.

He managed a tiny smile. "We have a few additional questions for Ivy," Sheriff Carter replied. "She's going to be detained a little while."

"Detained?" Devon suddenly asked and sat forward with a look of concern. "You mean arrested?"

"Nope," he casually replied and played with his pen while appearing almost bored. "Just detained."

As she stared at the sheriff, she was beginning to think she may have been wrong. Maybe he was just a clueless idiot.

"She didn't kill Paula," Devon firmly insisted. "You know she didn't."

"I didn't say she did," he announced then cocked his head slightly while eyeing her suspiciously. "Why would you assume I thought she had?"

Devon shifted in her chair while frowning. "Because you're naturally suspicious, and she was at the crime scene before we found Paula in the barn."

Sheriff Carter maintained his emotionless stare, but she swore she saw a hint of a smile at what he perceived to be a compliment.

"I'd have to be pretty stupid to think Ivy killed Paula before you arrived at the farmhouse," Sheriff Carter announced. "It was obvious Paula had been dead a few days already." He gave her a curious look. "What time did you leave Ivy on Saturday night?"

"It was about twelve-thirty, but she was drunk nearly to the point of passing out, and I had her jeep," Devon informed him. "She couldn't have gone anywhere even if she wanted to."

"I have to follow up on every possible lead," Sheriff Carter informed her. "Jamie and Tamara were Ivy's only real competition for that acting job. Witnesses said Paula was bragging that she had the job after her earlier audition in the back seat of Burt's sedan."

"What about Burt?" Devon demanded. "Couldn't he be killing off the women he's been promising this job? According to Marlene and Ivy, he's the one who lured them to that farmhouse."

"No, Devon," Sheriff Carter announced in a calm tone. "Someone *claiming* to be Burt Danson called and lured them to that farmhouse. Ivy confessed she wasn't sure it was actually Burt's voice on the phone."

She practically lunged forward. "Well, what about Karl? Jamie broke up with him a few days earlier. He must have been pissed at her," Devon exploded. "He could have been the one making phone calls and luring women to their deaths. Maybe Paula overheard something that got her killed."

"We're still looking for Karl. His roommate said he'd talked about taking off for a while after he'd lost his job with Larry's Construction," he announced then shifted in his chair. "Burt Danson doesn't have an alibi for Jamie's murder, but there weren't any phone calls made to the bank or the diner from his cell phone or the phone in his hotel room. Although we haven't ruled him out, his motive for actually killing women he auditioned would be hazy." He hesitated a moment while staring at her then raised his brows. "As a more interesting theory; we suspect one of the applicants may be cutting out the competition. Permanent like."

Devon was starting to feel overwhelmed by his questions and strange offering of information regarding the case. She wasn't sure if he was attempting to get her to confess something that would put Ivy in a bad light, or if he was just incompetent as most of the town suspected. She didn't believe he was incompetent, so she had to assume he was fishing for some reason and using her as the dangling worm on the hook.

"If that's the case, Tamara hated both women," Devon insisted in a defensive tone. "She'd be a more likely suspect than Ivy. Jamie and Paula were her friends back in high school. Tamara's sudden disappearance could just be part of her plan to frame someone else and generate sympathy. This town loves a good victim."

There was an awkward silence as the sheriff stared at her. He drew a deep breath. "Honestly, I'm not counting on finding Tamara alive."

She stared at him a moment as her mouth fell open with surprise. Devon immediately fidgeted and her defensiveness returned. "Ivy was called to that farmhouse. She'd received a phone call from a man the same as Jamie had," Devon informed him as her anxiety increased. "You know damned well she could have been the next intended victim."

"I'm not ruling that out either."

Devon was becoming frustrated with his line of questioning. It was possible that Sheriff Carter was after something, but she was certain he was enjoying watching her squirm.

"Why am I here, Sheriff Carter?" she finally demanded, becoming impatient.

He studied her a moment while remaining completely relaxed and showed little emotion. "Why?" he asked almost mocking her. "Because you know all the key players in this tale of murder and your mind is as sharp as a razor's edge." He leaned back in his chair while studying her. "I knew if I pissed you off just enough, you'd confirm or shoot down my theories." His mocking smile returned. "Do you honestly think there's anyone in this office who's smart enough to give me that sort of feedback? They're all one-trick ponies around here."

She stared at him with surprise. "You just wanted to bounce ideas off me?" Devon practically gasped then shook her head. "Why didn't you just ask?"

He suddenly snorted a laugh. "If there's one thing I've learned about your family," Sheriff Carter announced almost humored, "it's that you're all a bunch of level-headed thinkers who are good at keeping your mouths shut. Light the fuse, and you're a bunch of powder kegs waiting to explode. I appreciate your insights into the murders. I'll be in touch."

Devon stared at him in disbelief that she'd been played. He toyed with her emotions so she'd rattle off every theory regarding the murders. She wasn't sure if she respected him more for his devious mind or if she wanted to scream and punch him in the face. Why did she suddenly feel like her father?

§

Devon entered the diner a little while later with an annoyed look on her face. She waved at Marlene and looked for an empty table, but the diner was pretty full. Brant sat alone in a booth toward the back of the diner. Devon smiled more naturally and approached his table. She paused before Brant's booth and stared at him while he read the paper.

"Good evening."

Brant peered over his paper, appeared surprised to see her, folded his paper, and slid out of the booth while offering a sympathetic smile.

"Devon," he announced timidly. "How are you feeling?"

"I'm doing much better," she insisted. "It's been a rough day, but at least Sheriff Carter is letting Ivy go. I'm the first to admit that he's smarter than most people think, but sometimes he can be a real idiot." She groaned and ran her fingers through her hair. "I'd rather not talk about the murders anymore today."

"Fair enough," he announced while nodding then indicated the vacant seat across from him. "Care to join me for dinner?"

"I'd love to."

She joined him at the table then fidgeted slightly while reliving the events of her traumatic day. She attempted to push those thoughts from her mind.

"So did the zombies survive?"

"Yes, they'll live to frighten another day. Though I'm afraid the sets will need some major repairs," he informed her with a defeated sigh. "But I did buy a generator. No more power outages. It should keep the new sump pump working if there's another storm."

"I could come back to the museum with you and help clean up," Devon offered.

"I really appreciate the offer, but I'm afraid I have to attend a party at Tyler's beach house tonight," Brant announced then frowned. "He *insisted*."

"Oh," she groaned with disappointment.

"At least someone's enthusiastic about their work," Brant teased then studied her expression. "Wouldn't you rather spend a quiet evening at home?"

"Not particularly. My parents are going to grill me all night about what happened today at the farmhouse," she informed him. "I need to escape for a while. Honestly, I feel like I want to run away."

"You could always come with me to Tyler's party at his beach house," he joked then chuckled in his throat. "That might make you appreciate being interrogated by your parents."

She enthusiastically sat forward while staring at him. "Is that an actual offer?"

Brant was slightly surprised by the question then offered a sincere smile. "If you really want to go, but don't get too excited," he remarked. "Business parties are typically boring."

Her expression suddenly dropped. "Oh, that has the sound of formal wear," she remarked then frowned with defeat. "I don't even *own* a dress."

"The wardrobe closet at the museum is full of dresses," he informed her then hesitated. He seemed to drift off a moment as if in another world then looked back at her and offered a pleasant smile. "I'm sure you could find something suitable in there if you really want to come along."

She only took a moment to consider the thought then grinned with enthusiasm. "I'd love to," she announced suddenly feeling relieved. "Take me away from this awful place, Dr. Sheffield."

He chuckled at the comment. "Consider it done."

Chapter Thirty-two

The two-story beach house was nestled against the sand and appeared to be worth millions. It contained large windows and multi-tiered decks on the beachfront side. The beach was secluded, indicating Tyler owned most of the surrounding land as well. The house was well lit both inside and out for another lavish party. Wealthy couples socialized on the multi-level deck and within the large living room. Classical music could be heard even on the beach. Brant and Devon entered the house filled with neatly dressed men and women who were drinking fancy cocktails and socializing.

Devon looked stunning in the simple, black dress with a daring slit up the left side and matching high heels. She'd borrowed the dress from the museum's vast wardrobe closet and had to hope it had been cleaned since last worn by an actual human. Devon linked onto Brant's arm and looked around while feeling insecure.

"Do you know anyone?" she whispered close to his ear while leaning on his shoulder.

"Not a soul," he replied and gave a polite nod to the people they passed.

She eyed him with surprise then laughed. As they walked across the crowded room, several men turned their heads and watched them pass.

Devon uncertainly clung to Brant's arm and whispered, "They're staring."

"Men frequently stare at beautiful women," he casually informed her while grinning.

She gave him a surprised look then smirked. "Stop," she teased.

Tyler socialized with several of his guests on the far end of the room. When he saw them, he excused himself and approached while grinning deviously.

"I thought you abandoned me," Tyler announced to Brant then eyed Devon and chuckled. "But I see you had a better reason to be late."

"Don't get too excited," Brant announced casually. "Devon was bored, and I needed motivation to attend yet another party."

"Sure, if you say so," Tyler teased and chuckled. "Let's get Devon a drink then I want to introduce you to some wealthy investors I've been schmoozing." Tyler motioned for them to follow him.

Brant eyed Devon and drew a deep breath. "Welcome to my hell," he announced and sighed. "The only thing missing from this trip to purgatory is the devil himself." He then considered the comment and smiled at her. "But I'm sure you'll meet my mother one day."

Devon leaned on the balcony railing later that evening and watched the waves crash to shore as the wind whipped through her hair. She smiled contentedly and enjoyed the almost peaceful view. Several couples walked along the beach and stole kisses in the moonlight. She almost envied them, wishing she had someone to take on a romantic stroll. If she were honest with herself, she wanted someone to hold and kiss her. Her thoughts strayed to Brant and how handsome he looked in his expensive suit. She was suddenly thinking about more than a few stolen kisses.

"Dull party, huh?" a familiar male voice announced, interrupting her fantasy.

Devon spun toward the familiar voice and saw Martin standing on the balcony a few feet behind her. His expression immediately dropped when he realized it was his sister.

"Devon?" he practically gasped while staring at her. "What are you doing here?" His brows raised as he looked over her attire. "And dressed like that?" He suddenly cringed and looked away while shielding his eyes. "Talk about embarrassing. I can't believe I was checking out my sister!"

"Martin," she announced, just as surprised to see her brother. "I didn't know you knew Tyler."

"Tyler?" he asked and finally looked at her.

"He owns this house," she informed him. "He's Brant's business partner."

"I came with a friend. We're party crashers," he informed her in a slightly jovial tone. "The club pickens were a little stale tonight."

She shook her head and withheld her laugh. "You're amazing."

His eyes suddenly narrowed as he stared at her. "Are you dating your creepy boss?"

"No, he just brought me along for the ride," she insisted.

He cast a look at her in the dress. "I'd say he brought you along for his image," he teased then looked around. "So where is he? I'd like to meet him."

"He went for drinks," she informed him. "He'll be back shortly."

"You wait for him," Martin announced. "I'll find my friend and introduce you."

"Sounds great," she replied.

Chapter Thirty-three

Devon stared at the ocean and enjoyed the view from Tyler's balcony. She rarely got to the coast, although being without a car may have had something to do with that. She wasn't sure how long she was preoccupied with the romantic view before a champagne flute was extended before her. She turned to see Brant holding the glass of champagne. She smiled warmly and accepted the drink.

"Sorry I took so long," he announced with apprehension. "I ran into a guy I'd met last week, and I couldn't get away."

"That's okay," she replied then beamed enthusiastically. "You'll never guess who I ran into tonight."

"Who?"

"My brother. He's here," she insisted while laughing at how ironic running into him had been. "He said he'd meet us out here."

"Good," Brant announced cheerfully and casually leaned on the railing. "That means I don't have to go back inside and socialize."

"You really don't like these formal parties, do you?" she teased.

"I've been to enough of them to know how they all end," Brant informed her with a defeated sigh. "Drunk as hell or bored out of my mind." He raised his brows. "Sometimes both."

They remained on the balcony engaged in jovial conversation for nearly an hour. Brant told her stories about his rich, overbearing parents, and she told him stories about the ranch hands and their deviant behavior. She was having such a good time; she didn't notice her brother hadn't returned. When it finally dawned on her, she glanced at Brant's watch then frowned.

"I get the strange feeling my brother's met Miss Right-for-tonight and skipped out on the party," Devon informed him.

"He shares that personal stuff with you?" Brant asked with some surprise.

"It's a little-kept secret that he's a major league stud," she teased.

Brant looked at the beach then back at her with a pleasant smile. "Would you like to take a walk on the beach?"

"You don't have to ask twice," she replied and kicked off her shoes.

It was the invitation she'd been waiting for. They walked down the steps and into the soft sand. Devon took advantage of the moonlight and clung to Brant's arm while they walked.

"I've had a wonderful time tonight," she announced cheerfully.

"Sure you did," Brant scoffed and chuckled.

"I did, seriously," she insisted while subconsciously caressing his arm. "It's a beautiful night, and the champagne went down easy."

"So you're drunk?"

"I am not. I'm just enjoying myself," she insisted while grinning. "You seem to be having a fairly good time yourself."

"I'll admit, I enjoyed it more than I thought I would," he replied then looked at her. "Perhaps it's the company I'm keeping."

Devon offered a warm smile. Brant almost immediately frowned and stopped her near a large rock that offered a shadowy area away from prying eyes. She looked at him and noted something was bothering him.

"Is something wrong?" she asked.

"Yesterday afternoon, we both had a little too much to drink at lunch during the power outage," he remarked. "Do you remember our conversation in the dungeon stairwell?"

She stared at him a moment and attempted to recall the events leading up to the moment they'd found Jamie floating dead among the wax zombies. It all came rushing back to her, and she suddenly gasped while staring at him with horror on her face.

"Were we really going to dress like pirates and have pretend sword fights?" she gasped.

He stared at her a moment, fidgeted slightly, and then nodded. "I'm pretty sure that was the plan," Brant remarked without taking his eyes off her.

Devon let out a relieved sigh and held her chest. "Thank God we didn't go through with that," she announced. "Could you imagine how embarrassing that would have been?"

Brant managed a tiny laugh and seemed to relax a little. "Yes, it could have been very embarrassing," he remarked timidly while avoiding looking at her. "It's probably best if we pretend that conversation never happened. We all say stupid things when we drink."

"Definitely," she agreed then heaved herself onto the large rock and hugged her knees to her chest.

Brant's eyes strayed to the revealing slit on the side of her dress. He immediately looked away and hid his smile. Devon looked out to the ocean and felt her heart pounding at the rest of the conversation he politely chose not to bring up. With everything that had happened, she'd erased that entire seduction scene from her mind. As the details came flooding back in a tidal wave of lustful thoughts, Devon attempted to keep from blushing. She couldn't believe the things she'd said and what she was willing to do. She finally looked at him when she thought she could contain her embarrassment. Their eyes met briefly. Her thoughts immediately strayed to the wild, sexual encounter she so badly wanted. Her sexual fantasies with her boss were becoming more frequent, wildly intense, and mildly disturbing.

Brant immediately fidgeted as if reading her thoughts and glanced at his watch. "It's getting late," he announced. "I'd better take you home."

Her heart sank at his sudden urge to leave, but she certainly couldn't protest. How would that look? Devon slid off the rock with Brant's assistance. He helped steady her when she hit the sand, and she found herself momentarily in his arms with her hands pressed against his chest. She could almost hear her drunken seduction echoing from yesterday afternoon as images of a spontaneous sexual encounter with her boss flooded her senses. It wasn't just a drunken sexual fantasy. She actually wanted to have wild sex with the strange, handsome man she barely knew.

For a moment, Devon wondered what was wrong with her. She'd never entertained such erotic thoughts before, and why would she? Considering she'd never been with a man before, it wasn't as if she was craving something she was missing. It had to be Ivy's fault for sharing so many details about her wild encounters.

When she snapped out of her trance, she realized she was still in Brant's arms, and they were staring into each other's eyes for a long time without speaking. Something seemed to snap within him. Brant placed his hand on her face and kissed her warmly but aggressively as if he too had been reliving yesterday's seduction scene. Devon was taken by surprise by the heart-stopping kiss and tensed. She was about to return the kiss when a drunken couple was heard laughing from somewhere nearby and startled them. Brant pulled away, appeared embarrassed, and then attempted a smile.

"I, uh," he fumbled nervously. "We'd better go. It's late, and we both have work in the morning."

Devon felt her heart sink, but she managed a smile and nodded mechanically in agreement. With that passionate kiss now burned into her mind, she'd never stop the wild, sexual fantasies.

Chapter Thirty-four

Wednesday morning arrived without warning and with equally little sleep. Despite that Devon was still tired from her evening out, she was feeling enthusiastic and almost giddy. Her brief kiss with Brant played out in her mind a thousand times and even in her dreams. It was just one kiss. Perhaps it meant nothing, but she couldn't get Brant off her mind. Devon hurried into the workshop and smiled cheerfully at Ross as she slipped into her lab coat. She was a little anxious about seeing Brant that morning and the awkwardness last night may have caused, but she was optimistically enthusiastic.

"Good morning, Ross," she announced cheerfully then looked around for Brant as her heart pounded with anticipation. "Where's Brant?"

"Tyler sent him on a business trip."

Devon's heart suddenly sank, and she felt almost numb. She sat on a stool before the counter and didn't know what to say. She couldn't lead on to Ross that she was devastated. A business trip out of the blue? Was it a coincidence?

"I thought Tyler handled all the business related stuff?" she finally asked while attempting not to sound disappointed.

"Tyler decided he needed to stay behind and do some wax creations of his own," Ross remarked with noted sarcasm.

"Oh?"

"He'll be working in the evening the next few nights," Ross informed her. "On the bright side; you'll be working mornings with me until Brant returns."

"How long will Brant be gone?" she asked not the least bit interested in Ross' bright side to the story.

"Three days," Ross announced while groaning. "I'm on a countdown."

Devon sighed with defeat. She wondered if Brant's sudden business trip was so he could avoid her and what he might perceive to be an awkward moment between boss and employee. She no longer knew what she was feeling or what to think. She just knew she needed to take the next three days to wipe any sexual fantasies involving her boss from her mind.

"Tyler will also be checking in from time to time," Ross informed her. "I think he's afraid we'll be screwing around."

She eyed him sharply. "In your case, he'd be right," Devon teased.

"Helps pass the time and makes for a fun work environment," he announced defensively. "I don't know how people can be so serious all the time. It's not natural."

"It's called being an adult," she informed him then laughed. "But I don't have to worry about that because you'll never allow that to happen to me."

Ross pulled the black, horse-drawn hearse carriage while clutching a buggy shaft in each hand. He had the bridle around his neck with the plume proudly displayed on top of his head. Devon sat in the driver's seat with the reins in one hand and the buggy whip in the other. She playfully tapped Ross with the whip as he pulled the hearse carriage into the witch display. Once it was in place, he fell to the ground while panting. Devon jumped off the hearse carriage and approached him on the ground. He looked up at her.

"You know, you could have pushed," he informed her with some irritation.

She grinned at him. "Where would the fun in that be?" she teased.

Ross pulled himself to his hands and knees and stood with some exhaustion. Devon approached the back of the hearse and removed several severed heads on stakes. Each head depicted haggard looking women with looks of horror on their faces. She then removed a wax woman wearing an old black dress from the back. Ross stared as she removed the wax woman and several other set displays packed in the hearse.

"No wonder that thing was so damned heavy," Ross protested. "You loaded it up first!"

She gave him an innocent look. "Why make more than one trip?"

"Why?" he demanded. "Because I was the one pulling that thing loaded with props as well as you, your highness." His brows raised. "News flash, Devon dear, you aren't as light as you look."

She raised a skeptical brow, insulted by the comment. "Maybe you're not as strong as you think you are," Devon announced.

He frowned while glaring at her. "You know I love you," Ross remarked. "But some days I like you less than others."

It took nearly an hour, but Ross and Devon finally finished the display depicting one witch being burned at the stake, which included fake, automated flames, while surrounded by angry men and woman. Along the front of the nighttime set were the severed heads of suspected witches on stakes sticking out of the ground. In the background, two female witches attacked unsuspecting men. Ross and Devon stood back and admired the scene. Without looking at each other, they exchanged a high-five.

Chapter Thirty-five

Kids played in the park on the sunny Thursday afternoon. The park was located in the center of town with a gazebo not far from the courthouse end. It was a central location to have rallies and assemblies since there was plenty of space for residents to set up folding chairs. There was a small area containing kiddy swings, a jungle gym, sandbox, and various other kiddy rides. A concrete walkway crisscrossed through most of the park and circled the elegant fountain. Ross and Devon approached the fountain, sat on the edge, and watched the children playing nearby.

"Thank God Brant's back on Saturday," Ross announced already looking exhausted. "Did you get a look at that new wax woman Tyler made?"

"I suppose he's trying," she remarked with a sigh. "A little too much makeup."

"A little?" he announced with surprise while staring at her. "I don't know if she's supposed to be a prostitute or a cartoon character."

"Nothing a little turpentine can't cure."

He shook his head as his eyes widened at the comment. "I'm not touching Tyler's work," Ross announced. "He'll have my head on a stick and mounted in the witch display. Let Brant deal with offending him."

Ivy hurried across the park and joined them by the fountain. It was only a short sprint from the bank. She was out of breath but smiling.

"Sorry, I'm late."

"We're used to it," Ross teased then looked around with concern. "So where's Tony? Can't have lunch without the food."

They saw Tony approaching from the opposite end of the park carrying a plastic bag. Ross jumped to his feet and hurried to greet Tony, although it wasn't exactly Tony he was happy to see. Devon and Ivy moved to a nearby bench as the guys approached. Ross routed through the bag and handed out their salads.

"I think you should pick up the food tomorrow, Ross," Tony insisted while watching his friend tear through the wrapping on his sandwich.

Ross muttered something inaudible while devouring his hoagie.

"I'll take that as a yes," Tony announced then looked at Devon and Ivy and offered a pleasant smile. "Did I miss anything good?"

"I just got here myself," Ivy replied.

"Ross and I were just counting down days until Brant returns," Devon remarked.

"Tyler's that bad, huh?" Tony asked.

"He's just not much of an artist. His work needs some help," she replied then drew a deep breath and groaned, rethinking her last comment. "His new wax woman looks like a streetwalker."

Tony laughed at the comment. They saw Dorothy pushing Chelsea in her wheelchair not far from them. All four briefly stared.

Ross immediately returned to his lunch although with less enthusiasm. "Someone should keep Dorothy away from makeup as well."

Devon, Ivy, and Tony all stared a moment longer. Chelsea wore bright colored lipstick, dark eyeshadow, and an excessive amount of blush. She was dressed in a brightly colored, flowered shirt with large, fake pearls around her neck. Dorothy pushed her daughter toward them and paused.

"Nice day for a picnic lunch," Dorothy announced while smiling pleasantly despite all she'd been through in recent days.

All four nodded.

She then turned her attention to Tony. "The funeral was lovely," Dorothy announced then fidgeted. "I'm sure Jamie would appreciate what you'd done. She looked, uh, peaceful."

"Thank you."

Devon found herself staring at Chelsea, who was only a few feet from her. The makeup and bows in her hair were hideous. Chelsea looked more like a clown than a young woman. She had once been the most beautiful girl in town. Her long blonde hair was now cropped to shoulder length, which was probably more manageable for her poor mother, but there was no reason to treat the young woman like some porcelain doll. Since Chelsea had been two grades ahead of Devon in school, she didn't know her all that well. However, she did remember she was as smart as she was beautiful.

As Devon stared at the girl who could do little more than stare hypnotically at nothing in particular, Devon wondered if there was anything left of Chelsea inside her non-functioning shell of a body. Devon finally looked away and no longer felt like eating. Dorothy bid them an enjoyable lunch then pushed Chelsea along the walkway across the park.

Devon watched them leave and shook her head, feeling almost enraged. "Why does she insist on doing that?" she scoffed under her breath, surprising her friends.

"Doing what?" Tony asked.

"Dress her like a rag doll with all that makeup," Devon muttered and set her salad aside. "It's so disrespectful to that poor girl."

"Hard to believe she was once the most beautiful girl in town," Ross remarked and seemed to have less enthusiasm for his sandwich.

"Chelsea?" Tony asked with surprise.

"Oh, yeah. Before her accident, she was a raving beauty," Ross announced and sank into thought with fondness. "I remember every boy in school chased after her." He then eyed his friends and turned slightly serious. "Of course, I was a grade below her. I knew I never stood a shot, but in our few encounters, she was always nice to me."

"I remember hearing about Dorothy's rage over her wanting to date," Ivy added and shook her head. "Dorothy and Chelsea got into some terrible fights. If there ever was a man-hater, it's Dorothy."

"For such a god-fearing woman," Devon muttered.

"Chelsea and Jamie got into it a good number of times too," Ross interjected. "Jamie was working her way to becoming a slut even back then."

"Devon and I were in the same grade as Jamie. She was always stealing someone's boyfriend," Ivy scoffed with annoyance. "That's why Tamara hated her so much. I heard she slept with almost all of Tamara's boyfriends after we graduated high school."

"I seemed to have missed a lot not growing up here," Tony remarked while eying his friends. "Not to change the subject, but what actually happened to Chelsea?"

"She'd fallen off the bridge near the resorts back when it was all woodland," Devon informed him. "A lot of kids hung out around there after school."

"It was a big time date spot back then," Ross reported then cast a look at Devon. "But she didn't fall; she was pushed."

"Not the stranger theory again," Ivy groaned then shook her head. She turned on the bench to face Ross where he sat on the grass near them. "It was never proven she was pushed from the bridge by the man who murdered Christine."

"Well, it certainly wasn't suicide like some claimed," Ross boldly announced. "Chelsea was an attractive young lady. She had everything to live for. She did *not* try to kill herself."

"Doesn't always mean anything," Ivy boldly interrupted. "Being pretty and popular doesn't mean she wasn't depressed. If she had wanted to date and her overly religious, manhating mother was against it that could cause some serious issues."

"They found someone else's blood on her shirt. Although it was never publicly reported, I think Sheriff Carter has forensic proof that it was Christine's blood," Ross announced with annoyance, prepared to fight the issue to the death. "She also had scrapes on her arms and legs from sticker bushes."

"Yeah, she fell from a bridge," Ivy insisted, defending her theory. "Of course she had scrapes. There were rocks everywhere."

"They were sticker bush scrapes on her arms and legs," Ross insisted defensively. "You don't get sticker bush scrapes from rocks. There were, however, sticker bushes in the woods where they found Christine's body. Ergo, she witnessed the murder, and the killer chased her to keep her quiet. When he had the opportunity, he pushed her off the bridge."

"Ipso facto. I've gotten sticker bush scratches without being chased by a killer," Ivy announced.

Devon groaned and rubbed her temple, having heard her friends argue their cases many times before. Tony eyed Devon with surprise. She made a face and shook her head, having no way of ending their debate.

Tony finally looked at Ivy and Ross. "Okay, kids, fight nice," he scolded. "Going all Latin cliché isn't going to solve anything."

Chapter Thirty-six

Thursday night at the tavern was meant to be ladies' night, although most women avoided the bar. On the night when mixed drinks were half priced for women, which was meant to drive in more female customers, male patrons arrived in flocks to socialize with the women. The stench of desperation from the swarm of men essentially chased most of the women away. Now, Thursdays were just sad and depressing, leaving only the hardcore drinkers. Joe sat at the bar in his usual spot while Stan hovered over him with little better to do.

"I can't believe Paula's gone," Stan remarked while sadly shaking his head then appeared curious. "Did they find the guy who did it?"

Joe straightened and avoided looking at his bartender friend. "No, not yet," he remarked. "Sheriff Carter couldn't find his ass if it was on fire." He then eyed Stan. "I'll find the guy though. I intend to find him and make him pay."

"Well, if you need a hand with that, let me know," Stan announced and straightened. "Your sister was my friend too."

"I may just take you up on that," Joe remarked and offered a strange smirk.

Stan sighed and looked around while frowning. "Place just isn't the same without Paula. Our only lady on ladies' night."

Joe glanced at the clock on the wall. It was quarter to midnight. He didn't even finish his beer when he stood and placed some money on the counter. Stan gave him a strange look.

"What? You're leaving already?" Stan asked with surprise.

"I have business to attend to," Joe informed him, showing little emotion.

"Business? At midnight?" Stan asked while appearing curious. "What sort of business would you have at midnight?"

Joe grinned and raised his brows. "The slightly shady sort of business" he announced.

"The kind I best not know about, huh?" Stan remarked with a curious look.

"Yeah, that kind," Joe remarked. "I'll see you tomorrow, Stan."

Stan grinned and chuckled. "Yeah, see you tomorrow," he announced. "Good luck. Let me know if you need to borrow my car and a shovel."

Joe chuckled then left the tavern. He glanced at his watch and then hurried onto the back road in the direction of his house. It was possibly the first time he was making the return journey sober, allowing him to walk a little faster. He turned down his private drive and made the long trek toward his house at the end of the dirt driveway. A car's headlights seemed to appear mysteriously behind him. As he turned, dismayed by the closeness and sudden appearance of the headlights, the red sports car's engine revved and the bright headlights gained on him at an amazing rate. Joe's eyes widened in horror as he attempted to leap out of the car's path.

The car clipped him, sending him flying across the dirt driveway. Joe rolled several times then lay motionless on the road. The car skidded to a stop, was thrown into reverse, and raced backward. The tires squealed as the car came to a stop alongside him. Joe groaned but was barely conscious. The phantom grabbed him under the arms and heaved him into the trunk of the car. Joe slowly came to, saw the phantom, and immediately lunged for him. The phantom punched him in the face and slammed the trunk shut.

§

Joe woke within the trunk of the sports car and could see the sun rising through a rusted hole near the taillight. He lay on his back and kicked the trunk with both feet, attempting to jar it open. A strange grinding sound startled him. An electric saw blade penetrated the trunk. Joe jumped with surprise.

"Hey, let me out of here," he cried out. "What the hell are you doing?"

The electric saw stopped after making a triangle cut through the metal. Joe kept his distance while attempting to look out through the small opening. Liquid poured in through the opening. The stench of gasoline was unmistakable as it soaked him before he rolled away from the liquid.

"Christ, man," Joe yelled while attempting to slip out of his gasoline-soaked shirt. "This isn't funny! I won't tell anyone, I swear!"

A brilliant red light appeared near the opening. Joe jerked and slid against the back of the trunk while staring with horror as the flare was dropped through the opening. The gasoline immediately ignited, setting the interior of the trunk and Joe into flames. Outside, the phantom casually walked away from the sports car as smoke wafted from the trunk. Joe's agonizing screams quickly subsided.

Chapter Thirty-seven

The diner was crowded as it was most Friday evenings during the dinner hour. Most older locals preferred the diner to the more expensive restaurants at the resort area on the other side of town. The younger generation preferred the resort clubs and the food court at the newly constructed mall. Ross and Tony sat at a booth after they'd finished their meal and watched with mounting tension as Marlene set the bill on the table between them. The two men exchanged looks and refused to make a move for the bill.

Marlene returned to the counter as Brant entered. He approached the counter, offered a pleasant smile, and received his 'to go' order. Marlene did her best to flirt with the shy, handsome man. Brant attempted to pay his bill and leave but couldn't seem to complete the transaction as Marlene continued with her obvious seduction scene. She finally accepted his money, allowing Brant to make his escape. Ross and Tony were now locked in a battle of wills as they pushed the food bill across the table in a silent attempt to get the other to pay.

"You've gotten free lunches from me all week," Tony insisted while glaring at his friend. "The least you can do is pay for dinner."

Finally admitting defeat, Ross dug into his pocket and revealed some bills. "You're becoming a real nag; you know that?"

Marlene approached their table and smiled while refreshing their coffee. Tony immediately declined before she could pour more into his cup.

"Sheriff Carter was in here earlier," Marlene informed them. "Karl's still at large. Something tells me the sheriff doesn't think he did it," Marlene announced with disappointment. "I hoped it had been him. I don't like having an unsolved murder hanging over our town."

"Yeah, I was rooting for it to be Karl too," Ross remarked.

"I overheard Sheriff Carter and Deputy Havens discussing the murders," Marlene informed them. "Supposedly, someone saw Jamie's car driving on the backroads early Friday morning."

"That's right," Ross remarked. "They never did find her car." He eyed Tony and Marlene. "That almost proves it was Karl, doesn't it? He probably stole Jamie's car and made his getaway."

"I don't think so," Marlene informed him. "It was really weird. Whoever saw Jamie's car said it was being driven by someone wearing a phantom mask and what they thought to be a purple cape."

Ross stared at her a moment with some surprise and nearly choked on the words. "As in white mask, burnt faced phantom?"

She nodded then immediately cringed. "Creepy, huh?"

Tony gave Ross a strange look. Ross shifted uncomfortably in his chair. Tony immediately took his cue and blurted out the first thing that came to mind.

"Maybe Joe killed Paula," Tony suggested. "His sister was friends with Jamie too. There could be motive there, right?"

"That abandoned farmhouse is a long way to go from his house without a car," Marlene insisted. "They took Joe's license away after his last drunk driving accident, and he had to sell his car to pay the fines." She disapprovingly shook her head. "Honestly, Tony, you're behind on town gossip."

"My clients don't gossip much," he teased.

"Do you ever consider dating live girls?" Marlene asked while raising a clever brow.

"On occasion."

Ross rolled his eyes. He didn't seem to like when others were the ones cracking jokes. That was his department.

"How about meeting me for drinks at the tavern after work?" Marlene asked. "I get off at ten."

Tony appeared surprised by the invitation, fidgeted a moment, and then offered a pleased smile. "I, uh, well, I'd like that."

Ross stared at both with disbelief.

"Great," Marlene announced while practically turning giddy. "I'll meet you there around eleven."

Marlene turned and walked away with an added spring in her step.

Ross immediately leaned across the table and stared at Tony with near horror. "You made a date with *Marlene?*" he gasped.

"Yeah, so?" Tony remarked and cast a look after the waitress. "She's an attractive woman. I don't know in what universe a woman that attractive would want a guy like me, but I'm not going to turn her down."

Ross shook his head and leaned back in his seat. "Have you ever asked yourself why a woman that gorgeous is still single?" He leaned across the table, practically lunging for his friend. "Bypassing the fact that Marlene is a bit of a psycho bitch, her overly protective brother is one of those biker guys with tattoos covering half his body," he informed him. His eyes then widened. "I heard they're still picking her last boyfriend out of the tread of his hog."

Tony stared at Ross with his mouth hanging open. "The guy the size of a tank that I've seen riding through town? That's her brother?"

Ross nodded then shook his head. "I'd be willing to bet you a thousand dollars he'll be at the tavern tonight," he announced. "And his eyes will be on you and his sister."

"My first date in months," Tony groaned. "I should have known it was too good to be true." He leaned across the table and spoke softly to Ross. "Should I not show up?"

"Are you insane?" Ross practically cried out in a whisper as his eyes widened. "He'll break you in two if you do that!"

Tony leaned back in his seat and groaned. "So if I go out with her; her brother will kill me, but if I don't go out with her; her brother will kill me."

Ross casually nodded. "Yeah, you're pretty much screwed either way."

§

Marlene walked out of the diner that night with another waitress. They waved to each other then separated and went to their own cars. Marlene opened her car door and climbed inside. She started the car and fumbled within her purse as the other car pulled away. She removed her lipstick and turned the rearview mirror in her direction. In the mirror, she saw the white phantom mask staring back at her. She gasped and grabbed for the door handle.

A nylon rope circled her neck, and the phantom pulled back on it. Marlene clutched the rope and attempted to pull it free. The owner of the diner could be seen through the window still cleaning the grill. She slammed her hand on the horn to get his attention, but there was no sound! Marlene gasped and struggled against the rope. She finally slumped over the steering wheel out cold. The phantom leaped from the back seat while keeping low to avoid being seen by the cook inside the diner and opened the driver's side door. He pulled Marlene from the front seat and dragged her into the back seat. The phantom then jumped into the driver's seat and drove away from the diner.

§

Marlene slowly woke and immediately realized she was tied to an old, wooden chair within a mostly dark, dank basement. The basement was within a home at least one hundred years old. It had a dirt floor, low ceiling, and an old coal stove that hadn't been used in years. The sole light source was a single light bulb on a chain near the rickety, old stairs. Marlene immediately went into panic mode and attempted to scream through the duct tape across her mouth, but it was no use.

She fought against the duct tape binding her wrists to the arms of the wooden chair but couldn't free herself. The chair was so old; it creaked with every movement. She stopped struggling a moment and looked down at the old chair. Despite that her ankles were duct taped together, they weren't bound to the chair. She attempted to stand while picking up the chair, which was attached to her wrists. She teetered a moment then was able to maintain her balance.

Marlene shut her eyes, drew a deep breath, and cast herself and the chair to the dirt floor. One of the wooden legs splintered, although it didn't break off. She inhaled deeply and again attempted to stand with the chair. She teetered a moment and again caught her balance. A shadow fell over her from the dim light of the sole light bulb near the stairs. She immediately looked in front of her and saw the phantom standing only a few feet before her. She attempted to scream through the duct tape. The phantom pushed her backward with just enough force to knock her into the chair and the chair to the floor. The splintered wooden leg cracked and nearly gave out.

The phantom revealed a large hunting knife. Marlene let out a terrified gasp and attempted to rock the chair. Before the chair toppled, the phantom grabbed her by the throat and held her immobile. She gasped and wheezed beneath his gloved hand. He plunged the knife forward into her abdomen. Marlene muffled a painful cry. He pulled the knife free allowing her blood to pour out and saturate her shirt. Marlene gasped for several minutes while the phantom stood over her and watched her bleed out. Her eyes finally rolled back as she exhaled her last breath.

Chapter Thirty-eight

Devon hurried through the displays and nervously looked at her watch. It was Saturday morning, and she was late for the first time since she started working at the museum. She stopped and stared at the newest display with a werewolf. The woman within the display was caked with makeup. Her brown wig needed more work, and the clothes were wrong for the time-period. Devon rolled her eyes and continued toward the workshop. She entered the workshop and stopped within the doorway. Brant sat on his stool before a wax woman and painted her fingernails. He looked like a manicurist in a nail salon. Devon smiled warmly and approached.

"Thank goodness you're back," she announced. "Sorry, I'm late."

Brant glanced at her briefly and smiled. "And not a moment too soon. I didn't know Tyler had you working this morning."

"I didn't think you were coming back until this afternoon."

"Actually, I was back last night," Brant informed her. "I'd spent half the night working on some displays." He gently cleared his throat. "I see Tyler was busy with some waxworks of his own."

"Yes. He thinks he's found his calling," she teased. "What would you like me to do this morning?"

"Repair Tyler's creations before they make me physically ill," he announced then reluctantly sighed. "But we'll wait until he leaves. Afterward, we can finish restoring our zombie flood victims and return them to their display."

Devon couldn't deny she was slightly tense to see Brant again. She could almost feel the tension between them, particularly with the way Brant *didn't* look at her. She didn't want to bring up the beach house party in hopes Brant would eventually say something. The longer they remained in the room together without him mentioning it, the more she realized he was trying to forget about an uncomfortable moment.

§

Devon rolled a wax woman strapped to a dolly into the werewolf display. The werewolf display was a creepy wooded scene with small hills, rocks, and fake trees. It made the dolly harder to push with her wax reconstructed woman. The frightening werewolf was already set up in an attacking position with large teeth exposed. As Devon rolled the werewolf's victim closer to the creature, she was chilled at the sight. The teeth and snout were stained with fake blood from the victim already on the ground not far from where she was to place the new victim. Devon looked from the sharp, bloodstained teeth to the mildly torn victim on the ground. The wax woman had her throat ripped out with enough fake blood to make Devon nauseous.

It wasn't her place, but she felt the kills should be less gruesome. Parents might complain about the gory detail Brant seemed able to bring to life with makeup and paint. She arranged the newly arrived victim in her place before adjusting her dress and hair. She patted the woman on the shoulder.

"Good luck," Devon announced under her breath to the wax woman.

She was about to push the dolly from the display when she gave the victim on the ground another glance. Her wounds were extremely realistic and beyond chilling. It was almost too much. Devon crouched alongside the dying wax woman and studied the torn flesh. The blood almost looked wet. Devon held her breath and reached out to touch it. Blood suddenly spurt from her neck. Devon cried out and fell onto her backside. She heard Ross laughing. She looked across the display and saw her friend with the remote control.

He gave her a serious look and pointed a warning finger. "The sign says do not touch the displays," he threatened.

She glared at him and sprang to her feet. "What if I *touched* the dickhead who created the display?" Devon lashed out.

Ross raised his brows. "That sounds like sexual harassment to me," he announced. "Although it's possible Brant might enjoy it."

She shook her head in disgust and brushed the fake dirt from her lab coat and pants. "Payback is a bitch Ross," Devon informed him.

"I look forward to it," he announced then laughed evilly. He blew her a kiss and ran from the display before she could chase him.

§

An hour later, Brant kneeled beside the grave in the cemetery display and fixed the clothing on the female zombie sticking out of the ground. He sat back and gave the wig an added toss. Just then, he heard a low, creepy moan. A zombie appeared above the tombstone near him. Brant jumped with surprise and fell onto his backside. He stared at the zombie then looked behind him. Devon stood near the doorway holding the remote control. She laughed at his expense. Brant stood while hiding his smile and brushed off the fake dirt.

"I suppose I deserved that."

Devon approached Brant and looked at the female zombie. The zombie wore an old flowered dress with a lacy collar.

"Are you seriously going to leave her dressed in this?" Devon asked.

Brant eyed the zombie with some surprise. "Yeah, why not?"

"Looks like something my mother would wear," she retorted.

Brant studied the wax woman a moment longer then frowned. "Yeah, mine too. You're right. It goes." Brant unbuttoned the zombie's dress while shaking his head. "I've undressed more women today--"

Devon moved closer and watched him fumble with the tiny buttons. Brant glanced at her and appeared slightly embarrassed.

"That sounded bad," he muttered.

Devon handed him the remote, which he placed in his jacket pocket. She watched him a moment longer then shifted uncomfortably at the obvious tension while she was in the room.

"I was hoping we could talk about the other night," Devon announced timidly.

Brant avoided looking at her while fumbling with the dress. Although he acted casual, he was extremely tense. "Okay," he remarked timidly.

Devon continued to watch him work. She placed her hand on his and stopped him from working on the buttons. He hesitated and met her serious gaze.

"There's a tremendous amount of tension between us since the party," she informed him. "You have to be feeling it too."

Brant immediately fidgeted and became flustered. "I'm sorry about what happened on the beach," he blurted out his apology as if it had been weighing heavily upon him. "I didn't mean to make you uncomfortable, especially after what happened at your father's ranch. I was stupid and impulsive. Please don't quit."

His rambling apology surprised her. She stared at him a moment longer while holding her breath.

"I don't want you to apologize, Brant," she gently informed him.

She became uncomfortable and stared at him a long moment, unable to express herself. Brant stared back in silence as if attempting to read her expression. Devon forced a smile and waved him off.

"Never mind," she remarked timidly. "It's not that important."

Brant caught her hand, forcing her to stop and face him. They stared into each other's eyes a long moment. Brant took an aggressive step toward her, pulled her against him, and kissed her passionately. Devon appeared surprised but quickly relaxed and returned the kiss before he had a chance to reconsider. Brant broke off the kiss and pulled away while looking into her eyes.

"I'm really bad at reading women," he replied timidly. "Was that the correct response?"

Devon smiled with embarrassment and nodded. Brant's smile brightened. He kissed her again and with more urgency. She clung to him and returned the kiss, barely able to contain her rising passion. They heard someone approaching and immediately jumped apart. Devon was becoming tired of people interrupting her brief romantic moments. Brant returned to the female zombie and continued with the dress. Devon grabbed a hair pick, turned to one of the male zombies, and pretended to be working.

Tyler entered the cemetery set while smiling cheerfully. "Ah, here you are."

"Hey, Tyler," Brant announced while attempting a casual appearance, although he was breathing heavier than usual.

"I'm only going to stay for a couple of hours," Tyler informed him. "I have some business to attend to in the city. I think I have a line on some wax people from another closed museum."

"That's great."

"Yeah, well, I'll be here until five o'clock," Tyler replied and sighed as if bored. "I have a project I'd like to finish."

Tyler disappeared from the display. Both watched him leave then looked at each other from across the room. Brant approached Devon. She smiled and tossed the hair pick over her shoulder. Brant once more pulled her into his arms and kissed her. Tyler was heard within one of the nearby sets. Devon broke off the kiss and smiled with embarrassment.

"I, uh, was thinking," she announced timidly, "maybe I could come back *tonight* to finish my shift. Ross has the night off, and you could probably use the help."

Brant stared into her eyes and gently brushed the hair from her face. A sly smile crossed his face. "I was thinking about working late myself."

Devon slowly moved out of his arms, although both were reluctant to release the other.

"I'll be back around six," she gently informed him while offering a warm smile.

"I'll see you then," he responded timidly.

Chapter Thirty-nine

Devon entered the dimly lit museum at five-thirty that evening and paused in the foyer. There were rose petals sporadically lining the walkway leading into the displays. Devon contained her eager smile and followed the petals through the museum. They continued down the dungeon stairs, scattered along the stone steps leading into the dungeon. Devon was overwhelmed with desire as she followed the rose petals through the horror displays and finally to the church display with its fake candles flickering their romantic glow. Brant was playing out their fantasy, and she had no intention to disappoint him. Devon paused just inside the display and took a moment to nervously adjust her hair as her heart pounded with anticipation of her first time.

As she crossed the church display, she saw a red, satin comforter spread out over the altar. A bottle of champagne chilled in an ice bucket on the edge of the altar along with two crystal glasses. A dozen long-stemmed, red roses were tied with a red ribbon and lay on the altar alongside the champagne flutes. Devon couldn't contain her childlike grin. She was swept away by the romantic gesture. She walked toward the altar with nervous anticipation then stopped when she saw Brant lying on the floor on the other side of the altar. Something felt wrong. She quickened her pace, stepped around the altar, and saw blood soaking through Brant's white lab coat as his bloodied hand clutched his bleeding abdomen. He wasn't moving! Devon stared frozen with horror then cried out as she ran for him.

§

The city hospital was moderately congested with mostly minor medical emergencies. Sprains and lacerations seemed to be the early evening theme. The waiting room was nearly filled with crying children and farmers who'd had disagreements with farm machinery. Martin held Devon to his shoulder where they sat in the waiting room and watched nurses and doctors pass in the hospital corridor. A doctor finally stepped out of the emergency room and approached them. Martin nudged Devon. She straightened, resisted springing to her feet, and looked at the doctor. She feared if she stood and received bad news her legs would give out beneath her.

"Your friend's going to be fine," the doctor announced with a warm, tender smile.

Devon's eyes shut as she gasped a sigh of relief. Martin gave her a warm hug.

"Thankfully, the knife went in on a slant." The doctor held up the bloodstained remote control contained in a plastic bag. "Apparently hitting this first. Probably saved his life. He had it in his lab coat pocket."

Devon had never been so relieved to see that damned remote control. Martin released her as she stood on slightly weak legs.

"Can I see him?"

"We'll be moving him up to ICU in a few minutes," the doctor informed her, "but you can visit him before he's transferred. I must warn you; he's going to be groggy from the anesthetic and painkillers."

Devon nodded with understanding then followed the doctor into the emergency treatment room. He led her to one of the rooms and indicated the closed door. As the doctor walked away, Devon slowly opened the door and stepped into the room. Brant was motionless on the emergency room gurney with oxygen and IV lines sticking out of his arm. She approached, paused alongside the gurney, and gently touched his hand.

"Brant?"

Brant's eyes rolled open then closed. He squeezed her hand and smiled. "Devon," he gasped. "I had the worst dream."

"Everything's going to be fine," she gently assured him and sat on the edge of the gurney. "You'll feel better in a couple of days."

Brant closed his eyes. "I dreamt the phantom tried to kill me."

She stared at him with surprise. "The phantom?"

§

The sun was setting over the old farmhouse. Blue and red lights flashed from the sheriff's police cruiser while Sheriff Carter stood before the burned red sports car. There was still enough left of the vehicle to recognize it as Jamie's car.

Sheriff Carter shook his head with anger clearly on his face. "What the hell is going on in this town?" he demanded.

Deputy Havens approached with a crowbar in his hand and eyed the sheriff. "Want me to pop the trunk?"

Sheriff Carter reluctantly nodded. "May as well," he announced with a sigh. "I know it won't be good, so let's get the unpleasantness over with."

He followed his deputy to the burned car and watched as he easily forced the trunk open with the crowbar. Both peered into the blackened trunk and stared at what was almost certainly the remains of a body. The body was so badly burned, there was little left beyond bone and some particles of flesh. Deputy Havens grimaced and looked away while Sheriff Carter just frowned.

"Yep," he announced with a sigh. "About what I expected."

"Do you know who it is?" Deputy Havens asked while casting peeks at the gruesome find.

"I'm pretty sure that's Joe Jarred," Sheriff Carter replied. "Stan called and said he was concerned when Joe didn't show up Friday night. He left the tavern early on Thursday. Well, early for him." The sheriff looked around then indicated the barn. "Paula was found dead in the barn, so I'm almost positive that's her brother."

"I'll call the coroner," Deputy Havens announced and hurried to the cruiser to get away from the gruesome scene in the trunk.

Chapter Forty

Monday morning. Ross' clunker of a car was parked in front of the museum, being the only vehicle in the parking lot. Within the basement, Devon followed Ross around the werewolf set while he attempted to work. Devon had little interest in working that morning as her nerves were already frayed beyond repair. Ross refused to look at her and appeared unusually tense while working on the display.

"I'm telling you, Ross," she insisted. "He said the phantom attacked him."

"And now he doesn't remember a thing," Ross announced while casting a look at her. "I don't think you can rely on what he'd said after coming out of surgery. The guy was on cloud nine."

"Why won't you believe what I'm telling you?" she demanded.

"Because it already looks like an inside job. The police don't need any more help pointing the finger at one of us," Ross insisted then finally turned to face her. "But, of course, you're not worried, because you came to the museum for a romantic rendezvous. They'd never suspect you."

"I'm just as much a suspect as anyone," she insisted. "They could easily think I planted the entire thing after the fact."

"They'll discover Brant purchased the flowers himself just a few hours earlier," Ross informed her. "Face it; you're completely exonerated."

"They'll go after Tyler's alibi first," she insisted. "He's his business partner."

"He also has an alibi," Ross interjected with some annoyance. "He left early, picked up a female companion at four o'clock, and drove with her to the city. They were in each other's company the entire evening. Sheriff Carter says Brant was stabbed no earlier than five o'clock." He eyed her. "You probably just missed the killer on your way in. Any earlier and you would have been a witness; possibly a dead one."

"You must have been somewhere between five and five-thirty."

"Yeah, I took my motorcycle out for a ride along the coast," he informed her. "I was gone from three until six o'clock with no witnesses. Plenty of time for me to have come here and stabbed Brant."

"Stop being so dramatic," she announced. "You have absolutely no motive to want Brant dead."

"I'm sure they'd come up with something if they tried hard enough," Ross remarked.

"Anyone in the basement could've taken the mask and cloak from the wardrobe closet," she reminded him. "Aren't there multiple costumes?"

"Yeah," Ross remarked while raising his brows. "And we're suddenly lite two."

"Two are missing?"

Ross nodded with some irritation.

"If he saw someone in the phantom costume, it could have been just about anyone," she insisted.

"Yes, but there aren't many people in town who know Brant," he insisted. "Out of those few people, who'd really want him dead?"

"Maybe he saw something he shouldn't have," she deducted. "Someone slipped Jamie's body in the basement. Perhaps the killer came back for some reason, and Brant caught him."

"Let the phantom thing go," Ross firmly insisted while glaring at her. "Brant doesn't remember anything that happened about the attack. The police will come up with their own information." He indicated the display. "Can we get back to work?"

Ross returned to his work and refused to comment further. Devon stared at him with some surprise, uncertain what to make of his reaction. Why was he so defensive? Why did he think he'd be the prime suspect? It didn't make any sense.

§

The dark jungle display had an almost romantic rainforest appeal. Devon turned on the speakers for the jungle sound effects as mood music while she worked. At first glance, the display appeared void of life. She used the wall controls to begin the animatronic sequence. The tall grass moved from several directions as something stalked the walkway, which would contain visitors. Several creatures leaped out of the tall grass, which would hopefully scare the visitors. Devon pressed a button on the wall panel and stopped the creatures, so they were exposed. The four-foot tall, nearly black creatures were a cross between a velociraptor and a sea monster. They had reptile eyes, sharp teeth, and long claws. Devon approached the exposed creatures while attaching her tool belt. She paused before one of the amazingly lifelike creatures and held up a long, pointy tooth.

"Don't worry," she announced. "The dentist has arrived. Just say ah." Devon was about to replace the wax creature's tooth when she hesitated and gave it a serious look. "And no biting."

She placed a little cement glue on the end of the tooth and stuck it into the creature's mouth where the tooth had broken off. Devon held the tooth in place while waiting for the glue to set.

"Honestly," she announced. "How did you break your tooth in the first place?"

She eyed the creature then considered the question. How had it happened? The display was actually the one scene that didn't involve wax men or women. In this scene, the visitors were the intended victims. A cheap scare, perhaps, but it was actually rather ingenious. Since the displays weren't set to motion detection mode, it was unlikely the frightening alien creature somehow managed to take a bite from Brant's attacker while passing through. Although impossible, if that had been the case, it certainly would have been karma at its finest.

§

Monday afternoon. Ross and Devon stood by the back counter within the workshop and watched Tyler apply paint to the male wax head. Tyler appeared to be enjoying himself while whistling a lively tune. Ross and Devon looked from the unrealistic wax head to each other and raised their brows in silent question.

"Someone has to tell this guy his work sucks," Ross muttered.

"You go right ahead."

The phone rang near where Ross stood. He was quick to snatch it from the wall.

"Hello, Wax Motel," Ross announced cheerfully into the phone.

"Ross," Tyler scolded.

They heard someone outside the workshop. Both Devon and Tyler turned toward the door as it opened to see Sheriff Carter within the doorway.

"I'm sorry to intrude, but I knocked upstairs, and no one answered," Sheriff Carter announced. "I guess you didn't hear me down here."

"Good afternoon, Sheriff Carter," Tyler announced as he stood. He wiped his hands on a rag and approached the sheriff. "How can we help you?"

"We're looking for your partner, Brant Sheffield," he announced while showing little emotion.

"Brant?" Tyler practically gasped with surprise. "He's still in the hospital."

"His parents took him home yesterday, but they told us he'd left this morning without saying anything to them," Sheriff Carter replied then raised a skeptical brow. "We tried his house next door, but there was no answer. Had he returned here?"

Devon stared in silence, concerned as to why the sheriff was looking for Brant. They'd questioned him extensively about his attack, but this felt different. Ross remained on the phone but listened to the conversation with Sheriff Carter.

"No," Tyler replied and appeared curious. "What's this about, Sheriff?"

"We found some new evidence," Sheriff Carter announced. "We'll need to search his house and the museum." He extended a paper. "We have a search warrant."

"New evidence?" Tyler asked with surprise. "If you remember correctly, someone tried to kill him Friday night.

Surely you don't think Brant had anything to do with killing those women."

Devon held back her horrified gasp. Ross stared at Sheriff Carter as well and nearly dropped the phone. He turned, cut his phone conversation short, and immediately hung up.

"Brant picked up dinner at the diner the night Marlene disappeared. Annie said Marlene was flirting with Brant from the moment he walked into the diner," Sheriff Carter informed them. "Just before closing time, a witness claimed to have seen the phantom running through the alley near the diner. If I'm not mistaken, this museum has a phantom display."

"That's not much to go on, Sheriff," Tyler informed him.

Sheriff Carter cocked his head and glared at Tyler. "That's because I wasn't finished," he announced while placing his thumbs in his gun holster. "Marlene's car was found stashed in the cornfield not far from here. We found a paint pen like those you use here in the museum with a bunch of fingerprints on it. I'm willing to bet they belong to Brant."

"We all use those paint pens," Tyler insisted. "I'm sure you'll find all our prints on it."

The comment didn't sway Sheriff Carter's opinion. His expression remained emotionless. "We'll start with Brant's house next door," he informed them.

All three watched Carter leave the workshop.

"That's ridiculous," Ross proclaimed. "Brant couldn't have murdered those women."

"He certainly didn't stab himself," Devon remarked and insecurely rubbed her chilled shoulders when she thought about the way she found Brant in the church display.

Brant's wound was nearly critical. The plan was for her to return at six o'clock that night. Had she been on time rather than early, Brant would have died from his injury, so it certainly hadn't been self-inflicted.

"Of course, he didn't kill those women," Tyler insisted while attempting to hide his irritation. "They won't find anything to support that outrageous theory." He shook his head and sneered. "Pompous sheriff wouldn't know his ass from a hole in the ground. Blame the outsider. All these small towns are the same." He frowned and shook his head in disgust. "Let's break for lunch. I need a drink."

Chapter Forty-one

Sheriff Carter and his two deputies had been searching Brant's house for a better part of the afternoon with little to show for their effort. It was starting to look like a witch-hunt. Deputy Havens stepped out of one of the second-floor bedrooms and looked down the hall where Sheriff Carter was jotting notes on his tablet.

"Sheriff, you'll want to see this," the deputy announced.

Sheriff Carter approached the bedroom and stepped inside. The bedroom was void of furniture and was mostly empty except for a few boxes on the floor. To Sheriff Carter's surprise, black and white, 8x10 glossy photos were taped to the wall, lending a creepy mood to the room. They were professional headshot photos of the women who had applied for the acting job with Burt Danson. On each of the dead women's photos was a bold, red 'x', possibly drawn with a paint pen. The deputy handed Sheriff Carter the empty, leather folder containing the initials B.D.

embossed in gold. Sheriff Carter accepted the folder and stared at it.

"This belongs to Burt Danson. He reported it missing when I questioned him about the murders," Sheriff Carter remarked then immediately frowned.

"I also found this in the closet," Deputy Havens announced and picked up a plastic bag containing the phantom cloak, mask, and hat. He held a second bag in his other hand containing the bloodstained hunting knife. "The knife has blood on it."

The sheriff frowned. "Get that to the boys in forensics after we finish searching the house," the sheriff ordered then shook his head. "We'll need to put out a warrant for Brant's arrest."

Sheriff Carter left the room already in a foul mood and headed down the main stairs. As he reached the bottom, his second deputy appeared from the basement stairs looking flustered.

"Sheriff, down here!"

As the deputy ran back into the basement, Sheriff Carter ran after him. He thundered down the rickety steps and reached the old, dimly lit basement containing a low ceiling and a dirt floor. The deputy led him across the basement to the old coal furnace with a coal storage stall alongside it. The stall was now being used for split wood for the fireplace. The old coal chute was big enough to dump the firewood into the stall from the outside. The deputy had already removed several pieces of wood to reveal Marlene's decomposing body with a single knife wound to her midsection.

The sheriff shut his eyes and shook his head in disgust. "I was really hoping we'd find Marlene alive," he remarked.

"Looks like she's been dead a couple of days," the deputy reported.

"Probably killed shortly after she disappeared," the sheriff remarked.

The deputy shined his flashlight a few feet away to an old, wooden chair. There was dried blood on the chair and a small dark stain on the dirt floor beneath it.

"I'm guessing she was murdered there and then dumped in here to hide the body," the deputy informed him.

Sheriff Carter shook his head with anger. "We need to find this bastard and stop him."

§

Half an hour later, Sheriff Carter stepped off Brant's porch and approached his police blazer parked in the driveway. Devon hurried across the museum parking lot, crossed the lawn, and cut off the sheriff's path to the vehicle.

"I heard you're issuing a warrant for Brant's arrest," she gasped with surprise.

Sheriff Carter seemed stunned by how quickly she'd learned about the situation. "Gossip in this town certainly travels fast," he muttered then nodded in response. "Yes, we're going to bring him in for questioning."

"He didn't kill them."

"We're dealing with a sick man, Devon," the sheriff announced while giving her a stern look. "If you see him, call us immediately."

"What possible motive would he have?" she demanded and folded her arms across her chest. "He didn't even know those women."

"Sexual frustration, feelings of inadequacies, rejection," Sheriff Carter replied. "Paula embarrassed him at the tavern in front of several witnesses. Now she's dead. We also found a phantom mask and cloak in a bedroom closet along with the knife he used to stab his victims."

"Someone planted that stuff there to frame him," Devon insisted without hesitation. "Why would he hide the phantom costume and knife in his own house, implicating himself, when he could simply return them to the museum where they could implicate just about anyone?" She shook her head in disbelief. "Come on, Sheriff. Think about it. You're being played."

He stared at her with surprise then shook his head. "What's gotten into you? Why are you so defensive about him?" Sheriff Carter demanded then considered the question as his eyes lit up with understanding. "Oh, that's right. The flowers and champagne." He cocked his head while staring at her. "You and your boss were romantically involved."

Devon felt her cheeks redden, but her mood turned foul as she folded her arms across her chest. "Except for his run-in with Paula, he'd never even met the other women," she insisted. "What would he even know about the acting job, the women who auditioned for it, or Burt Danson?" She then threw her arms in the air. "The guy spent most of his time either in his museum or at his parents' house in the city. Only ten people in town have ever even met him. Hell, even Ivy and my own brother haven't met him, and they pick me up and drop me off just about every day. You expect me to believe a guy who doesn't know anyone has a grudge against them?"

"Tell that to Marlene," Sheriff Carter snapped in anger and pointed at the house. "We just found her body in the basement."

Devon's eyes widened as she placed her hand over her mouth to hold back her terrified gasp.

Sheriff Carter drew a deep breath and attempted to collect himself. "Do yourself a favor and stay out of this," he informed her.

He walked past her, got into his blazer, and drove away. Devon watched him leave then ran trembling fingers through her hair while cursing under her breath. The coroner's wagon pulled up just moments after the sheriff had left. It was true! They found Marlene dead in Brant's house!

Chapter Forty-two

It was late afternoon. Devon sat on the sterile counter in the funeral home prep room alongside Ross, who leaned against the counter. They watched Tony prep the deceased, elderly client on the metal table.

"What makes you so sure your boss didn't do it?" Tony asked as he carefully applied makeup to the dead man's face. "As an objective party, I think it's possible he could be a killer." He glanced back at them. "Neither of you know him that well."

"He's not the killer type," Ross insisted a little defensively.

"Neither was Norman Bates," Tony countered in all seriousness.

"He's not some closet psychopath," Devon announced with frustration. "This sexual frustration theory just doesn't come into play."

"Be realistic, Devon. The man can't even look a woman in the eyes," Tony remarked. "When it came right down to it, he couldn't even take the town slut to bed. What more proof do you need?"

Devon hesitated and drew a deep, nervous breath. "Brant and I were becoming very familiar that morning before he was attacked."

Tony suddenly stopped and stared at her. "You and Brant?" he gasped.

"There was no reservation," she insisted. "If it hadn't been for Tyler interrupting, he wouldn't have hesitated to take me right there." She shifted uncomfortably. "He'd planned a romantic evening for us the night he was stabbed."

Tony wiped his hands on a rag and leaned against the metal table. He was surprised and suddenly engrossed in the conversation.

"I think she's right," Ross remarked. "He went through a lot of trouble setting up a romantic interlude in that church display."

"Sounds more creepy than romantic to me," Tony muttered then turned serious. "Have they picked him up yet?"

"No one knows where he is," Ross announced with a sigh. "His mother said they had an argument, and he walked out."

"Kind of odd that he didn't return to his house or the museum," Tony remarked.

"I doubt he knew the police were looking for him. He probably went somewhere to recover from his ordeal and escape his mother," Ross remarked. "I certainly wouldn't be in any big hurry to return to the place where I'd been stabbed."

Devon eyed Ross and sank into thought. A strange smile crossed her face, which she immediately hid from her friends.

"Well, I think if he's innocent, he should turn himself in and explain the mask and knife they'd found in his house," Tony informed them. "Finding Marlene murdered in his basement isn't helping his case either. He has to come forward or people will assume he's guilty. On vacation or not, if they post it in the paper that he's wanted for questioning, he should return if he's innocent." Tony returned to his client.

Ross peered at the dead man then gently cleared his throat to the uncomfortable subject. "So, uh, you doing Marlene?"

"Just the prep," Tony replied with some discomfort. "Her mother said it had always been her wish to be cremated."

"Doesn't this job give you the creeps?" Ross asked. "I mean, you asked Marlene out the other day, and now you're going to be prepping her dead body."

"They're just people who've passed on," Tony insisted then cast a look at Ross. "Creepy is displaying life-like wax bodies in scenes of horror. That museum has all the appeal of a morgue."

"I'll gladly take that as a compliment," Ross replied while laughing.

"You would."

§

Devon and Ross left the funeral home and headed into the empty parking lot. She abruptly stopped him halfway to his car. Her strange smile had returned as she stared at her friend. He noted her grin and gave her a puzzled look.

"That phone call yesterday was Brant, wasn't it?" she demanded, mildly excited. "You told him the police were going to search his house. You warned him."

"Be serious, Devon," he announced while fidgeting. "I could get into a lot of trouble if I'd do something like that."

"I'm not going to turn you in. I want to find Brant the same as you," she announced. "I think he's innocent too, remember? Where is he?"

"I don't know," Ross insisted and groaned. "I didn't want him to tell me where he intended to go. That would be aiding and abetting a fugitive."

"You've done that already."

"Acht, not technically," Ross announced while raising a clever brow. "They had nothing to really go on when I spoke to him."

Devon fidgeted while running her fingers through her hair. "I hope he's all right."

Ross stared at her and the lost look on her face. He seemed oddly serious. "You were really going to turn in your virgin card, huh?"

She drew a deep, nervous breath and forced herself to meet Ross' gaze. "I know he's kind of shy and maybe a little nerdy," she remarked gently. "But something about him turns me on."

Ross placed his arm around Devon's shoulder and pulled her to his side while guiding her toward his car. He sighed deeply. "Yeah, he has that effect on me too," he announced then immediately cast a look at her.

As if on cue, she glared at him. Ross smiled and chuckled.

"Come along, you slutty, dirty girl," he announced. "We have important sleuthing to do."

Ross released her to open the passenger side door for her. The rusted car door creaked loudly. She was about to get into the car when Ross caught her arm, stopping her. She eyed his serious look.

"You intended to get down and dirty on the church altar?" he suddenly asked. "What goes on in that place when I'm not around?"

She rolled her eyes and got into the car. He pointed a warning finger at her.

"I swear, if I ever catch you doing it with him in the torture chamber, there's going to be hell to pay," he boldly announced then shut the car door.

Chapter Forty-three

Dorothy sat in a plush chair before Chelsea's wheelchair and repeatedly brushed her daughter's golden hair. Chelsea stared off at nothing and remained emotionless, showing no sign of brain activity. Dorothy heard a strange rustling sound outside the house. She stopped and looked at the big, bay window to the darkness beyond it. She then heard a gentle breeze blowing against the shrubs outside and immediately relaxed. She resumed brushing her daughter's hair.

"I think we'll go with flowered barrettes tomorrow," Dorothy informed her. "One on each side. They'll look beautiful in your hair."

Only a moment passed before she heard a thud from upstairs. Dorothy looked at the ceiling with a fixed stare. She set the brush down on the chair and nervously stood. Dorothy removed an old golf club from alongside her chair and approached the stairway. She looked up the stairs a moment and listened, but she didn't hear anything. She slowly walked up the steps while clutching the golf club. A floorboard creaked beneath her feet. She immediately paused while making a face then continued to the second floor.

As she reached the top of the stairs, she saw her bedroom door gently sway. She was certain the window had been closed, so nothing should have moved the door. Dorothy hesitated a moment then cautiously approached her bedroom and looked into the dark room with her golf club firmly in her hand. She felt inside the inner wall for the light switch and turned on the light. The room suddenly brightened, almost startling her. Dorothy's eyes immediately fell upon her queen-sized bed where Tamara's dead body lay on top of the frilly comforter.

Tamara was covered in her own blood from a large, gaping wound to her lower abdomen. She appeared to be partially gutted, although the blood was dried and there was none on the bed. Dorothy held back her scream while shaking her head. On the wall above the bed was the word *killer* written in blood. Dorothy screamed at the sight, ran from the room, and thundered down the stairs. She ran into the kitchen, grabbed the phone from the wall near the counter, and pushed a button. She turned toward the kitchen doorway and darted looks around her while clenching the phone cord.

A shadow moved within the living room. Dorothy gasped while dropping the phone, clutched her golf club, and cautiously entered the living room. She didn't see anyone except Chelsea, who sat in her chair with her usual fixed stare. Dorothy looked around the room while breathing heavily. She darted for the living room phone on the end table alongside her chair and snatched it from its base, realizing too late that she hadn't hung up the kitchen phone.

To her surprise, there was a dial tone. She looked back at the kitchen with concern. Someone must have hung up the kitchen phone! She dropped the phone and ran for the front door. Dorothy pulled on the doorknob, but the door was still locked and bolted. She tossed her golf club aside and fumbled with the lock and deadbolt. A floorboard creaked behind her.

Dorothy whirled around to the somehow terrifying sound. The phantom stood before her, his eyes piercing into hers. Her eyes widened as she screamed hysterically. The large knife thrust forward, stabbing her in the throat to silence her scream. The bloody knife was fiercely pulled back allowing blood to streak across the wall. She clutched her bleeding throat while gasping. Chelsea remained immobile in her chair with her usual fixed stare, unaware of what was happening. Dorothy attempted to scream while spitting up blood. The phantom slammed her against the door to keep her from falling as he repeatedly and violently thrust the dagger into her abdomen.

The phantom continued to stab her in her abdomen over and over until she finally slipped from his hand and slid down the door, collapsing in a bloody heap on the floor. There was blood strewn across the entire foyer from the brutal assault. The room fell silent except for the clock ticking on the wall. Chelsie sat in her chair staring at nothing, unaware of the vicious attack that had just ended her mother's life. The phantom, covered in Dorothy's blood, approached her in her chair and stared at her with the bloodied dagger still clutched in his gloved hand. With his left gloved hand, he gently touched her cheek, leaving a small bloody streak on her face. Her eyes lifted possibly for the first time in seven years.

The following morning, police blazers blocked the driveway to Dorothy's house and yellow police tape roped off the front yard. Several townspeople gathered by the tape and strained to see what had happened. Low murmurs came from the crowd. Within the house, a photographer took photos of Dorothy lying on the floor in a bloody heap. There were dozens of stab wounds to her body surrounded by her own blood. Sheriff Carter stood in the corner of the living room near the plush chair and stared down with an angered look on his stern face. Deputy Havens walked down the stairs while scratching his head. He wore a slightly sickened look as he approached the sheriff, who still hadn't moved.

"The coroner is convinced Tamara died the same day she went missing," Deputy Havens informed him then shook his head. "The girl's been dead a week. Someone kept her body stashed somewhere all this time just to put it in Dorothy's bedroom. This is insane."

The sheriff didn't take his eyes away from the corner and maintained his stare at Chelsea's empty wheelchair lying on its side. His anger had reached its boiling point while he kept his back to Deputy Havens.

"I don't care how you do it, Havens," Sheriff Carter launched in a low, cold tone. "Even if you have to search every house in this damned town, I want Chelsea found."

"Yes, sir."

§

The following afternoon, Ross and Devon sat inside the funeral home parlor while reading the morning paper. Ross shook his head and muttered something. The parlor doors opened startling both.

Tony entered looking mildly disturbed and eyed his friends. "Sorry I've kept you waiting so long," he announced although he was clearly distracted.

"They still haven't found Chelsea," Ross informed him with noted hostility. "How could anyone possibly harm a girl in her condition?"

"I think it's sick," Tony launched and immediately fidgeted. "I'm afraid I've kept you waiting for nothing. I have to run over to Dorothy's place and get another dress. Her sister called and changed her mind again. The funeral's tomorrow night and no one from the family can pick up the dress."

"They're certainly in a hurry to plant the old girl," Ross remarked. "Didn't the police just release the body this morning?"

Tony nodded and appeared frustrated by the entire situation. "The killer certainly left a mess," he announced while exhaling a shaken breath. "Embalming her was a nightmare. Thankfully, there was no damage to her face, so they can still have an open casket." Tony attempted to collect himself. "Her sister's family is leaving the day after tomorrow for a month-long tour of Europe. They opted to have the funeral right away, so they wouldn't have to postpone their trip."

"How compassionate of them," Ross muttered.

"You're going to Dorothy's place?" Devon asked while giving him a curious look.

"Yeah," Tony replied with a sigh. "I find it a little unsettling after what happened. They just took down the police line."

Devon and Ross eagerly stood.

"We'll come with you," Devon announced a little too quickly.

Ross nodded without hesitation.

"You will?" Tony asked with surprise then suspiciously eyed them. "Why?"

"We just want to have a look around," Devon announced while attempting to act casual.

Ross nodded again.

"You mean snoop," Tony remarked with a huff then sighed while throwing his arms in the air. "All right. I'd rather not go there alone anyway. Just don't do anything that will get me into trouble."

Chapter Forty-four

Tony led Ross and Devon into Dorothy's house through the garage door, which led into the kitchen. The front door remained sealed, even though the coroner had finished his investigation. Devon wondered why the front door remained sealed if they were finished. They followed Tony into the living room. All three immediately stopped when they saw the foyer area strewn with blood. There was blood spattered on the walls, pooled on the floor, and streaked down the door. Since no one was living in the house, the crime scene cleanup crew hadn't been through yet.

Devon immediately clutched Ross' arm while staring at the grisly scene. Ross clutched her hand nearly tight enough to cut off her circulation. He was possibly more horrified than she was. Tony ran his fingers through his hair, drew a deep breath, and then led them to the stairs, which took them closer to the spilled and spattered blood. Devon and Ross clung to each other as they neared the mess by the door.

"Poor Dorothy," Devon whispered as they headed for the stairs, unable to tear her eyes away from the gruesome scene. "No one deserves to die like that."

Ross practically dragged her up the stairs, not wanting to see the graphic image any longer.

§

Once in Jamie's bedroom, Ross and Devon sifted through drawers and poked around in the closet. Devon removed a box filled with junk from the shelf in the closet. As she set it on the bed, Ross immediately joined her. They removed items from the box and studied them with interest. Ross removed a framed picture of Jamie and Chelsea.

"What a shame," Ross remarked. "Two attractive girls; both lives ending in tragedy."

"Except Chelsea was a sweet girl and Jamie was a troublemaker."

"If it hadn't been for the accident, Chelsea certainly would've given Jamie some fierce competition with the guys."

Devon sorted through loose pictures in the box then removed a small, black velvet box from the bottom. Ross stared as she opened it. It contained a small, diamond engagement ring.

"Do you suppose that was from Karl?" Ross asked while raising his brow.

"I don't remember them ever being engaged," Devon informed him. "Karl never came across as commitment minded."

"Someone else proposed to Jamie?" Ross asked then laughed. "Typical of her not to give the ring back."

Devon placed it on her finger and eyed it. It was rather a tight fit. "Tiny too. Jamie would have to wear it on her pinkie."

"Maybe she stole it," Ross remarked then tilted his head with a curious look. "Or received it as hush money. That girl did drive a nice car for someone who barely worked full-time as a waitress."

"Just makes me wonder who'd ask her to marry him besides Karl," Devon remarked while deep in thought. "I know she had a ton of boyfriends, but they were usually the temporary type."

"There are plenty of motives for someone to want Jamie dead."

"Is it possible Dorothy killed Jamie in anger over this acting job?" Devon asked. "You know she's totally against women flaunting themselves. She's so self-righteous. She considered the others to be trashy women. Ivy too. Karl may have figured out that she'd killed Jamie and sought revenge on her."

"But why take Chelsea?" he asked. "It's not as if she's a material witness."

"I don't know."

"You know, you may be on to something," Ross remarked. "All the women killed had two things in common. They all auditioned for the same acting job, and they were all close at one time. I mean, apart from Dorothy."

"But how does Brant fit into all of this," Devon practically demanded. "Was he just meant to be a scapegoat? And why Brant? No one really knows him. If you're going to frame someone, you need to make sure they don't have alibis for the murders. So who, apart from you, me, and Tyler, knew Brant's movements enough to frame him?"

"Tyler has an alibi for two of the murders," Ross announced. "If he didn't, I might believe he had something to do with it."

"Tyler knows less people in town than Brant," Devon remarked. "Even if he didn't have an alibi, what possible reason would he have for killing women he didn't even know?" She shook her head. "There has to be some connection with the victims all being friends."

"Ivy wasn't their friend," Ross remarked. "You and Ivy didn't hang out with them in school."

"Yes, but we don't know that Ivy was targeted," Devon informed him.

"She was called to that farmhouse where we found Paula dead," Ross corrected. "I think she was an intended victim."

"Maybe we were meant to think that," Devon replied. "Why didn't the killer show up? We certainly didn't scare him off. Ivy was there a good half hour before we came along. He had plenty of motive and opportunity to kill her before we arrived."

"It feels like it should be Karl," Ross announced while shaking his head. "They need to track him down and question him--not Brant."

Devon sank into thought then eyed Ross while grimacing. "It's a long shot, I know," she announced, "but they never found that guy who killed Christine seven years ago. What if it's him? I mean, we don't know who this stranger was. He could have known Christine's friends and despised them."

"They said they didn't recognize the guy," Ross corrected. "They said he was a stranger."

"What if they lied?" Devon remarked. "What if the guy who killed Christine was some poor bastard they teased endlessly? They were good at bullying."

"If that were the case, why wouldn't they tell the police who killed Christine?" Ross practically demanded. "Why protect his identity, Inspector Clouseau?"

"Maybe he had something incriminating on them," Devon announced while raising her brows. "What about that, my dear Mr. Stringer?"

Ross frowned. "Okay, I would have accepted Mr. Watson, but I'm no Mr. Stringer."

Tony walked into the room with a dress draped over his arm and a slightly sickened look on his face. "Uh, I think the sheriff withheld some facts about Dorothy's murder."

"What makes you think that?" Ross asked.

Tony nodded them from the room. They sprang to their feet and hurried after him. All three entered Dorothy's bedroom and saw the blood-tinged comforter and the word *killer* written in blood on the wall above the headboard.

"There was another body," Devon gasped.

"Who?" Ross asked while staring wide-eyed at the writing in blood.

"I don't know."

"Tamara is still missing, and no one's seen Joe," Ross offered and looked at his friends.

"But why leave a body in Dorothy's bed?" Tony asked while shaking his head. "Why killer written in blood?"

All three stared at the scene in silence.

Tony suddenly drew a deep breath and looked at them. "Anyone else ready to leave?" he asked.

Chapter Forty-five

Friday couldn't have come soon enough. It had been a long, tiring week and this was the first time Devon couldn't wait to leave her new job. Up until now, she had enjoyed her work at the museum, but with Brant missing and wanted by the police, she just couldn't shake her feelings of anxiety. Devon pushed a hand truck containing a wax man depicted with a painful expression on his face into the torture chamber. She gently slid him off the hand truck then moved him into place along the wall. His arms were in the air with his wrists limp. She easily connected the shackles to his wrists, took a step back, and studied the new addition.

Somehow, Brant had managed to work the wax creation perfectly without an inch to spare, so the shackles were tight against his wrists, and his dirty, bare feet just touched the floor. She was about to leave when she paused and looked around the torture chamber, taking it in. It was a gruesome display that would surely give adults nightmares. There was even a warning posted outside the entrance, so that visitors would be warned of the gory displays. Her job would be to add more blood to the set once all the figures were in place. She noticed a woman had been added to the display, which she found surprising. She didn't think they were putting women in the torture chamber. Not that women weren't tortured back in the medieval days, but she was certain Brant and Tyler decided against it.

Devon approached the lone woman stretched backward across the wheel. She was bent painfully with her wrists tied above her head and her ankles tied together near the bottom. Devon stared at the look of anguish on the woman's once attractive face. She seemed to be crying out in terror. Her eyes immediately traveled to the woman's tattered clothes, noting her rather large, exposed breast. The amazingly detailed breast was so lifelike, it made Devon squirm. She immediately felt her cheeks redden and harbored some anger at the audacity of the decision to have some big-breasted woman displayed half-naked. Why did men always have to go there?

She shook her head then was about to turn and leave when she paused. Devon turned back toward the woman, tugged on her tattered dress and covered the exposed breast. She gave a satisfied nod then took her hand truck and passed through the torture chamber. She eyed the man torn in two on the stretching rack.

"Catch you later, Oscar," she announced and left the room.

§

Fondly dubbed the snake pit, Devon entered the display that was literally filled with wax snakes. She cringed at the entirely too realistic reptiles dangerously close to the walkway, which was lined with fake torches, making it look as if the fire was keeping the snakes back. Ross worked in the middle of the *pit* and put the finishing touches on a wax man and woman drowning in the snakes. Devon paused on the walkway and eyed Ross. He saw her and waved her to join him.

"Thanks," she announced while making a face, "but I'm good right here."

"I need your help," he announced.

She grimaced and attempted to tiptoe through the fake snakes. "Whose idea was this display of terror anyway?" she practically demanded.

When she was nearly halfway to Ross, the snakes began to move, and the room was filled with the sounds of hissing and rattling. Several large cobras lifted their hooded heads. Devon screamed then glared at Ross while he watched her and laughed.

"Come on," he again insisted.

"Turn them off," she cried out, refusing to move.

Ross frowned and turned off the animatronics with the remote control. "Party pooper."

§

Devon sat in the workshop and implanted long strands of reddish-brown hair into the head of a wax woman while Tyler stood over her shoulder and watched with great interest.

"You do excellent work, Devon."

"Thanks," she replied then resumed working on the wax head.

She didn't know how much longer she could tolerate Tyler standing over her shoulder. She was starting to feel like a prison inmate with the guard watching her every move. Devon didn't know why she felt such a creepy vibe from Tyler. He didn't actually do anything to make her feel that way. She couldn't write it off as a rich boy wanting to play the role of an artist, because that's exactly what Brant was doing.

"Brant has taught you well," he announced then sank into thought and sat on the counter near her. "I'm worried about him. I hope nothing's happened to him. It's not like him to take off."

"He probably doesn't even know the police are looking for him."

He cocked his head while glancing at her then offered a tiny smile. "Nice try, but it's been in all of the papers," Tyler insisted then sighed. "I'm really worried about him." He then glanced at her and appeared curious. "You haven't heard from him, have you?"

"Not since his parents took him home from the hospital," she remarked.

"If you have, you can tell me," Tyler announced while giving her a sympathetic look. "I won't say anything to the police. Brant's not just my business partner; he's also my friend."

"I'm sure he'll be back soon and straighten everything out," she insisted while also trying to convince herself of that.

Tyler placed a hand on her shoulder and pointed to the wax woman's eyes. "This is just so realistic," he announced then grinned. "You've really come a long way in a short time."

"Thank you."

"I have a lot of ideas for the museum displays," Tyler announced and finally stood, giving her more room to work. "I was thinking we could discuss them over dinner tonight."

Tyler turned toward her from behind and gently massaged her shoulders. Devon immediately tensed to his touch. She knew better than to assume it was just a friendly shoulder massage.

"I, uh, have plans for tonight," she remarked and hoped that'd stop his hands.

"Oh?"

Ross entered the room with a burst of energy while wearing a big grin. He clapped his hands together excitedly and began to dance around the room. Tyler removed his hands from Devon's shoulders and moved away from her. That he didn't want Ross to see his hands on her shoulders confirmed her suspicions regarding his intentions.

"Put on your dancing shoes, Devon," Ross announced enthusiastically. "We're going to party hearty." He did a little dance that was mostly embarrassing. "Time to get this weekend started!"

Devon turned and smiled while watching Ross embarrass himself with his goofy dancing. She had to admit; his timing was perfect.

§

Limousines were parked in front of the exclusive Ruby Club located within the city. Well-dressed men and women entered the glittery club and enjoyed the party atmosphere. Devon had little choice but wear the borrowed, black dress. She linked onto Ross's arm as they entered the club. It was the first time she'd seen Ross in anything other than jeans and a t-shirt. Tony and Ivy entered behind them. Ivy wore a red, spandex dress and her hair was meticulously styled. There were people at the bar drinking and even more on the dance floor. Everyone in the club was dressed in their finest. The four walked across the club and found a table that had just opened.

"I'm going to the bar and order some drinks," Ross announced. "I'll be right back."

Devon hurried after him, stopped him just short of the bar, and smiled knowingly. "Okay, Ross. What's this all about?" she practically demanded. "It's not like you to willingly suggest an expensive club like this. The cover charge is more then you make an hour."

Ross reluctantly sighed. "On the night Jamie was murdered, Brant said he was at his parents' house, but he'd left early because he and his mother got into a fight. Supposedly he came here," he informed her. "Jamie didn't leave the diner until six o'clock, so they're estimating her time of death between six-thirty and nine-thirty. I thought we'd come here and see if we could establish an alibi for him for that two-hour window from seven-thirty until nine-thirty."

"How did you know Brant got into a fight with his mother?" she asked. "I never told you that."

He immediately fidgeted. "Uh, an anonymous phone call told me to check this club for a bartender named Ozzy."

"You *were* talking to Brant!" she exclaimed as her eyes lit up.

Ross motioned for her to keep it down. He looked around with some uneasiness. "Just briefly," he announced in a hushed tone. "He was around people during Jamie's estimated time of death. It's the only alibi we can produce for him."

They approached the bar and found the bartender named Ozzy. Ozzy was a big man in his late twenties. He had long red hair pulled back into a ponytail and a neatly trimmed beard. His appearance was almost frightening to those who didn't know him.

Ozzy casually leaned on the bar. "Yeah, he was here that night. I remember him well," he remarked. "One of the few patrons wearing a tuxedo. Great tipper. Comes in here a lot of Friday nights. Likes to sit in the corner. Quiet. Keeps to himself."

Several customers ordered drinks, keeping Ozzy and the other bartenders busy. Ozzy poured several drinks and made change for the customers while they questioned him about that night.

"So he was here that Friday night--all night?" Ross pressed.

"Yeah, until about one-thirty. He nearly passed out at the bar," Ozzy replied. "He'd been drinking with another man at the bar that night. The guy called him a cab."

"Can you tell me who he was with?" Ross asked with renewed enthusiasm.

"I've seen the guy a couple of times, but I don't know names," Ozzy replied. "He was with the other guy from about ten o'clock until they left half an hour before closing. I remember it well. They were depressing me with talk about women. Your man was interested in some woman, but he was afraid she'd never be interested in him, and the other guy lost the woman he loved."

"Would you be willing to tell the police he was here the entire time?" Ross asked.

"Sure. He gives great tips."

Ross looked at Devon as Ozzy walked away. "He was at his parents' house until six-thirty, and it took fifteen minutes to get here. He has the bartender as a witness from seven until one-thirty," Ross announced. "It'd take him at least forty-five minutes to return to town. I'd say it'd be impossible for him to have murdered Jamie."

Devon smiled happily and hugged Ross.

Chapter Forty-six

The following morning, Devon had her horse tied in the crossties in the center of the barn while she brushed him. She intended to spend the entire morning taking a lengthy, well-deserved ride. She needed to clear her head and stop thinking for a few hours. Martin appeared in the barn doorway still wearing his clothes from the night before. He folded his arms across his chest, leaned against the doorframe, and smiled wearily while watching her.

"You're up early," he announced pleasantly.

She eyed her brother, noted his exhaustion, and grinned deviously. "I could say the same about you," she teased. "I didn't hear you come in last night. What time did you get home?"

"Five minutes ago," he remarked while grinning.

She raised her brows suggestively and noted his enthusiasm despite his weary condition. "One of *those* nights, huh?"

"Possibly the best night I've had in years," he remarked while grinning.

"Really?" she asked with surprise then gave him her full attention. She noted the look on his face and the sparkle in his eyes. She didn't remember the last time she'd seen him looking that way. Perhaps she'd never seen him looking that way. "Does this mean you're in love?"

"Never know," he replied with a shrug although his smile told a different story. He was obviously on cloud nine.

"Think we may actually meet this one?" she prompted, hoping he'd finally found the right woman. Nothing would make her happier.

"Well," he fumbled slightly, although his smile never disappeared. "You know I don't like to bring young ladies around since they rarely work out. I promise, though, you'll be the first one to meet the love of my life when I'm sure."

"I'd better be," she announced.

"Going out for a ride?"

"I've neglected my poor horse lately," she replied and patted the horse's thick neck. "He needs to stretch his legs." She cast a serious look at her brother. "Marlene's wake is this evening. Are you going?"

Martin groaned and fidgeted while straightening. "You know how I feel about funerals and dead people on display," he announced. "It creeps me out."

"Well, you're in luck then," Devon announced. "Marlene was cremated yesterday, so there won't be a viewing; just a memorial."

He sighed softly. "Considering our brief romantic history, I should probably pay my respects," Martin remarked. "If you're taking the scenic ride, stay away from the hired men. They've been acting odd the past week. I think they're up to something."

"When aren't they?" she remarked then hesitated. "Remember that summer Marco had his girlfriend living in the bunkhouse for nearly two months?"

Martin chuckled. "Best kept secret on the ranch," he announced.

Devon continued to brush her horse then sank into thought. She hesitated then turned toward her brother with a serious look on her face. "Tell me something, Martin. Do you remember Jamie being engaged?"

"Jamie?" he asked with surprise. "No, I don't recall ever hearing about that. Why do you ask?"

"Ross and I were poking around in Jamie's room after Dorothy's death, and we found an engagement ring in a junk box in the closet," Devon informed him. "Judging by the karat size, I'm guessing it was given to her by someone of limited means."

"Really?" Martin remarked then appeared momentarily surprised as he considered the comment. "It's possible she may have been engaged to some guy briefly when she was younger then dumped him as usual. Not to speak ill of the dead, but you know how Jamie was." He brushed it off with little interest. "I doubt she was murdered by some jilted lover from years ago. Forget about the murders for a while and enjoy your ride. I need to get some sleep." His cheerful smile again returned. "I have a busy night ahead of me."

She laughed knowing exactly what sort of night he had ahead of him. "Pleasant dreams, lover boy."

That night, a thunderstorm was heard in the distance. Despite the approaching storm, Devon slept peacefully as the curtains gently blew inward from the increasing winds. A shadow moved along the balcony past her open window. Just then, a floorboard creaked causing Devon to stir. She listened a moment. When she didn't hear anything, she nuzzled her pillow. The shadow passed over her as a dark figure moved closer to her bed. Devon woke and shot up in bed with a gasp to see Brant sitting on the edge of the bed near her. He was wearing faded blue jeans, a cotton shirt, and cowboy boots.

"Please, don't scream," he practically gasped. "I saw the assortment of shotguns your father keeps in the downstairs cabinet."

"Brant," she softly cried out with surprise and looked him over.

"I know I'm taking a chance coming here," he announced timidly, "but I had to see you."

Devon threw her arms around Brant's neck and clung to him. He uncertainly returned the embrace and buried his face in her neck.

"I guess you aren't as mad as I thought you'd be," he muttered into her neck.

Devon pulled away, gave him an angry glare, and repeatedly smacked him on the chest. "You'd better believe I'm mad," she cried out in a whisper. "I was worried sick."

"I meant about the murder accusation," he replied timidly and offered a concerned look. "I was afraid you might believe I killed those women."

"I know better," she announced then grinned with enthusiasm. "Ross talked to that bartender. He's agreed to testify that you were at the club all night." She grabbed his hands and held them. "You should be cleared by Monday morning."

He gave her a confused look. "What bartender?" Brant asked. "What are you talking about?"

"The one you told Ross about. The bartender at the Ruby Club," she announced while holding back her laugh. "You were there the night of Jamie's murder."

Brant stared at her and remained puzzled. "I haven't spoken to Ross since the day they'd searched my house," he remarked.

She was momentarily stunned by his words. "That doesn't make any sense," Devon remarked. "Who would call Ross and tell him to check out that club and mention the bartender by name?"

"Truthfully, that idea never even occurred to me," he replied and appeared embarrassed. "I was pretty drunk that night. I don't even remember calling a cab to take me home."

Devon brushed off the conversation then touched his shirt while giving him an approving once-over. "Look at you. You look like a cowboy," she announced then met his gaze. "Where have you been hiding out?"

"In the bunkhouse with your father's ranch hands. I think they mostly felt sorry for me," he announced. "I've been herding cattle with them the entire week."

She stared at him surprised to hear he'd been hanging out at her ranch all week. It was no wonder the ranch hands were acting strangely.

Devon smiled and laughed. "You can be devious when you want to be."

He drew a deep breath while staring into her eyes. "Maybe," he replied timidly, "but that's not what brought me to your bedroom window."

Devon stared at Brant a moment then smiled warmly. She gently ran her hands along his chest and slipped her arms around his neck. He didn't look away from her while anticipating her next move. Devon was almost humored by his shy nature. She leaned closer and kissed him warmly on the lips. Brant wasted little time returning the kiss and pulled her against him. The warm, tender kiss swiftly turned passionate and aggressive as both released pent-up desire. Devon finally broke off the kiss and affectionately caressed his face while staring into his eyes through the dim lighting.

"This is the part where you throw me down to the bed and make love to me, cowboy," she informed him then grinned slyly.

Brant stared at her a moment with surprise then groaned with desire.

"Yes, ma'am."

He practically tackled her to the bed, not wasting a moment. Thunder rumbled loudly as the rain poured down outside the window, but neither seemed to notice.

Chapter Forty-seven

Devon entered the doctor's office waiting room Monday morning and approached the nurse seated at the front desk. Since they were a small town, the older nurse was also the secretary. To someone unfamiliar with their town, they may not have realized Gina was a registered nurse since she dressed in a flowered print shirt and polyester pants. Devon looked around the empty waiting room, surprised the office was empty.

"Quiet today," Devon remarked.

"I like quiet," the older nurse announced while smiling pleasantly.

Gina was in her early sixties and had been Dr. Sherman's nurse since he first opened his practice decades ago. Dr. Sherman delivered most of the babies in town straight through Devon's generation. Gina was only a tick over five-foot and possibly shrinking. She was a round, stout woman with her long, gray hair worn in a granny bun. Well, she was a granny, so it was only fitting. The older woman leaned on the desk and smiled pleasantly at Devon.

"How can I help you, dear?" Gina asked. "Doc had a house call, but if you'd like to wait, I'm sure he'll see you when he gets back. His schedule is wide open."

"Yeah, that'd be great," Devon announced then fidgeted. "I, uh, actually wanted to discuss birth control options with Dr. Sherman."

Gina suddenly grinned. "Oh, you're seeing a young man? That's wonderful."

Devon exhaled and relaxed slightly. "I didn't expect much support," she announced then fidgeted. "You know; since I'm not married."

Gina laughed while covering her mouth. She then waved off Devon. "Honey, I may be old, but I know what it's like to be young. Get out there. Test the waters!" She then stood and approached the filing cabinet behind her. "I have a few brochures you can look at while waiting for Doc." She removed some brochures then returned to the desk. "Of course, he may recommend you see an OBGYN for that."

Devon accepted the brochures while staring at the older nurse. "Oh, yes. I hadn't considered that. Ivy has a female doctor she sees in the city."

Gina threw her hands in the air while smiling cheerfully. "You can make an appointment with her doctor then. Cut out the middleman, so to speak."

"Thanks," Devon replied with relief. "I'll do that."

"Anytime, dear," she announced then raised her brows. "So--who's the young man? You know how I love good gossip."

"Oh," Devon remarked and immediately fidgeted. Since Brant was still officially in hiding, it seemed a good idea not to mention him by name. "You haven't met him yet. He's not from around here."

"I understand," she announced dramatically. "So many young people these days are spending a lot of time in the city. Half the young people in our town are engaged to guys and gals living in the city." Gina sighed and appeared almost defeated. "I just hope some of them decide to stay in our little town. I so love seeing little ones running around the park."

Devon considered the comment and tilted her head. "You hear all the good gossip, Gina," she remarked, playing on the woman's ego.

"Absolutely," she announced with glee. "This is gossip central. Well, next to the tavern and the hair salon."

"Did you remember Jamie ever being engaged?" Devon asked.

Gina straightened in her chair and gave the question serious consideration. "No, I don't think so. If she had been, she didn't tell anyone about it." Her eyes then widened. "Dorothy would never have allowed it. She wasn't exactly fond of men."

"I suppose she had reason to be protective," Devon remarked and considered the comment. "With her husband running off like that."

"But there comes a time when a mother needs to step back and allow her daughters to make their own mistakes," Gina announced firmly. "It's part of growing up."

"I'm sure she felt some guilt about Chelsea," Devon replied, almost surprised she was defending Dorothy on anything. It may have had something to do with seeing the brutality of the crime scene that made her sympathetic toward the woman.

"Between us," Gina announced while leaning forward on the desk. "Dorothy was a bit of a hypocrite. I mean, she claimed to be so religious then to even suggest aborting a healthy baby." She shook her head. "Breaks my heart when I think about it. It's a shame we can't practice what we preach."

Devon allowed the comment to sink in then realized what Gina was saying. Had Jamie been pregnant and Dorothy insisted she have an abortion? Could that be the significance of the engagement ring? Now the jilted lover scenario seemed almost plausible. Unfortunately, nearly everyone who knew about Jamie's secret life was already dead.

§

Devon got a ride home with Ivy later that afternoon. She waved to Ivy as she turned her jeep in the driveway and drove away from the farm. Devon headed for the house then paused on the porch and looked at the bunkhouse in the distance beyond the barn. She wondered if Brant was out working cattle with the rest of the hands. More importantly, she wondered if he would scale the balcony and slip into her room again tonight. Since he'd be going to the sheriff today to clear his name, she was uncertain what would happen tonight, but she couldn't deny she was giddy with anticipation. Devon entered the house and paused by the hall table where the mail lay sorted in piles for her and her brother.

She saw an envelope with her name scribbled across it. Oddly enough, it contained no return address and the stamp wasn't canceled. She eyed it suspiciously, picked it up while looking around the quiet house, and then opened the envelope. It read, "Meet me at the museum seven o'clock tonight. Urgent. Come alone!" Devon stared at the note without a signature and sank into thought. The note seemed odd, considering Brant was working on clearing his name. He had already made plans to visit the sheriff's office later that day armed with the bartender from the Ruby Club as his witness and his lawyer, so why the mystery? She couldn't deny the recent rash of murders weighed on her mind.

Is this how the murdered women were lured to their deaths? Or was it simply Brant attempting to be romantic? Did she dare show up alone as the note requested? Devon studied the strangely prepped envelope. The note was almost certainly hand delivered, which meant it had to come from Brant. He obviously added her address and the stamp to make it less suspicious if her parents found it first. It had to be Brant; didn't it?

Chapter Forty-eight

Devon entered the museum just a little before seven o'clock that night with Ross directly behind her holding a baseball bat in his hand. He closed the front door behind them and gave her a serious look.

"Are you sure you don't want me to go along?" he asked with concern.

"Yes, I'm sure," she replied. "Just stick with the plan."

"If something doesn't seem right," he announced. "Scream like hell and run for the dungeon stairs. I'll clock anyone chasing you."

"Thank you, Ross," she replied timidly. "I'm sure it's just Brant, but I appreciate the backup."

Ross managed a weak smile then sat on the nearby bench in the lobby. Devon left Ross and headed along the walkway. She nervously looked at the displays as she walked toward the back then headed down the stairs to the basement and paused at the bottom of the steps. She looked around cautiously then continued past several horror displays. Despite having Ross as her backup, she was still feeling anxious. There was a light coming from the church display that still hadn't been touched. Obviously, since it was the only lit display that was where she was meant to go.

She approached the room with some apprehension after her last encounter with the church display. Devon eyed the fake candles and silk flower arrangements around the room. She was already having feelings of déjà vu. As she walked further into the display, she saw a beautiful blonde woman wearing a full, white, wedding gown and veil on top of the altar. She wasn't sure when Ross or Tyler had completed the altar display, but it was beautiful.

The woman's wedding gown train was draped elegantly over the side of the altar, her veil cascaded along her body, and her hands were neatly clasped over her abdomen. She had a small bouquet of wildflowers grasped in her hands. Devon nervously looked around the room, but she didn't see anyone. She slowly approached the display, marveling at the work someone had put into the scene. It certainly wasn't Brant. Was Ross up to something? She suddenly stopped when she recognized the woman on the altar. It was Chelsea! Her hair was neatly pinned up, and her makeup was carefully applied. She was a vision of beauty. She was dead. Devon held back her gasp. Her eyes then strayed to the familiar, small diamond ring that was proudly displayed on her left, ring finger with a gold wedding band below it.

She heard a door gently shut. Devon turned around with surprise. Martin stood by the door dressed in a black tuxedo and had a blank expression on his face. He walked toward her with a glass of champagne in his hand. Devon remained still and stared at him. Her brother walked past her and paused before the altar and the dead woman. He placed his hand on Chelsea's, revealing the matching wedding band on his left hand. Martin stared at Chelsea a moment in silence.

"Seven years ago, Chelsea and I were going to run away and get married after she'd graduated high school. I loved her more than life itself. She was the first woman I'd ever made love to." He hesitated and drew a deep, labored breath. "And I haven't been with another woman since." Martin finally looked at Devon. "She was pregnant with our child."

Devon held back her gasp while staring at her brother, attempting to make sense of what he was telling her about his past.

"Last month, after Joe was fired from the ranch, I had a few drinks with him in the tavern," Martin announced in a solemn tone. "He was so drunk; he started talking about his sister's feud with Jamie." He stared into Devon's eyes with a serious, frightening look. "Paula told him Jamie killed Christine in the woods that day. I had left Chelsea at the bridge less than half an hour before she witnessed her sister killing Christine. The three of them chased her to the bridge, and what started as a threat rapidly turned into Chelsea's *accident*."

"Oh, my God," Devon gasped.

"I lied about my one-night-stand with Marlene. I overheard her saying something about Chelsea that concerned me, so I took her out, got her drunk, and encouraged her to gossip. Marlene told me that Dorothy terminated Chelsea's pregnancy shortly after the accident," he remarked in a calm tone although the anger could be seen in his moderately sedate eyes. "I had foolishly assumed she miscarried from the fall."

Martin finished his drink, set the glass on the floor, and turned to face Devon while straightening proudly.

"I killed Jamie, Tamara, and Paula for robbing me of my one true love. The woman I wanted to spend the rest of my life with. When I found out Dorothy destroyed the only part of Chelsea I could have taken with me, I made her suffer for what she'd done." He hesitated and drew a deep breath. "I swear on Chelsea's soul; I didn't kill

Marlene. Someone must've had a score to settle with her and used my murder rampage to their advantage. It's all in my journal. You'll find it on your bedside table."

Devon was now down to tears. "Oh, Martin," she gasped. "You could have told the police about Chelsea. It didn't have to be this way."

"It wouldn't have done any good," he replied. "Maybe they could have persuaded her friends to point the finger at her for Christine, but there's no proof Jamie intentionally threw Chelsea from the bridge. Honestly, I don't care if it was intentional or accidental. I just wanted to see them pay."

"What about Joe?" Devon gasped softly while feeling her body tremble. "You didn't--? Not for me."

"Joe was a two for one deal," Martin admitted proudly while raising his brows. "When Ross blabbed what actually happened that day in the barn, I wanted to kill Joe. It wasn't until he attempted to blackmail me for killing Paula that I decided he had to go. I didn't count on him actually remembering our drunken conversation. Joe's death was no big loss, I assure you."

"And Brant?" she asked with surprise. "Did you try to kill Brant? Why did you frame him?"

"That wasn't me, I swear. I'll admit; I did dispose of Jamie's body down here, but it wasn't my intention for Brant to be blamed. In fact, when I learned how much he meant to you, I tipped Ross off to the Ruby Club. I was the one Brant spent the evening with drowning his sorrows. When I ran into him at the beach house party, I had to take my leave. I didn't realize that was your boss and couldn't risk him connecting any dots," Martin informed her. "I knew he was innocent. My journal will clear him as well." He drew a deep breath while staring at her. "You were my only reason for living, Devon. I just want you to be happy. Chelsea and I will be together forever now. This is the way it has to be."

"What do you mean?" Devon suddenly gasped with alarm. "What have you done?"

"Just a little poison cocktail."

Devon gasped with horror. Martin clutched the altar for support.

"It's okay, Devon," he gently informed her. "I'll finally be happy. Chelsea and I will be together forever. We'll finally be free."

"No, we need to get an ambulance."

Martin snorted softly and, with all his strength, approached her. He gently touched her face.

"It's already too late, I assure you," he announced while smiling weakly.

Devon sobbed softly while shaking her head. Martin held her in his arms then released her and wiped away her tears.

"I love you, Devon," he announced. "But it's time for you to go. I only have a few minutes left, and I'd like to spend them alone with Chelsea."

She sniffed and wiped her tears while staring into his eyes. "I love you, Martin."

Martin smiled warmly and turned toward the altar. He clutched the altar for support and took Chelsea's hand. Devon slowly backed away and turned for the walkway. She knew she needed to get to the phone in the workshop. Perhaps, she could still save her brother. Save him for what purpose though? He'd brutally killed nearly half a dozen people and would need to pay for his crimes. Letting him go the way he wanted would be the compassionate thing to do. As she headed for the walkway, she heard a thud. She turned and saw Martin lying on the floor alongside the altar. She ran back and fell to her knees alongside him. Devon clung to Martin and sobbed.

Chapter Forty-nine

There was a large gathering at the ranch after Martin's funeral. Despite what had come out about Martin, dozens of people from town showed up to express their condolences to the family. Although no one condoned Martin's behavior, they knew the family had a long way to go with the healing process. The twelve ranch hands were dressed in their finest jeans and flannel shirts to attend the wake at the main house following the viewing at Tony's funeral home.

Devon's friends were there to support her as well, which she was grateful. She needed her friends more than ever to deal with the crushing blow of losing her brother. Even more so, the fact that someone she had admired since she was able to walk could do the horrible things he'd done. Tyler had accompanied Brant to the farmhouse. It was his first introduction to Ivy, and he was particularly taken with Devon's friend. Devon wanted to warn her about Tyler, but she just couldn't bring herself to have a normal conversation. She particularly avoided Ross, because he would try to make her feel better, and she didn't want to feel better.

Brant remained by her side throughout most of the wake, which she appreciated, but she needed some time alone and was frustrated when she couldn't escape people attempting to cheer her up. She eventually ended up standing by the paddock fence petting her horse. Even her horse attempted to cheer her up by lipping her cheek when she stood still and silent for too long. She looked across the yard filled with cars and saw her father leaning against Tony's blazer with his head down. Devon drew a deep breath and finally approached her father. She leaned against the blazer near him but didn't speak. He placed his arm around her, pulled her to his side, and held her in silence. It was probably the nicest moment she'd had with her father in a long time.

"Seven years," her father muttered finally breaking the silence.

She pulled away and eyed him, wondering what he'd meant by the comment. "What about seven years?" she finally asked.

"Your brother loved that girl for seven years, and I never knew about it," he announced almost painfully. "To love someone that much and keep it hidden so deep inside. I guess I never really knew him at all."

"You knew him, Dad," she gently replied. "He just chose to keep that part of his life to himself."

"And it eventually destroyed him from the inside," he remarked then looked at his daughter. "I don't want that to be us, Devon. I don't want you mad at me and let it fester inside for the next seven years."

"I'm not--" She hesitated and met her father's gaze. "Yes, I'm mad at you. You took away the thing I loved most because you didn't want me to be one of the boys. You wanted me to be like mom; a dutiful wife and mother. That's not going to happen."

"You're wrong, Devon," he informed her and shook his head. "I don't believe a woman's place is in the kitchen. I never have. I don't want to see you attempting to fill a role that makes you miserable just because you were born a certain gender."

"You ordered me to stay away from the ranch hands," she reminded him. "You told me I could no longer work the herd. Don't deny it upset you when you had to fire Joe because you didn't want to lose a hard worker. That it tore you up inside to fire a man fulfilling the role your son didn't want."

He stared at her with surprise. "Yes, it upset me when I fired Joe because he was a great worker," her father boldly announced. "But I wasn't upset with you because of his weakness, Devon. I never blamed you for being in the barn that day." He drew a deep breath. "Honestly, I was mad at myself. I'd allowed you to engage with men I thought I could trust around my daughter. Joe betrayed my trust, and I was afraid I'd been mistaken about the others as well. I didn't want anyone else ever touching you again." He shook his head. "I just wanted to protect my little girl, and I failed. Keeping you away from them was my only way to protect you."

"You don't get it," she announced defensively. "You don't have to protect me. When things happen, I'll deal with them. I can't stop living just because I get hurt along the way."

"I know, and I'm sorry," he replied gently. "I don't want you carrying anger with you like your brother had. I want us to be honest with each other and have real conversations when things are bothering us."

Devon lowered her head. "I'll admit; I didn't handle our disagreements very well either."

"What do you say?" he asked and managed a smile. "Can we start over? You can even come back and work the ranch if you'd like." He then made a face. "You can even bring your odd boss along since I hear he's been playing cowboy while evading the police at my ranch like some outlaw."

She laughed nervously and managed a smile. "You heard about that, huh?"

"Yeah, the guys think they're so slick," he announced with a sigh then shook his head. "I know more than they think, but we'll keep that between us."

She laughed and hugged her father.

Chapter Fifty

Nearly a week had passed since Martin's journal, and confession had cleared Brant of killing Jamie and her friends. Unfortunately, Martin had an alibi for Marlene's murder, so that meant he was telling the truth about not killing her. Marlene's killer was still out there. Sheriff Carter sat behind his desk while staring at the whiteboard on the wall, which contained photos of the dead women and Joe. Marlene was now on the left side of the board by herself. Her murder was unsolved, which took him right back to his first suspect--Brant. Marlene's body was found in his basement, where it was proven she had been murdered. By his own admission, Brant was in the museum workshop from the time Marlene disappeared until her suspected time of death. He was alone the entire night. Carter shook his head with annoyance and slammed his fist on his desk, bouncing several items.

"Son-of-a-bitch," he muttered, leaned back in his chair and resumed staring at the board.

Deputy Havens poked his head into the sheriff's office. "Did you call me?"

"No," Carter muttered. "Unless your name is Deputy Bitch."

The deputy entered the office and stared at Marlene's photo all by itself pinned to the left-hand side of the whiteboard.

"Should we bring Brant back in for questioning?" Deputy Havens asked.

"No," the sheriff muttered into his knuckles while resting his chin on his fist. "With Martin's deathbed confession to the murders, the evidence against Brant is shaky at best."

"Marlene was killed in his basement, and he doesn't have an alibi from the time she left work until the moment she was killed," Havens reminded him. "It doesn't look good for him."

"Yes, but everything we found in the upstairs bedroom pointed to Brant killing the women Martin confessed he'd killed," Sheriff Carter reminded him. "Sure, the knife we found was used to kill Marlene, but it wasn't used on the other victims. We found the dagger Martin had used and another phantom costume in his bedroom at his father's ranch. It's obvious everything in Brant's spare bedroom was planted there to frame him. Martin didn't frame Brant, so that means whoever killed Marlene planted those things in Brant's house."

"So you don't think he killed Marlene?" Deputy Havens asked with surprise.

Sheriff Carter frowned without moving his mouth from his knuckles and continued to stare at the board. "Nope, I'm convinced he's innocent."

"So who killed Marlene?"

"I have no clue."

It was a little after six o'clock Saturday evening and another fun-filled night of work for Tony at the funeral home. It seemed a lifetime since he'd had a day off after the rash of murders provided additional work for the mortuary. Things were finally returning to normal until yesterday's death meant another weekend of work. Tony took it in stride and hummed while busily working on his most recent client spread out on the metal prep table. There was a knock on the interior prep room door, surprising him. Tony looked up as the door opened. As Ivy poked her head into the prep room, Tony covered his client out of reflex. He relaxed when he saw it was just Ivy. Tony laughed nervously.

"You startled me," Tony announced and leaned on the table. "I really need to lock the front door when I'm working in the prep room."

Ivy managed a timid smile and indicated the covered body. "Is it okay if I come in?"

"Uh, yeah, sure," Tony announced and smiled. "Mr. Rumsfeld won't mind."

She eyed the sheet then cringed. "Old man Rumsfeld?" Ivy nearly choked while seeming tense. "Didn't he, uh, shoot himself in the head with a shotgun?"

Tony grimaced and managed a tiny nod. "Yeah, it's, uh, well, sort of--" He groaned and shook his head. "Definitely a closed casket affair. You don't want to see it; trust me."

"Yeah, you're probably right," she announced then indicated the interior door to the kitchen. "Do you have a minute?"

"Yeah, sure," he replied and pointed to the door. "Make yourself comfortable in the kitchen. Just give me a minute to, uh, clean up."

She eyed the dark smears of old blood on his apron and nodded. "Sure," she replied and grimaced. "Take your time. Scrub thoroughly."

Ivy exited the prep room and entered the kitchen. She approached the stove and put water in the kettle to make tea for them. The kettle finally whistled, and she had just poured two cups of tea when Tony entered the kitchen. He leaned against the counter near her and eyed her almost suspiciously.

"So what brings you here this time of night?" he asked then raised his brows. "And a Saturday no less. Don't you and Devon have important partying to do?"

"She's working this evening, and I didn't feel like going out by myself." Ivy leaned on the counter near him and managed a tiny smile. "I was offered the part in the soap opera."

Tony's eyes suddenly lit up and he immediately hugged her. "Congratulations!" He pulled back just far enough to look into her eyes. "And without sleeping with some sleazeball. I'm proud of you."

She placed her hand on his chest and frowned. "I turned it down."

Tony released her and appeared surprised. "What?" he practically gasped. "Why would you do that?"

"Turns out the scenes won't be filmed at the resort," she replied. "The job is in New York City."

"Okay," he replied not understanding. "What's wrong with an acting job in New York? I mean, that's big time, right?"

She fidgeted slightly and avoided looking at him. "I've done a lot of thinking," Ivy announced then drew a deep breath. "I don't want some acting job that'll take me away from my family and friends." She stared into his eyes. "There's another reason."

"What's that?" he asked.

Ivy placed her hands on his face and kissed him warmly but passionately on the lips. She pulled back and stared into Tony's eyes. He stared at her with some surprise then smiled.

"Good reason," he announced then pulled her into his arms and returned the kiss.

§

Ivy and Tony fell apart on the bed beneath the sheets while panting after their wild lovemaking. Tony wore a permanent grin on his face while Ivy was pleasantly rumpled. Ivy moved against Tony and rested her head on his bare chest. Tony clung to her and caressed her shoulder. She affectionately kissed his chest while he watched her and attempted to control his rapidly beating heart.

"Can you call your mother and see if you can spend the night?" he teased.

She eyed him and laughed.

"Sorry," he remarked while grinning. "It's been a while since I've had a girl over."

"That long, huh?" Ivy giggled.

"I exaggerate," he replied then nodded. "But it has been a while."

"Unfortunately, I can't spend the night," she sadly informed him. "I have to drive my mother to the airport at an ungodly hour tomorrow morning." She then offered a sly grin. "On the bright side, I'm free the rest of the week until she gets back on Friday."

"Well, then I'll settle for the rest of the week," Tony announced cheerfully. "Do you have enough time for a shower?"

"I should probably go," she replied while frowning. "I'll see myself out."

"I understand," he replied then kissed her warmly but passionately before pulling back and grinning. "If you change your mind; I'll be in the shower."

Chapter Fifty-one

Devon arrived at the museum Saturday evening a little before seven o'clock. She entered the workshop and paused in the doorway, surprised to see Tyler sitting at the counter working on one of his hideous creations. He cursed and wiped some paint from the wax face before him. Devon looked around with bewilderment then approached while summoning a pleasant mood.

"Good evening, Tyler."

Tyler looked back with surprise. "Devon, I wasn't sure you were coming back tonight."

"I thought I'd get a few hours in," she announced. "I needed to get away from home for a while anyway." Honestly, she didn't want to think about Martin anymore right now. It was too painful. "Where's Brant?" she asked. "He said he'd be here."

"He had to run a few errands," Tyler replied. "He'll be back soon."

Devon walked toward the rack against the far wall and slipped into her lab coat. She took a seat at the counter before an awaiting wax head.

"Are you going to the city tonight?" she asked while starting her work on the wax woman's hair.

"More than likely," he replied then walked behind her. "Would you like to come along? I'm attending a friend's party. It should be great fun."

"I'm working tonight," she announced then looked back and offered a tiny smile. "My first night back after a week off."

Tyler sat alongside her and grinned. "I'm your boss, remember?" he teased. "I give you permission to take the night off."

Tyler placed his hand on her arm and affectionately stroked it.

Devon pulled her arm away and glared at him. "You know I'm dating Brant."

"Oh, come on," he announced and offered a slight chuckle. "We both know your thing with Brant will end the moment you meet his mother. She'll never approve of some small town girl." He raised his brows while staring at her. "Brant comes from a long line of wealthy snobs, and you're nothing like those people. My family, however, will welcome you with open arms."

He again attempted to touch her arm. She sprang up from her chair and glared at him.

"Leave me alone," she snapped and hurried from the room.

§

Devon entered the mummy display with a rag and a can of turpentine. She needed to cool off before another confrontation with Tyler. Hopefully, Brant would be back and that would be the end of it. The carefully wrapped mummy was in a stalking position while a frightened woman was braced against a pillar in the ancient tomb setting. There were fake gold trinkets, statues, life-sized idols, and several wax archaeologists with horrified expressions upon their faces. There was a frightened woman apparently begging for her life from the horrifying mummy not far from the woman positioned against the pillar. As beautiful as the standing woman was, the begging woman was hideous and caked with makeup.

Unfortunately, she was one of Tyler's creations, easily recognized by the heavy and unrealistic makeup. Devon placed some turpentine on the rag, crouched alongside the begging woman, and attempted to clean her excessively painted face. Devon wasn't sure how many layers of paint she removed before finally reaching the base coat. Once she finished removing the excess makeup from the begging woman, she sat back on her feet and eyed the woman braced against the pillar only a foot or two away from her. She noticed the woman's legs below the light brown skirt she wore.

There was a strange indent on her calf that traveled a few inches downward. Devon ran her finger along the indent and studied it a long moment. It looked almost like a scar that had been covered over. She again looked up at the wax woman and felt as if something was off. Devon stood, moved closer, and studied the beautiful woman's face. Something about her seemed familiar, although she had worked on a lot of wax figures in recent weeks, particularly since they'd received the large shipment from the closed museum.

She stared into the wax woman's eyes a long moment then eyed the dark hair. The dark hair didn't seem right. Somehow, Devon felt the woman should be blonde. As Devon continued to stare at the wax woman's face, something suddenly clicked, and she knew why the face was familiar. She tore the hat from the wax woman's head then ripped the dark wig off with some effort, revealing golden blonde hair. Devon stared at Chelsea beneath the tan explorer's costume. She jumped back with a startled, horrified cry and backed into the mummy. She turned with a gasp, scaring herself.

As the mummy stared back at her through slits in the bandages, she saw something oddly familiar. Devon fumbled with scissors from her pocket, carefully cut the bandages around the head, and practically ripped the bandages off. To her horror, she saw her dead brother staring back at her. She dropped the scissors and gasped with horror as tears filled her eyes.

"No."

She couldn't tear her eyes away from Martin in his state of wax eternity. Her situation then dawned on her. Devon looked in the general direction of the workshop and stared a moment, wondering if anyone had heard her. She didn't wait to find out. She took one final look at her brother then ran from the display, away from the workshop, and toward the stairs. She raced up the stone dungeon steps, bolted to the front desk near the main entrance, and grabbed the phone. She punched in several numbers and nervously stared down the walkway as if expecting someone to chase after her. She heard a male voice on the phone.

"Deputy Havens," she gasped. "Oh, thank God! I need you to come out here right away--"

The line went dead. Devon felt her heart skip a beat then pound wildly. She hit several buttons but didn't get a dial tone. Was it a coincidence that the phone went dead? She doubted it. Devon ran for the main entrance, bolted through the door, and ran across the parking lot to Martin's blazer. She threw open the door and jumped inside. She felt her pockets and realized she'd left her keys in the workshop. She screamed with frustration and slammed her hands on the steering wheel. She sprang from the car and looked around the vast farmland to the distant lights of town beyond the cornfield. She was completely isolated. She then saw lights from Tony's funeral home just a cornfield away.

"Tony," she gasped then ran across the parking lot for the road.

Devon ran alongside the cornfield toward the awaiting funeral home while casting several looks behind her. She found it strange that no one was following her. She was almost certain someone should have been following her.

Chapter Fifty-two

Devon ran across the funeral home parking lot and noticed Ivy's jeep was parked out front. She wasn't sure why Ivy was at the funeral home that time of evening, but she was relieved for the additional support. She ran onto the elegant funeral home porch and tried the door only to discover it was locked. For the first time in his entire career, Tony locked the front door! Why would Tony lock the door while Ivy was visiting? It wasn't as if they were doing something requiring privacy. She pounded on the door several times, but there was no response. What the hell were they doing in there?

She looked around with concern, half expecting someone to be chasing her. Devon was almost surprised when she didn't see anyone, but she still didn't feel safe. She ran from the porch and hurried to the back of the funeral home, which was where Tony spent most of his time prepping clients. He had to be there. She reached the back door to the prepping room and pounded violently while screaming. The door was almost immediately unlocked and opened. Tony stared at her with some surprise and confusion.

"Devon?" he practically gasped. "What's wrong? Are you all right?"

"No," she cried out.

Devon grabbed him, pulled him inside with her, and immediately slammed and locked the door. Tony watched her with confusion and some concern. She cast her back against the door and sobbed while burying her face in her hands as she sank down to the floor.

Tony kneeled before her and gently touched her arm. "Hey," he announced in a soothing tone. "Are you okay? What happened? Did someone hurt you?"

Devon looked at him with a completely shaken expression. "You have to call the police," she gasped coming back to life. "They need to go to the museum right away."

"What? Why?" he gasped. "What happened? What's going on?"

"Tell them--tell them they're using dead people in their displays," she practically cried out then stared into his eyes with horror. "I found Chelsea and Martin in the mummy display."

Tony stared at her as if he hadn't heard her correctly. "Are you serious?" he nearly choked.

"Please, just do it."

"You think Tyler and Brant--?"

"Tony, please," she begged while fighting her tears and frustration.

Tony nodded and hurried across the room to the wall phone. Devon exhaled a deep, shaken breath and stared at the sheet-covered client on the metal table. Today just wasn't the day for seeing more dead people. She knew Tony's job, but somehow she found it unsettling right now. As she stared at the covered client on the table, she saw the chest rise. Devon's eyes suddenly widened in horror. She slowly stood and continued to stare. She could barely hear Tony talking on the phone over the sound of her heart pounding in her ears. Devon uncertainly approached the table and stared at the sheet-covered body. The head beneath the sheet turned to the side.

Devon gasped with alarm, catching Tony's attention while on the phone. He turned and looked at her. Devon snatched the sheet and whipped it off the body. Ivy clutched the nylon rope around her neck and pulled it free while loudly gasping just before she passed out. The horror of seeing her friend lying on the metal table was almost too much. Although she was alive, it made no sense. Devon looked at Tony with a horror she had never known. Tony tossed the phone down and bolted across the room toward her. Devon screamed and jumped backward into the counter, almost uncertain which way to go. Her friend was lying helplessly on the table, but her own life was hanging on the line. Tony snatched the discarded rope from the table near Ivy.

"How could you?" she cried out with horror, although she knew she should be running. How could she run? She couldn't just leave her immobile, nearly unconscious friend alone with the man who tried to kill her.

"Believe me, Devon," he announced while staring at her. "I didn't want this to happen."

Tony lunged for her with the rope. Devon bolted for the nearby door and attempted to unlock it when the rope circled her neck from behind. Tony pulled on it. Devon clutched the rope and gasped for air. For a moment, she was paralyzed with fear. A thousand thoughts raced through her mind in the moment she thought she was going to die. She decided it wouldn't be today. Devon went against instinct and released the rope. She rammed her elbow backward into Tony's mid-section with all of her strength. Tony gasped as the air was knocked from him, forcing him to back up a step and release the rope.

Devon turned toward the counter, grabbed a sharp, tube-like instrument, and clutched it in a threatening manner. Tony moved toward her despite the dangerous object in her hand. She screamed in fear and anger while plunging it into his shoulder. He cried out with surprise and pain before stumbling backward. Ivy suddenly wheezed while sitting up on the table. Devon rushed to her side and aggressively pulled her from the table. Ivy's feet hit the floor, and she immediately collapsed to her knees.

"Ivy! Get up!" she screamed at her friend, even though she knew it wasn't Ivy's fault she was in a weakened condition.

Ivy clutched Devon's arm and attempted to do as she said.

Devon pulled on her arm while screaming. "Get up, damn it! Get up!"

Tony pulled the instrument from his shoulder, allowing blood to fly from the object as he screamed out in agony. "God damn it!"

He clutched the sharp instrument in his hand and leaped for Devon. Devon screamed, released Ivy, and jumped backward, out of his path. Ivy collapsed to the floor. Devon hit the counter, momentarily dazing herself, and then bolted across the room.

"Why'd you have to get involved, Devon?" Tony cried out. "Do you think I really wanted to hurt you? Any of you?"

Devon scanned the room, not sure which way to go and what to do about Ivy, although she seemed to be his intended target at the moment. If she kept him busy, perhaps Ivy would be able to escape.

"Then don't," Devon cried out.

"I'm in too deep," Tony informed her. "I can't back out now." He shook his head while giving her a half-crazed yet sympathetic look. "I'm sorry."

Tony raised the bloodied instrument and prepared to lunge for her when they heard pounding on the door near her. The door vibrated.

"Devon? Tony?" Ross cried out from the other side of the door. "What's going on in there? Open up!"

"Ross!" she suddenly screamed while feeling her heart racing with fear and hope. "Help us!"

Tony leaped for Devon to silence her. She screamed and caught his wrist, preventing the instrument from piercing her, although it was dangerously close to her throat. Ivy weakly clutched the metal table for support and attempted to pull herself to her feet. There was a thunderous rumble from outside the door followed by Ross' loud curse. Devon screamed as Tony overpowered her, moving the instrument closer to her throat. The sound of splintering wood was almost deafening as the door frame cracked. Tony released Devon, who fell backward to the floor, and he turned toward the nearly broken door. As Tony bolted for the door, it flew open with enormous force and struck the opposing wall, shattering the thick, frosted glass. When he saw Devon on the floor, without hesitation, Ross charged into the room. Devon scrambled to her feet as Tony appeared behind Ross.

"Behind you!"

Ross spun around with only a split second to spare as Tony plunged downward with the sharp instrument. Ross cried out with horror, stumbled backward to avoid the sharp tube, tumbled over Ivy, and crashed backward onto the floor. As Tony lunged for Ross, Ivy coiled her leg back from her position on the floor and kicked Tony's knee. Tony cried out in pain, stumbled sideways, and crashed into the counter. Devon and Ross grabbed Ivy by either arm and pulled her to her feet with so much force, she was momentarily airborne. Without hesitation, they practically dragged her out the funeral home door.

Chapter Fifty-three

Ross and Devon pulled Ivy across the front parking lot as she stumbled to keep them from dragging her. They carelessly threw her into the back of Ross's beat up, old car. Devon jumped into the front passenger side while Ross ran to the driver's side and started the car. Surprisingly, it started on the first try. The car's engine revved with a loud roar, and the back tires immediately burned out on the driveway. The car rocketed backward into the street, narrowly missing the mailbox. The back end of the car swung as it burned out on the road and headed in the direction of the museum. Devon looked behind them then at Ross, who clutched the steering wheel with a death grip. He looked in the rearview mirror then glanced at Devon.

"What the hell was that all about?" he suddenly cried out now entering panic mode. "Why did my best friend try to kill me?"

Devon looked past Ross toward the museum as they prepared to fly past it at high speed. She saw Brant's car was now in the parking lot. Devon peered out the window with a look of horror.

"Ross, stop!"

Ross slammed on the brakes causing the car to skid and screech to a grinding halt. Devon and Ivy were flung forward then bounced backward.

"What?" he cried out.

"Brant's car," she gasped. "He's back. If he discovers what I found, he could be in danger!"

"Damn it, Devon," he cried out while glaring at her. "Tell me what's going on."

"They're using *real* people in the displays."

Ross stared at her with horror. "What?" He shook his head. "No, that can't be. You must be mistaken."

"Tony was supplying the museum with embalmed bodies," Ivy assured him and gingerly rubbed her bruised neck. "There was a body on Tony's table this evening. He said it was old man Rumsfeld, so that I wouldn't peek under the sheet." She drew a deep, nervous breath. "Well, I peeked anyway. It was Marlene under the sheet. Embalmed and ready for delivery."

"Marlene?" Ross gasped with surprise. "But she was cremated."

"No," Ivy insisted. "I assure you, she wasn't. They wanted her for the museum."

"Who are they?" Ross demanded. "Tyler? Brant? Both?" He shook his head then shifted the car into reverse. "You know what? I don't even care. We need to get the police."

The old car burned out on the dark road, spun around, and flew in the direction they'd just come. They saw the headlights of another car approaching in the near distance.

"We have to warn Brant," Devon insisted.

"Are you insane?" Ivy cried out. "He could be in on it!"

The headlights veered into their lane. Ross cried out and swerved harshly while slamming on the brakes. The car squealed and spun wildly. All three screamed as Ross' old car shot into the cornfield and plowed down a section of cornstalks. Devon, Ross, and Ivy screamed as cornstalks crashed against the sides of the car and into the windshield. The car bucked as the brakes attempted to take hold and came to a stop. Ross looked behind them. The black hearse skidded to a halt just outside the cornfield then raced for them, picking up speed with no intention of slowing. Ross looked away from the rearview mirror with horror.

"Oh, shit!"

Ross stepped on the gas forcing the car to burn out on the cornstalks. Devon and Ivy turned and looked out the back window. Both screamed when they saw the headlights gaining on them. The old car jetted forward, but it wouldn't pick up enough speed to outrun the already flying hearse. Ross spun the wheel and made a sharp turn. His car was old, but it could bank better than the larger hearse. Ross' car entered a small clearing with an electric pole directly before them. All three saw the electric pole and screamed.

Ross turned the wheel hard and narrowly missed the electric pole, losing his side mirror. The hearse entered the small clearing a split second behind them. As their car swerved, the electric pole was suddenly in front of the hearse. Tony gasped and attempted to turn the much larger vehicle. The hearse smashed into the poll with a tremendous crack. The poll was jarred, and the electric box on top sparked while crackling. Both women turned and looked through the back windshield while Ross watched through the rearview mirror.

"Serves him right!" Ross chuckled loud and evilly. "B-a-s-t-a-r-d!"

Ross' car suddenly sputtered and slowed. All three jerked with surprise. Ross shifted the car into neutral and turned the key as they came to a stop. The car's engine made a grinding sound but wouldn't turn over. Ross pounded on the steering wheel.

"Son-of-a-bitch," Ross cried out. "What a piece of shit!"

All three jumped out of the car. Ross stared at his car and watched as steam rose from beneath the hood. He kicked the tire.

"Rotten piece of shit!"

All three looked back. There was no movement from the wrecked hearse. The front end was pretty much smashed, indicating the driver was possibly fatally injured. Devon turned to Ivy and Ross.

"Go back to the funeral home," she instructed. "Call the police and tell them to come to the museum right away."

"Where do you think you're going?" Ross suddenly demanded as his eyes widened.

"I know Brant's not involved," she insisted. "He could be in serious danger. I have to warn him."

"Devon, you can't go back there," Ross pleaded. "I like the guy too, but he could be involved. If he is, he'll kill you too."

"And if he's not, by the time Carter arrives, it could be too late for Brant," she informed him. "I have to do this."

Devon turned and ran.

Chapter Fifty-four

Devon crouched in the cornfield and watched the dark museum a moment while considering her next move. When the hearse hit the electric pole, it must have knocked out power along the entire road. She then heard the sound of a small engine from within the museum. Some lights came on, although there weren't many. Someone pounced beside her. Devon spun with a gasp while Ross stared at the museum.

"Kind of dark," he announced then looked at her. "What's the plan?"

Devon frowned. "I don't have one."

"Fine, then we'll use mine."

She stared at him with surprise. "*You* have a plan?" Devon gasped.

"We'll slip in through the basement door and remain low until we see what's happening inside," he informed her. "A little on the cautious side, but you know I'm a coward by nature."

She knew that wasn't true. He proved his bravery tonight. "The basement door is locked," she reminded him.

Ross removed a set of keys from his pocket and grinned. "Not for long."

She stared at the keys with surprise. "Where did you get those?"

"Brant gave me a set of keys to accept a couple of deliveries," he informed her. "He never asked for them back. I thought I'd hang onto them, you know, in case I met that special lady who shared my fondness for the torture chamber."

"You're a sick bastard, Ross," she announced. "But a crafty one. Let's go."

§

A single emergency light dimly lit the workshop giving the room an eerie glow. The outer basement door slowly opened to reveal Devon and Ross. They peeked into the workshop but didn't see anyone not made of wax. Both hurried inside and simultaneously jumped when they saw the wax English policeman guarding the door. Devon sneered and smacked Ross on the shoulder. He frowned and gestured defensively. They darted behind one of the counters. Devon looked toward the inner door. Nothing moved. Ross glanced at the counter and saw the remote control on top. He snatched it and sat on the floor a moment.

"I have an idea."

Devon glared at him with concern. "Whatever it is-- no."

"Trust me," he announced while grinning deviously. "Wait here."

Ross sprang to his feet, playfully rumpled her hair, and then crept across the workshop. Devon frowned, ran her fingers through her mussed hair, and watched him while shaking her head.

"This isn't going to end well," she muttered then hurried after him.

§

Ivy quietly entered the dark funeral home dimly lit by moonlight poking in through the open curtains. She hurried across the front, left parlor. She'd been inside the funeral home enough times to practically know her way around in the dark. She stumbled into the leather sofa, hitting her shin, and bit her lip to prevent the painful yelp. She endured the pain then fumbled with the phone on the end table and dialed the police while watching the front door. She nearly jumped when Deputy Havens answered the phone.

"Hello? Deputy Havens?" she gasped and was relieved to hear his voice. "Thank God! It's Ivy. I'm at the funeral home," she informed him then paused while he responded in return. "I'm okay, but Ross and Devon are in trouble."

She heard the front door open. Ivy held her breath while staring beyond the parlor doors with wide, horror-filled eyes. Deputy Havens spoke into the phone, but she feared answering him. She heard the front door gently shut. Ivy slipped behind the sofa while clutching the phone and peered at the parlor doorway. Tony stepped into the doorway holding a tire iron in his hand. Despite that the room was only dimly lit by moonlight, she could tell he'd been injured in the crash. Blood seeped from his temple and from the corner of his mouth. Judging by the way he clutched the crowbar, he was angry. He scanned the room and saw the phone was missing from the base. His eyes then strayed to her where she hid behind the sofa. Ivy's eyes widened as fear spread through her.

"Havens, help," she whispered into the phone. "He's going to kill me!"

Ivy threw the phone to the floor, sprang to her feet, and bolted across the room. Tony didn't move from the doorway leaving her trapped. Ivy eyed the phone receiver on the floor. She could hear Deputy Havens speaking from the other end.

"Why are you doing this, Tony?" Ivy cried out, hoping Deputy Havens heard her on the other end. "You're supposed to be my friend!"

"Friends?" he questioned then snorted a laugh. "We were never friends. None of you were ever my friends. You, Ross, and Devon used me every chance you had."

"That's not true!"

Tony clutched the tire iron and slowly walked toward her. Ivy backed across the mostly dark room and into a table. Tony yanked the phone cord from the wall then approached her and raised the tire iron above his head.

"Don't you understand?" he demanded. "I have no choice. I've involved myself in something I just can't get out of!"

"You were removing bodies from their caskets and delivering them to the museum," Ivy cried out. "Then you buried the empty caskets for appearance."

"I guess you and Devon have been comparing notes," he snarled. "You shouldn't have looked under that sheet, Ivy. None of this would be happening if you hadn't looked under that sheet."

As Tony was about to strike, Ivy reached behind her and fumbled with a vase on the table. She picked it up and threw it at Tony. What turned out to be an urn hit him in the head and cracked open. Ashes of the dearly departed covered his face and body. Tony clutched his eyes and coughed on the dense ashes. Ivy saw her chance and bolted across the room through the divider doorway to the adjoining room. Tony wiped the ash from his eyes and ran after her.

Chapter Fifty-five

Devon wasn't sure how she lost track of Ross. He was able to move silently and swiftly through the dimly lit museum faster than she could. She thought he was looking for Brant, but she didn't see Ross anywhere. She was about to pass the torture chamber when something dawned on her. She slipped into the frightening room and darted into the shadows of the iron maiden. Devon looked across the room and saw the woman stretched backward on the wheel of pain. Her large, realistic breast was again uncovered, which wasn't surprising. Devon hurried across the torture chamber while keeping low and reached the half-naked woman. She stared at the wax woman only a moment before seeing it. She tugged on the woman's mane of tangled, black hair to reveal the blonde hair beneath and found herself staring at Jamie.

As she looked around the room, she realized they were probably all there somewhere. Jamie, her friends, and everyone else who had died recently. How long had this been going on? Since the purchase of the museum? Did that mean Brant had to be involved? She was suddenly no longer sure she could trust Brant, and maybe Ross had been right. She needed to find Ross and leave at once. Her need to warn Brant may have been a mistake. Devon hurried from the torture chamber and silently made her way along the walkway through the different displays. She needed to find Ross and get him out of there. Whatever plan he had in mind couldn't be healthy for either of them. She'd find him and go with Ivy's original plan of letting Sheriff Carter deal with it.

As Devon silently made her way through the dimly lit displays, she paused within the mummy set. Her eyes immediately strayed to Martin, who was now playing the role of the mummy. Martin's face was once again covered with tattered bandages, and Chelsea's wig and hat had been replaced. Someone had covered them to conceal their identity, and Devon couldn't automatically rule out Brant this time. She could hear voices from the nearby vampire display and had to get closer in order to hear their conversation.

Devon approached the end of the mummy display just near the vampire display and hid against the dividing wall. The voices were louder now, and she recognized them as Brant and Tyler. Both men were laughing, indicating neither may be involved or perhaps both were involved. She panicked when the voices silenced, indicating they could be parting company. A shadow approached, startling her. Devon hurried across the mummy display and slid behind the massive tomb. Tyler walked through the display and headed in the direction of the workshop.

§

Brant sat on the edge of the vampire's casket within the second half of the display and adjusted the clothes on the vampire within the casket. Devon cautiously crept through the display while looking around yet still keeping Brant within view. She paused while crouching down and keeping low within the first half of the display where the two vampires were attacking the villagers. She looked behind her to the sword Teddy, the wax villager, held.

"If you don't mind, Teddy," she announced softly while reaching up to the wax villager and silently removed the sword. "I'll be needing that."

The sword was relatively dull, but she was low on options. When there was no sign of Tyler, she knew she had to make her move. Devon straightened and revealed herself to Brant within the second part of the display containing the vampire in the casket. Brant saw her, smiled cheerfully, and immediately stood.

"Devon," he announced while grinning as he approached her. "I was worried you'd decided to take the night off."

Devon raised the sword, aimed it at his chest, and glared at him.

Brant stopped and stared at the sword with surprise. "What are you doing?" he asked.

Devon stared into his eyes without expression. "The murdered women are here," she informed him. "Their corpses are being used in your displays."

"What are you talking about?" he asked with surprise then hesitated and looked around.

"My brother's body is beneath the mummy wrap. I saw him myself," she informed him. "I'm convinced the others are here as well. I know the deal. Tony embalms them then removes them from their caskets after the viewing and delivers them to the museum for the displays. They were never buried."

"I--I don't understand. You know I wouldn't do something like that," Brant gasped with surprise. "What you're saying doesn't even sound possible." He tensed and again looked at the wax displays then met her gaze.

"Not possible?" she remarked.

Devon then eyed the handsome wax villager just behind Teddy. While keeping the sword aimed at Brant in one hand, she swiftly yanked the hair from the wax villager's head to reveal Karl. Although she was almost positive she had been right, seeing Karl encased in wax nearly jump started her heart. She put on a brave front and raised her brows demandingly while tossing the wig aside.

"Remember Karl?"

Brant stared at the familiar face of the construction worker he'd manhandled for threatening Devon. The stunned look on Brant's face was almost enough to convince Devon he wasn't aware of what was going on, but she couldn't convince herself to lower the sword she kept pointed at him. He finally looked at her, only briefly eying the sword in her hands.

"Devon, I know you're frightened and upset, but you have to trust me. Please, put down the sword," Brant announced in a slightly tense voice. "We're both in danger right now." He drew a deep, shaken breath. "You know I'd never do anything to hurt you." His frightened look turned tender. "I love you."

As Devon stared into his eyes, her expression softened. She wanted to believe he wasn't involved. She wanted to trust him even if it ended up costing her life. She slowly lowered the sword.

Brant relaxed then exhaled and attempted a smile. "You had me worried for a moment there," he announced then indicated the sword. "Even if that sword isn't sharp enough to give a papercut." He drew a deep breath and straightened proudly. "Have you called the police?"

"Ivy called them," she replied. "They should be here any minute."

Brant again looked around and appeared tense. "Then we'd better wait outside for them."

"Wouldn't be a bad idea--" Tyler announced from across the room.

Both turned toward the display archway where Tyler stood holding a gun aimed at them.

"Had your friend been able to complete her call to the police," Tyler replied. "Tony called me on his car phone and told me you and Ross were on your way here. He went back to take care of your friend."

"Then it's true?" Brant gasped with surprise while staring at Tyler. "You attempted to display dead people as your own wax creations."

"Why not?" Tyler announced while shrugging. "I've been doing it for years. It saved on expense and cut the work time in half."

"I don't know how you possibly thought you'd get away with it," Brant remarked while sneering at him. "Your creations are hideous. Someone was bound to uncover them and see what was beneath."

"That's where you're wrong," Tyler announced while grinning then indicated the beautiful female vampire alongside the male vampire. "That's my work. Creating bad wax men and women was for everyone else's benefit, so if my beauties were found beneath their waxy surface, you or Ross would be blamed. Sorry to inform you; I'm twice the artist you are, Brant."

"You tried to kill me," he gasped then turned angry. "When that didn't work, you tried to frame me for the murders."

"Once you were out of the way, I could bring in my new partner, Tony. He and I would create the most beautiful displays a museum has ever seen." He then offered an unsettling grin. "The murders gave me the idea to dissolve our partnership. Tony heard about the killer wearing a phantom costume, so he borrowed one, made sure people saw him in it, and killed Marlene in your basement." Tyler laughed. "Yes, you would have eventually stumbled upon my secret beneath the wax. I'm actually surprised you hadn't figured it out sooner," Tyler announced. "I couldn't allow you to see what lie beneath the makeup." He shook his head and sighed. "It would've worked out perfectly if it hadn't been for Martin coming forward and confessing to the killings. His journal exposed a second killer. Do you have any idea how much trouble he caused?"

§

Back at the funeral home, Ivy screamed and bolted across the casket display room while Tony blocked her only exit. She jumped behind one of the display coffins. Despite that they were only displays, the room was decorated with flowers as well as some lit candles. When he thought he had her cornered, Tony lunged for her. Ivy continued to scream and heaved several flower arrangements at him. Tony skillfully dodged the flowers and their heavy vases. She was now trapped behind the casket. She placed her hand on the closed casket lid and stared at Tony, waiting to see which way he'd go next. Tony removed a switchblade knife from his pocket.

"It'd be easier on you if you don't fight it," he informed her. "We could have done this the easy way if Devon hadn't interrupted earlier. This way is so messy and painful. After what we shared, I didn't want it to be painful."

"After what we shared?" she gasped then sneered. "You're a sick fuck!"

"And you came on to me," he reminded her in an almost mocking tone.

Ivy stared him in the eyes with a look of horror. Tony dived on top of the casket and slashed the knife at her. Ivy let out a sharp cry and pushed the casket forward with all her strength. The casket toppled off its hydraulic stand casting Tony to the floor. Tony cried out and shielded his face as the casket landed on top of him. Ivy heard a chilling, bone-crunching sound along with Tony's painful grunt. There was a moment of silence followed by a low wheezing sound.

Ivy stood immobile a moment and stared at the toppled casket on the floor. She nervously walked around it while keeping her eyes locked on the motionless object. She reached the other side and saw Tony crushed beneath the casket. He coughed up blood while attempting to speak. His eyes shifted to meet hers as blood seeped from the corner of his mouth.

"I'm sorry," he whispered then became motionless as the last breath left his body.

As Ivy stared at him, she heard police sirens in the distance.

Chapter Fifty-six

Within the vampire display, Brant stood between Devon and Tyler, who held the gun aimed at them. Brant's gesture to protect her from his partner was darling but pointless. Two shots and they would both end up dead.

"Think about it, Brant," Tyler announced while grinning. "You'll actually be a part of this museum forever. It'll be your greatest contribution and sacrifice to your dream."

"You're sick."

"Perhaps," Tyler agreed, "but with your share of the museum, I stand to be a wealthy man. These displays will bring a fortune." He chuckled then grinned. "I'll even put the two of you in a display together. You'd like that, wouldn't you?" Tyler appeared almost touched by his own suggestion. "Kind of a last romantic gesture. Maybe I'll mount the two of you in the church display, where you almost got it on. It'll be beautiful."

They heard a woman's shrill scream echo throughout the museum. Devon and Tyler jumped with surprise, although uncertain where it originated. Brant appeared confused but not startled. There were several screams that immediately followed. Low groans and beastly snarls soon added to the special effects of the nearby displays. The vampire behind Brant straightened and turned toward them. As the vampire hissed, Tyler cried out with surprise and fired at the wax creature. His shots missed the moving vampire and struck the female vampire standing not far from the male.

The bullets tore through her waxy surface and revealed dried, decayed flesh. The vampire turned toward the frightened villager and appeared to bite him. A male scream came from a speaker near the wax villager, so it sounded as if the scream came from him. The room was suddenly alive with movement as more objects went into motion. Brant shifted his eyes slightly. Devon turned with surprise. Tyler's fear turned to anger as he waved his gun at Brant.

"Stop it," he cried out with anger. "You're not fooling me!"

Brant raised his hands, revealing empty palms. "It's not me," he announced. "The control panel is on the wall by the door."

As Tyler turned toward the doorway to see who was at the controls, Brant snatched the sword from Devon and lunged for Tyler. Tyler spun around but was a little too slow. Brant swung the sword for Tyler, cutting his arm with the dull blade. Tyler dropped the gun and clutched his bleeding arm. Unfortunately, the blade wasn't sharp enough to do any serious damage. Brant and Tyler both leaped for the discarded gun. As Brant snatched the gun, Tyler straightened and ran from the room. Brant ran after him.

Tyler ran along the corridor near the phantom display with the phantom posed before the organ where loud, evil music seemed to come from the pipe organ. Brant was heard running along the corridor not far behind. Tyler gasped and hurried across the display. He approached the pipe organ and saw a space behind it where he could hide. The phantom suddenly glared at Tyler. Tyler's eyes widened, and he cried out. Tyler bolted away from the pipe organ, but the phantom leaped into Tyler's path. Tyler again screamed. The phantom clutched his throat with both hands and choked him. Tyler gasped and fell to his knees while attempting to loosen the phantom's grip. Brant appeared near the display and stopped.

"No, please, don't," Tyler cried out.

"Let him go, Ross," Brant casually announced.

The phantom looked at Brant, revealing Ross on the unmasked side, and released Tyler's throat. He took a step back while staring at Tyler and removed his white, half mask.

Ross smirked and wickedly raised his brows. "Scared ya, didn't I?" He laughed evilly like some old movie villain.

Tyler appeared surprised while staring at Ross. Brant approached them and motioned Tyler to his feet with the gun. Tyler clutched his chest and slowly straightened. Devon hurried onto the set with the sword in her hand and walked up behind Tyler. Tyler continued to stare at Ross and Brant with anger on his face.

"You tricked me," Tyler cried out while clutching his chest. "You never told me the displays moved and made sounds!"

Brant shrugged. "It didn't seem important at the time."

"I think I should play the phantom when we open," Ross announced.

Tyler pulled a large knife from his lab coat and raised it above his head. He was about to plunge it into Ross when Devon cried out. Ross spun toward Tyler and saw the knife only inches from him. Devon lunged forward with the sword and ran the sharp, pointy end into Tyler's back straight through his chest. Tyler gasped as his eyes widened and looked at the blade sticking out of his chest. As his eyes rolled back, he sank to his knees and collapsed to the floor. Brant and Ross stared at Tyler with surprise and shock.

"Oh, my God," Devon cried out, realizing what she had done.

Brant rushed to Devon and gathered her in his arms. Ross continued to stare at Tyler then looked back at Devon. She clung to Brant and sobbed softly.

"Remind me to never piss you off," Ross announced in a serious tone.

Devon pulled away from Brant and happily hugged Ross. Ross smiled warmly and returned the embrace. They heard the faint sirens outside followed by movement upstairs. Devon quickly pulled away and stared at them with a concerned look.

"Tony went back for Ivy!"

Thundering footfalls were heard running through the displays. Sheriff Carter and Deputy Havens approached them with their guns drawn. Ivy was only steps behind them with several other officers.

"Ivy!" Devon cried out then ran past the police and hugged her friend.

"I was afraid he'd killed you," Ivy exclaimed.

Devon pulled away from her friend and stared at her with concern. "What about Tony?"

Ivy shook her head. "I gave the bastard what he deserved," she announced while sneering. "He won't be coming back."

"Damn," Ross cried out. "You girls are dangerous!"

Chapter Fifty-seven

While awaiting the coroner and reinforcements with cadaver dogs, Devon, Ross, and Brant walked through the dungeon displays with Sheriff Carter. Ivy chose to remain upstairs with the deputies rather than review the gruesomeness of the evening. They entered the mummy display and approached the mummy. Devon stood before the mummy and drew a deep, shaken breath.

"You don't have to do this," Ross announced gently to his friend.

She extended her hand to him. Ross handed her a pair of scissors. Devon cut the bandages from the mummy's face to reveal her brother looking perfectly preserved in his wax casing. She trembled and took a step back while fighting her tears. Brant pulled her into his arms and held her. Ross appeared slightly sickened and looked away. Sheriff Carter just stared at Devon's dead brother. He removed his cowboy hat, shut his eyes a moment, and shook his head. Carter drew a deep breath and looked back at Devon, who found herself staring at her dead brother. Sheriff Carter stepped into her line of sight, keeping her from seeing him.

"Where are the others?" Sheriff Carter asked in an attempt to keep her focused and her mind off her brother encased in wax.

Devon indicated the woman against the pillar and nodded. "That's Chelsea."

Sheriff Carter approached the frightened wax explorer woman and carefully removed her dark wig. He stared at Chelsea then shut his eyes and groaned softly.

"Jamie's in the torture chamber tied to the wheel," she informed him while shivering at the thought. "And Karl is in the vampire display."

"Tyler shot a woman in the vampire display," Brant informed him. "The bullet tore through something I'm convinced was old, dried flesh."

Sheriff Carter suddenly looked at Brant. "What do you mean 'old dried flesh'?" he asked with surprise.

Brant drew a deep breath and held it a moment. "The wax figures he claimed to have bought from a closed museum were created from dead bodies as well," Brant informed him. "He admitted he's been doing this for decades."

Sheriff Carter shut his eyes and groaned. "Son-of-a-bitch," he muttered under his breath. He cast a look back at Devon. "Were there any other wax people giving you a bad vibe?"

Devon nodded with some apprehension. "A lot of them, Sheriff."

"That's terrific," the sheriff muttered then skimmed several pages of notes within his notebook before giving up and tossing it over his shoulder. "Ivy said she found Marlene's embalmed body at the funeral home. If we have Marlene, Jamie, Karl, your brother, and Chelsea, it's only logical to assume Tony brought Tamara and Paula to Tyler as well." He shook his head and looked around. "They must be down here somewhere." He looked at the three.

"Any idea where they'd be while we're waiting on the cadaver dogs?"

"They would have been placed while Brant was missing," Ross informed the sheriff. "Tony and Tyler must have been working overtime to get them into displays while Devon and I weren't around."

"Just enough confusion with the reconstructed wax figures that Ross and I wouldn't know who'd done which ones," Devon added.

"Tyler confessed he was one hell of an artist," Brant remarked. "While he did a few horrible wax figures for our benefit, he was probably working with Tony to get as many of the dead victims into displays without our knowledge."

"More were in place just about every morning," Devon remarked while frowning.

Deputy Havens hurried through the display to join them. "Sheriff, the coroner is here and so are the cadaver dogs."

Sheriff Carter eyed the three. "You may want to go upstairs and sit this out," he announced. "This could take a while."

§

It was later that night and the coroner and his men, along with cadaver dogs, were still investigating the museum. Devon, Brant, Ivy, and Ross sat on the bench in the lobby and watched the parade of coroner's people remove another stretcher containing a black body bag. It seemed like an endless parade of actual bodies hidden beneath waxy exteriors.

Brant moaned while clutching his head. "How many was that?"

"Twenty," Ross announced with little emotion. "But who's counting." He then shook his head. "Obviously, Tyler had been playing his little game for years with the help of countless morticians."

"Each time one of his wax museum's failed, he'd store the wax figures until he could find the next sucker to be his partner," Brant muttered. "Apparently, I was that sucker." He watched the stretcher pass and shook his head. "I was stupid enough to believe he'd bought those wax people from a closed museum. The crates containing actual bodies beneath the wax must have been the ones that were already packed up before we arrived at the museum." He then groaned. "I suppose I deserve whatever happens from this. I'm such a fool."

"Don't feel too bad, Brant," Ross announced and patted his shoulder as he frowned. "I'd changed wardrobe on several of those women and never knew they weren't just wax figures."

"That's because he made sure their private parts were hidden beneath a thick layer of wax," Devon informed them in a sedate tone. "He had to make sure no one ever discovered the bodies beneath them."

"I suppose an anatomically correct penis would give it away," Ivy muttered while holding her knees to her chest where she sat on the bench. She then eyed Brant. "Who do you suppose they were?"

"Bodies taken from other funeral homes that were stolen from their caskets after the viewing," Ross reported and shook his head. "Tyler said he was doing this for years. Who knows how long some of them have been encased in wax."

Brant finally straightened. "I think we should call it an evening," he announced with a defeated sigh. "We can go to my house next door. The bar is fully stocked, and there are plenty of spare rooms."

Ross stood while groaning with exhaustion and assisted Ivy to her feet. She appeared stiff and sore from her ordeal. Devon and Brant stood with even less enthusiasm. Brant caught Devon's hand and held her back as the others left so they'd have a moment alone. She looked at him then eyed his hand holding hers.

His look was serious as he stared at her. "I'm grateful you trusted me tonight," Brant admitted. "Given the situation, it would've been very easy for you to suspect I was involved." He managed a nervous laugh. "Honestly, you probably shouldn't have trusted me, but I'm glad you did."

"I was just hoping I wasn't wrong," she replied timidly then offered a warm smile. "When I thought about those rose petals on the floor, the way you made love to me, and that look in your eyes when you told me you loved me; I knew I had to trust my feelings."

Brant affectionately caressed her hand. "You certainly can't buy that kind of trust," he announced.

"What do you intend to do about the museum?" she finally asked with some concern. "Will you still pursue your dream?"

"There's a part of me that wants to pack it in and give up," he replied then sighed deeply. "I still have a few dozen wax figures I'd made from scratch, so I know they're salvageable. At least twenty from the closed museum aren't cadavers, so that should give me a pretty good start." He then eyed her and smiled. "I also have some motivated wax artists. We could probably make it work with extra hours, hard work, and dedication."

"You know Ross and I will do whatever it takes to get the museum up and running," she announced proudly while clinging to his arm.

"I don't really have the capital to pay for the amount of overtime we're going to need," he informed her while sighing with defeat.

"I'm sure we can work out something," she insisted, trying to keep him motivated. Devon didn't want him giving up on his dream.

"Perhaps if I made you and Ross equal partners in this venture, we could make it work," he remarked then eyed her and smiled. "What do you say?"

Devon stared at him with surprise. "Really?" she announced then became enthusiastic for the first time. "I'd love that." She hugged him briefly then pulled away and met his gaze. "I don't think you'll get much argument from Ross either."

"Thank you, Devon," he announced warmly while gently caressing her face and offered a timid smile. "Thank you for believing in me. No one has ever been there for me like you have."

She wanted to enjoy the compliment, but something Tyler said earlier made her uncomfortable. "How are you going to explain me to your mother?" she finally asked. "I'm guessing she won't approve of us."

Brant stared at her with some surprise. "Approve?" he remarked then laughed. "If she thinks there's any hope of you giving her that grandchild, she's going to treat you like a princess." He sighed with relief. "Finally, she can torture someone else for a while." He raised his brows and grinned. "I am so throwing you under the bus with my mother. In return, you can throw me under the bus with your father."

She managed a tiny smile and held back her laugh. "Sounds like a fair trade."

"Not really," Brant replied then grinned. "You're totally screwed."

Both laughed softly. Brant lowered his mouth to hers and was about to kiss her when he saw the coroner's assistant pushing another stretcher containing a body bag. He groaned lowly and pulled away.

"I think it's best if we head to my house and work out the details of our new partnership," he announced while frowning. "This place is starting to give me the creeps."

She eyed the black body bag on the stretcher as it was wheeled past. The endless conga line of body bags caused her to fidget. "No arguments there."

Brant hurried her from the museum.

The End

Other books by Holly Copella!
Reviews left on Amazon are appreciated!

"The Battle for Andrea Maria"

A cruise ship attack turns six survivors into overnight celebrities after they take credit for the heroic act of a stowaway who died saving them.

The cruise is just what Jess needed--a bit of harmless fun far from her daily grind. But what begins as a relaxing vacation turns into a desperate fight for her life when terrorists take over the ship and start piling up bodies. Teaming up with a mysterious stowaway, Jess attempts to send out a distress call but knows they cannot wait for help to come. If she or the few remaining passengers have any hope for survival, Jess must act now. The papers dub it "The Battle for *Andrea Maria*," but to Jess it is the moment she fought side-by-side with her enigmatic Romeo, saving the ship--and losing him. She thinks the story ends there, but really, the nightmare is just beginning...

"Insanely Deadly"

When the dead return to life, it's up to an admiral's daughter and a mildly insane, former war hero to save their small town.

Jetta Cross, a Navy Admiral's daughter, is tasked with keeping her father's comrade, a former war hero turned town crazy, grounded in the real world. Capt. John Hunter is still fighting the war in his head, where imaginary dead people are part of his world. When a viral outbreak brings about a zombie uprising, Hunter is left to his own devices. He must resume his role as a one-man commando unit in order to destroy the ravenous undead. With Hunter still fighting his own inner demons as well as the undead, the townspeople fear their zombie neighbors may not be the only threat. Stranded at the island's luxurious resort with a handful of workers, Jetta is forced to live up to her father's reputation and take charge of the deteriorating situation at the hotel. She must wage her own war against the infected before the government declares her hometown a total loss.

"Deadly Institution"

A town recluse suspected of killing his wife teams up with a young woman in order to stop a killer.

After being accused of murdering his wife, Konrad Asher turns his back on the town that once adored him. Ten years later, he still holds his grudge and the title of the most feared man in town. With the reopening of the burned mental institution, where his wife had died, former employees are now murdered one-by-one, throwing suspicion back on Asher. A young local reporter, Jacey, is forced to reveal her long-time friendship with the infamous recluse in order to clear his name not only in the recent murders but to exonerate him in the death of his wife as well. Will Jacey's relationship with Asher invite the killer closer to her? Or is the killer already in her life?

"Screenplays: The Island Collection"
"Jungle Princess", "A.L.F. Resort", "Brighton Island"

Discover how romance and fun in the sun can be downright *chilling*!

"Jungle Princess" is a romantic/thriller that leaves a teenage girl stranded on an island with two male shipmates and a creature of "unknown" origin. She soon discovers the island is home to an abandoned prison with several prisoners roaming free. What really killed over one hundred prisoners? And is it still out there--?

"A.L.F. Resort" is a romantic/thriller set on an island resort with Artificial Life Forms as the main draw. At this resort, all your fantasies come true...until a malfunction removes safety inhibitors on the A.L.F.'s. Zombies, biker gangs, and mobsters run amuck, turning fantasies into nightmares. A young reporter gets more of a story than she anticipates, but will she survive long enough to write the story?

"Brighton Island" is a romantic/thriller set on a private island. When the owner's niece brings her psychic friend to the mansion, his presence awakens the spirits' tortured souls. As the psychic attempts to solve the old murders, the niece is confronted with the possibility that she's next to join the mansion ghosts. Stranded on the island with a crazed killer, her uncle wages his own war to save them. Will his "shock and awe" tactics actually save them or get them killed?

"Death Displacement"

A grief-stricken man travels back in time to seek revenge on the woman who murdered his girlfriend but inadvertently falls in love with her.

Kane is about to marry the woman he loves. His life is perfect. A few weeks before the wedding, a vindictive woman from his girlfriend's past mysteriously arrives and kills her. He learns of a traumatic accident that happened five years earlier, which triggers Riley's hatred for his girlfriend. Distraught over his girlfriend's death, Kane uses an antique time machine to travel into the past in order to find and destroy the woman responsible. When he runs into Riley's younger self, he realizes she's not the monster she later becomes, and he can't bring himself to destroy her. With a little help from his oddball friend from the past, they formulate a plan to prevent the accident that sends Riley down her destructive path. Kane's plan backfires when he falls for the younger Riley. His new tortured existence is further complicated when future Riley, his girlfriend's killer, shows up with her own devious agenda that doesn't include him. Will he be able to stop the time ripple, which ultimately ends with his girlfriend's death? Or will future Riley take him out of the timeline forever--

"Dead Village"

After strange happenings isolate a small resort town from the rest of the world, nearly one hundred residents seek refuge at the closed hotel. Only eight survive the night. And that's just the beginning...

One day after the entire population of Fox Ridge Village disappears, a car wreck forces several unsuspecting crash victims to seek help at the closed summer hotel. Within the hotel, they discover the grisly aftermath of a brutal slaughter. Crash victims Vander and Devon, a reluctant clairvoyant, team up to solve the riddle of the "haunted hotel" and the mass hysteria plaguing the remaining survivors. By the time they discover the hotel's secret, they're already drawn into the hysteria. As the body count continues to climb, it's a race to isolate the source and bring everyone back to reality before they kill one another. Will Devon be able to communicate with the traumatized spirits before their fate becomes her own?

"Misfits, Inc."

A seemingly ordinary, young woman meets four misfits who claim she has given them supernatural powers.

While on a business trip to a remote island paradise, a bored secretary, Hailey, has her world turned upside down when her path collides with a psychic freak, Skyler. He attempts to convince her that they had met in his dreams, and she had chosen him as one of her four mystic warriors. After Skyler foresees a woman's death, they discover an unidentified creature has killed one of the guests. They are joined by a lounge pianist and a rich playboy, who also claim they had met her in their dreams. If Skyler's prophecies are genuine, the evil entity controlling the ravenous creatures needs to destroy Hailey to ensure its survival. Reluctantly accepting her fate, Hailey has to locate the last and most powerful of her chosen warriors, The Guardian. Their fate is in doubt when The Guardian turns out to be a self-absorbed, former cat burglar with a bad attitude. Can Hailey turn her company of misfits into an elite team of mystic warriors? Or will The Guardian's secret agenda destroy them all?

"Basement Dwellers"

A viral outbreak at a hospital leaves a mortician, sheriff, and coroner fighting for their lives against a horde of undead and the CDC.

After a massive car wreck leaves several survivors in critical condition at the local hospital, a surgeon uses experimental drugs on his critical patients and accidentally causes a zombie outbreak. When local mortician, Lexx, receives an infected corpse as her client, she becomes stranded in the hospital basement during CDC quarantine along with the local sheriff and the coroner. The infamous surgeon struggles to find a cure for his infectious blunder by using the other survivors as test subjects. Meanwhile, Lexx and the sheriff attempt to locate his missing sister, who's stranded somewhere in the battle zone that once was the emergency room. It's a race against time and the ravenous undead. Can they survive the undead before CDC sanitizes the hospital of all infection?

"Witness Protection"
Also available in audiobook!

After witnessing an execution, a resourceful young woman attempts to disappear while being pursued by a hitman and a handsome federal agent.

A helicopter pilot, Jackie Remus, reluctantly agrees to go on a date with one of her clients, but her date is unexpectedly cut short when she witnesses a man being murdered. After narrowly escaping with her life, she is placed into protective custody. When the safe house is breached, Jackie makes a daring escape from both the hired killers and the handsome FBI agent, who wants to return her to protective custody. With a little help from her sly and crafty friend, Monroe, Jackie is convinced she can disappear until the trial. While on her journey to meet with her friend, she solicits help from a few shady but lovable characters along the way. Although she manages to stay one-step ahead of the hired killers, the federal agent remains in hot pursuit. Will Jackie reach Monroe before she's captured by the FBI and returned to protective custody? Or will the hired killers silence her first?

"Town Darling"

After surviving a brutal attack that claims the lives of those she loves, a young woman seeks revenge on a corrupt town.

Going back home is never easy, but for Casey, it means returning to her corrupt hometown where she barely survived a brutal attack. Accompanied by two family friends, she seeks justice for the night that destroyed her life. Her physical scars are nothing compared to her emotional ones, forcing the local sheriff to believe that the town darling is back for revenge. As the conspiracy for her revenge appears to be leading up to the coveted town fair, the sheriff is determined to stop her from fulfilling her vengeful scheme...but guilt over his role on that fateful night continues to haunt him. Will his desperate need for Casey's forgiveness be his undoing? Or will Casey's desire for revenge destroy them both?

"Unconditional"

A young woman puts her life on hold to care for an unstable, highly skilled combat soldier, who believes someone is trying to kill him.

A botched military coup leaves a team of elite fighters injured with one clinging to life in a coma. When Harlan wakes from his coma, he's left with no memory of his past life. His commander's daughter, Indy, takes it upon herself to care for the fallen war hero. She's challenged with more than just his physical care as she combats with not only his memory loss but also his newly found desire for her. His infatuation with her becomes the least of her worries when he sinks back into his role of a combat soldier. Believing his life is in danger, his fighting skills surface, turning him into an unpredictable and dangerous man. Will his memory return to him before Indy is forced to commit him? Or will he finally find his nemesis, "the coyote", and possibly claim the life of an innocent person?

"Witness Protection 2"
The Return of Whiskey Tango Foxtrot

Believing she holds the clue to millions in missing laundered money, a young woman is placed into the protective care of a former Navy SEAL team.

Feeling sorry for her recently separated co-worker, Leeann invites Wiley to join her and her friends on their night out. Little does she know that finding her co-worker murdered is just the beginning of her nightmare. Leeann unknowingly holds the key to fifty million dollars in potentially laundered mob money. With hired killers pursuing her, the FBI places her into a different kind of protective custody. Former Navy SEAL team Whiskey Tango Foxtrot reunites to keep Leeann alive at their secret hideaway. What should be an easy assignment takes an unscheduled turn when secrets, lies, and betrayal threaten to derail their mission. Is the team prepared for a war on their own doorstep? Will Leeann's misguided trust endanger the lives of those sent to protect her?

"Deadly Institution 2"

When blackmail turns into murder, a young woman finds herself caught in the killer's crosshairs.

The small town of Stony Ridge is no stranger to scandal and persecution of the innocent. When a brutal killing shakes the town's prestigious country club, Jacey McMurray seeks help from a self-proclaimed vigilante, Konrad Asher. As her professional and personal worlds collide, Jacey fears the stress of the country club killings have finally taken their toll on Asher. Can a stressed out vigilante stop the killer before he strikes again?

"Witness Protection 3"
Alpha Mike Foxtrot

A helicopter pilot risks her life to help a team of retired Navy SEALs rescue two girls from a killer.

When former Navy SEAL team Whiskey Tango Foxtrot asks for a simple favor, Jackie reluctantly offers her air-taxi services. What could go wrong? What begins as a search and rescue for two girls turns into a fight for survival against a heavily armed drug cartel. Wanted by the law with the cartel in hot pursuit and their home base breached, the team is forced to call in a favor from a questionable ally. Unfortunately, their new safe house isn't what it seems. Without knowing who the real enemy is, can Jackie and the team save their young witnesses from the hands of a killer?

"The Pen Pal"

In order to save her friend, she must enter the mind of a serial killer.

When her best friend is abducted, no one believes Jolynn saw it in a psychic vision. With nowhere to turn, Jolynn reluctantly joins Agent Harris Slade and his team on their hunt for a sadistic serial killer known only as "The Pen Pal". Finally confronted with the killer, Jolynn realizes she must enter the mind of the psychopath in order to stop the brutal killings. But when her vision reveals a particularly disturbing death, can Jolynn sacrifice her lover for her friend?

"Awaken the Dead"

A grieving innkeeper struggles to keep her haunted hotel out of foreclosure.

After losing her parents in a suspicious boating accident, Harley Brandon is determined to keep the family hotel out of foreclosure. Unfortunately, the hotel ghosts have other plans. Built with tainted money, the century old Horizon Hotel thrives on a tradition of murder, scandal, and suicide. As the paranormal activity increases to alarming levels, Harley discovers the truth about the hotel and its residents. Can Harley save her friends from the hotel's frightening hidden secrets?

"Already Dead"
Supernatural Collection

From the already dead to the undead. Three supernatural tales of "things that go bump in the night".

"Bloodletting" - A vampire themed resort allows guests to *participate* in their Bloodletting Ritual to celebrate the island's legendary vampires.

"Reaper of Souls" - A young woman must outwit an evil sorcerer in order to save her brother or become one of his minions forever.

"Already Dead" - When Flight 220 crashes, ten passengers make it to an isolated island, but only one man lives to tell the lie.

"Witness Protection 4"
O-Dark-Hundred

A simple assignment turns deadly when a retired Navy SEAL team uncovers a plot to kill a notorious mob boss.

When Whiskey Tango Foxtrot embarks on a simple stalking case, they're not prepared for a trip to a private island paradise owned by an infamous mobster. With one of their own suffering from traumatic head injuries, the team is left scrambling to decide what is real or imagined. The situation escalates even further when they uncover an assassination plot where everyone is a suspect. Now targets themselves, can the team survive their trip to paradise?

"Witness Protection 5"
Outside the Wire

After suffering several casualties on their last assignment, a retired Navy SEAL team discovers their misery is just beginning.

When Whiskey Tango Foxtrot returns home after suffering a devastating loss, they're hit with even more bad news regarding the rest of their team. Their grief is cut short when they discover their names are all on the same hit list. Hunted by relentless assassins, the scattered team must decide whether to remain safely hidden or find the man who put the price on their heads. Against the wishes of her teammates, Jackie strikes out on her own in order to save a friend who wants her dead. In a kill or be killed situation, will Jackie's emotions finally betray her?

"Once Upon a Disaster"

A young homicide detective finds herself at the mercy of a hitman in the aftermath of an earthquake

While investigating the murder of a hitman, Detective Jade Wesson pursues a lead connecting the dead man to a break-in at a computer programming company. She's drawn into the world of nightclub owner and front man for the mob, Cody Riley. Her investigation keeps pointing to Cody's right-hand man and possible hitman, Vahn Lott. Despite her efforts to keep her investigation on track, Vahn has plans of his own for the attractive detective. When an unprecedented earthquake rocks their east coast town, Jade must put her life in Vahn's hands if she wants to survive. Can she trust a man who might be the killer she's hunting?

"The Murder of Emily Fisher"

After finding their favorite teacher murdered, the lives of two teenage girls are forever changed.

Everyone loved Emily Fisher. While walking home one afternoon, two teenage girls, Sidney and Trisha, stumble upon a gruesome murder scene. The brutal murder of Emily Fisher, a young, attractive schoolteacher, shocks the small town of **Marilina**. After graduation, Sidney moves far away from the memories of the small town while Trisha retreats deeper into denial. Eight years after the murder, Sidney receives a desperate call from her childhood friend, forcing her to return home. Trisha believes Emily's killer was falsely accused and she manages to turn the entire town against her while attempting to prove it. When Trisha receives a death threat, Sidney realizes there may be some credibility to her friend's wild accusations. Is Trisha's mental breakdown a result of childhood trauma? Or is the real killer actually attempting to silence her? In order to save her friend, Sidney must answer the eight-year-old question. Who murdered Emily Fisher?

"Castle Bloodshed"
Murder Collection

From a deadly island paradise to haunted castles. Three novella length tales of murder, mystery, and malicious intent.

"Castle Bloodshed" — A tour of Wesley Castle turns into a fight for survival as six stranded tourists discover the haunting secrets within the castle walls. A mystery writer teams up with an uptight butler in order stop a killer who may already be dead. Novella length paranormal murder mystery.

"Fleshies" — Is Uncle Rutger crazy? Five years ago, four business partners died within their newly purchased, fixer-upper castle. Their bodies were never found. The surviving partner, Rutger, claims a demon keeps him as its slave. Rutger's nephew schemes to save his uncle by sacrificing the lives of a group of stranded motorists and a high-profile novelist. Novella length supernatural murder mystery.

"Demon Island" — A group of strangers are invited to a remote island for the reading of a will. The guests soon discover they were brought to the island to be executed one-by-one. It's up to a private detective and a tenacious young woman to solve the murders and find a way to escape paradise. Novella length murder mystery.

"Brighton Island"

When a psychic visits a haunted island mansion, he inadvertently awakens the ghosts' tortured souls.

Something's not right with Simon. When Jacklyn brings her eccentric friend to her uncle's island mansion, she didn't expect him to slip into psychic overload. As Simon attempts to solve a decade-old, double homicide, Jacklyn is confronted with the possibility that she could be next to join the mansion ghosts. When they find themselves stranded on the secluded island, her Uncle Hyland wages his own war to save them from a flesh and blood killer. Will her uncle's "shock and awe" military tactics save them or get them killed? Can Simon bring peace to the tortured souls or unexpectedly join them?

"A.L.F. Resort"

A fantasy vacation turns into a nightmare when the resort's artificial life forms are compromised.

Welcome to A.L.F. Resort where you can live out your fantasies with safe, state-of-the-art artificial life form robots! When a young journalist and a photographer are sent to A.L.F. Resort to do a story for their magazine, Shay and Becka believe they've hit the jackpot of all work-cations. The engineers pull out all the stops to make their fantasies memorable. Unfortunately, the newly designed A.L.F., the Gen X, is smarter than his programming and creates havoc within Shay's fantasy. A computer malfunction removes their safety inhibitors and the A.L.F.s play out their own hostile fantasies. Zombies, bikers, and mobsters run amuck, turning fantasies into nightmares. Shay gets more of a story than she anticipates, but will she survive long enough to write it?

"Jungle Princess"

While stranded on a prison island, a young woman discovers a creature of "unknown" origin.

After their cruise ship sinks, Alex and two of her shipmates are stranded on a deserted, tropical island. Unfortunately, the castaways soon realize they're not alone. They discover an abandoned prison with over two dozen inmates living on the island's south side. While avoiding the prison on the far side of the island, Alex discovers a strange but loveable creature of unknown origin. When one of her fellow castaways is in trouble, Alex reluctantly seeks help from the prisoners. After the brutal murder of several inmates, their questions surrounding the abandoned prison are about to be answered. What really killed over one hundred prisoners? And is it still out there?

Coming Soon!
"Witness Protection 6"

ABOUT THE AUTHOR

Holly Copella has been writing since the age of twelve when her frustration at a book's poor plot drove her to author her own story. Over the last decade, she's written a number of screenplays, some of which she's now adapting into novels. Her fascination with zombies and other darker material lends an edge to her writing, which tends to lean toward horror. As a fan of Agatha Christie, she appreciates the craft of a good plot and the importance of creating significant characters.

Hailing from Pennsylvania, Copella lives in the Endless Mountains on a farm with her rescue horses and other animals. In addition to writing and reading fiction, she enjoys riding horses and traveling to Las Vegas and Disney World.

www.ingramcontent.com/pod-product-compliance
Lightning Source LLC
Chambersburg PA
CBHW071101250626
47159CB00002B/544